Powered

Mech Wars Book 1

Scott Bartlett

Mirth Publishing
St. John's

POWERED

Cover art by: Tom Edwards (tomedwardsdesign.com)

Library and Archives Canada Cataloguing in Publication

Bartlett, Scott

Powered / Scott Bartlett ; illustrations by Tom Edwards.

ISBN 978-1-988380-07-0

To Cecily, my heart.

CHAPTER 1

Mech

Jake Price swapped out his assault rifle's empty magazine for a full one, sucked in a quick breath, and leaned to fire around the low garden wall that served as his only cover. A tight burst, and then back again. His ammo was almost depleted.

The Ixan soldiers were closing in, and they'd already taken out the rest of Jake's team.

Of course, today wouldn't have gone half so poorly if his dropship pilot hadn't insisted on putting his team down in the middle of an open square bordered by Ixan snipers. Jake had lost half his people as they tried to sprint across the open space, zigzagging to give themselves a nonzero chance of survival.

Right now, his chance of surviving seemed pretty close to zero. But he'd been in tighter spots than this.

And he had to complete the mission.

Ripping a grenade from his tactical vest, he lobbed it at the approaching soldiers as he scrambled the other way, staying low to the ground and praying he wasn't kicking up enough dust to give away his location.

When he judged he'd put enough distance between himself and his original position, he flipped onto his back, ripped his pistol from its holster, and waited.

There. The Ixa started coming around the wall, fleeing the impending explosion. Jake inhaled, lined up his shot, and fired as he exhaled.

Boom. Headshot. *Boom.* Headshot.

Jake was already up and running as the grenade went off, rumbling through the ground and sending a wave of heat against his back.

His mission was to rescue a diplomat who'd been foolish enough to try negotiating with the Ixa. They'd taken him hostage, of course, and then the demands had started.

The Commonwealth needed to send a strong message: they weren't interested in entertaining Ixan demands.

And Jake was the messenger they'd chosen.

Intel had the hostage in a basement two streets over, and an indicator blinked on Jake's HUD, with a dotted line outlining a suggested route.

Screw that.

Following the AI's suggestion meant staying predictable. Instead, Jake tried a door, and when it wouldn't open, he slapped a charge just above its doorknob, taking cover behind a nearby dumpster.

The charge went off, and the door creaked open. *Perfect.* Now, if he could just...

"Jake." Someone shaking his shoulder. "Jake, come on. We've arrived. Time to work."

He opened his eyes to the gunmetal gray of the tiny cabin he shared with his father aboard their comet hopper.

As it often did, reality brought a resigned sigh to his lips. "I was about to get a hostage back from the Ixa."

"The Ixa aren't here. I'm here, though, and I'm telling you it's time to clock in."

"They could come," Jake muttered as he sat up, blinking rapidly to clear his grainy eyes.

"Not in time to get you out of work," Peter said with a grin. Then his smile fell away. "You were jolting in your sleep again. I think you're spending too much time lucid, Jake. It's not worth sacrificing your sleep for."

"It'll be worth it if the Ixa ever show up."

"Sure," Peter said, nodding. "Or the Gok, or Amblers, or maybe the Quatro will develop spaceflight to come out here and pester us. Until they do, though..."

"Yeah, yeah." His father wasn't mentioning what the single orbital telescope in this system had discovered: the fact that almost all of the nearby star systems had exoplanets with atmospheres filled with oxygen, carbon dioxide, and methane—which made it pretty likely those planets harbored life.

People living in the Steele System barely ever mentioned that. It made them uncomfortable, so they avoided the topic. They especially didn't mention that the flux of one star in particular often dropped to below the twenty percent level, for periods that ranged between five and eighty days at a time. On the system net, Jake had seen speculation that the unusual fluctuations could signify a Dyson sphere under construction.

Either way, Darkstream Security didn't dare explore the surrounding systems, for fear that it would alert their occupants—who might be much more powerful—to humanity's presence in the neighborhood. At least, Darkstream wouldn't do that until they achieved a much better foothold here.

Jake crouched beside his bunk to access the long drawer underneath it, pulling it out until the handle hit his father's closed drawer under the opposite bunk. Piles of neatly folded work shirts and jeans waited inside. His father made him fold them neatly every time he steamed them clean, and then Jake had to arrange the clothing according to outfits. Even when they were in transit between work sites, his father enforced neatness.

"Did we get any messages from Mom and Sue Anne?" Jake asked.

He glanced to see his father shaking his head. "Not this morning," Peter Price said softly, after a brief pause.

Jake nodded, reflecting that no news was probably good news. If Sue Anne's illness had taken a sudden turn for the worse, then they would have heard about it.

Even though they'd disembarked the comet hopper hundreds of times, Peter insisted they triple-check every clip and fastening on each other's pressure suits before leaving through the airlock.

With his helmet on, Jake sighed again, loudly, knowing his father couldn't hear. He hated this job. He'd never say that, because they did it to help Sue Anne, but this wasn't how he'd envisioned spending his life. Turning comets into habitats, for homesteaders so paranoid that it wasn't good enough

Darkstream Security had already brought them far away from every government in existence. No, the homesteaders still weren't satisfied—they still felt the need to get away from Darkstream itself.

Although the comet's surface was almost as cold as anything ever got—Jake's HUD told him minus two hundred and forty Celsius—the inside of the pressure suit could be made as warm as he liked. If he wanted, he could make it feel like his whole body was pressed against a radiator.

But that would make work even more unbearable, so he kept the suit's environment fairly cool.

"Come help me with the hose," his father said over the frequency they always used, walking over to the hopper's hull and keying open a square panel that took up much of the aft. The panel slid aside to reveal a coiled drilling hose. The thing was half a kilometer long and as big around as a man's ankle.

"Where are we setting up?" Jake asked.

Peter pointed. "That flat area over there."

As his father unwound the hose, Jake walked with its end toward the indicated spot. It was more shuffling than walking, actually. If you had too much bounce in your step as you crossed a comet, you could easily fly off into space.

His father had activated the water harvester before leaving the hopper. That device projected downward from the ship's keel, where it would heat the ice and collect the resultant water before it could freeze again. As water passed through the system, the ship would warm it further, till it was piping hot.

"That's far enough," his father said, and Jake lowered the hose to the ground. They'd have to wait thirty minutes for the ship to heat up enough liquid. In the meantime, Jake helped his father extend the hopper's antenna array from another part of the hull. The array would use step-frequency radar to gradually scan the comet's interior, so they could anticipate any problem spots during the drill down.

That done, it was time to stand around and wait. Even if he'd been able to go lucid, he doubted his father would have let him. But you needed an implant for that anyway, and all Jake had was the dorky-looking sleepgear.

His eyes played over their comet hopper, which didn't technically have a name, though he always thought of it as the *Whale*. The name fit: the thing was big. It had to be, to carry the equipment necessary to set up multiple comet colonies.

They were on a years-long voyage to establish several such habitats, hopping from comet to comet. Anything smaller than a mile wide didn't interest them, but luckily there were more than enough suitable candidates for colonization in what had originally been dubbed the Kuiper Belt 2, and those candidates passed near each other often enough to make the whole operation viable.

No one was sure whether the same was true of the Outer Ring, since it was far enough outside the normal sphere of operations that it made no sense to expand there until Kuiper Belt 2 was fully exploited, which it wouldn't be for a long time.

Eventually, everyone dropped the "2" in Kuiper Belt 2. No who'd followed Darkstream to this galaxy intended on having any more contact with the inhabitants of humanity's home system, and so using the same name wasn't likely to become a problem.

Even so, nowadays, most people simply called the circumstellar disk "the Belt."

Darkstream Security Ltd. supplied Jake and his father with the equipment and building materials necessary to erect each colony, in exchange for sixty percent of all resources extracted as well as fifty percent of the sales they made to homesteaders.

It was kind of funny to think about how the homesteaders wanted so badly to get away from Darkstream, and yet without the company they'd never be able to—

"Jake."

Jake's head jerked up, until he was looking at his father, whose hand was raised in a gesture recognizable as one used to manipulate a virtual interface.

"Yeah?"

"Radar found something odd. I think...I think there's something *inside* this thing."

"The comet?"

"Yeah. Take a look at this." With a flicking gesture, Peter sent the radar image to Jake's HUD.

So far, the antenna array had only managed to render part of the object buried deep within the ice of the comet, but Jake thought he recognized it nevertheless. He'd never seen one in person, of course, because they didn't actually exist.

Or so he'd thought. And yet, here one was. He'd piloted simulated versions himself, many times, while lucid. But here one was in *real life*.

An actual mech. Buried deep within the comet's ice.

CHAPTER 2

The Dusty Bucket

"The usual, Lisa?" Phineas Gage asked when she sauntered up to the bar.

Lisa Sato nodded, using her implant to summon the pile of silver and copper coins that represented her financial worth in credits. It hovered in the air, waiting for her to count out the right change from it. She did so, and pinched some extra copper from the top, dropping it onto the bar in front of Phineas.

The bartender grinned, eyeing the added coin through his v-lenses. Lisa believed in tipping generously. Darkstream paid its military operatives well—much better than most other employees, as well as most of those the company contracted with. Spreading the extra coin around a bit was the least she could do.

"Can I have your number, Lisa?" Bob O'Toole singsonged drunkenly from the bar's end.

She suppressed a grimace, avoiding O'Toole's gaze. The gross old man had never tried anything with her, and if he did he'd live to regret it. But he did have a knack for being annoying.

"Getting her number wouldn't help you one iota, Bob," said Tessa Notaras, who sat with her hands curled around a beer between Lisa and the old lech. "Even if you managed to get her number, IM address, and employee ID, she still wouldn't sleep with you."

Bob might have come back with something saucy, but Tessa had paired her words with a stern glare, and the drunk fell silent. Then Tessa turned to smile at Lisa.

Lisa smiled back. She'd often shared a drink with Tessa, and she liked the older woman a lot. Tessa always seemed to have something interesting to share, whether it was a rumor no one had heard yet, but which would inevitably be all over Habitat 2 by the next day, or an intriguing tidbit from one of the books she spent so much time reading on her implant.

Tessa had also worked for Darkstream, once, but now she seemed to revile the company. That made it a little awkward whenever Lisa's employer came up in conversation. Lisa had no idea how the ex-soldier made money now that she'd estranged herself from the biggest company in the system, but it didn't really matter. Tessa had come to play something of a "big sister" role to Lisa.

"Here you go, darling," Phineas said, plunking a whiskey sour on the bar top in front of her.

Lisa raised the glass to her lips, sipped in some foam, and tilted the tumbler toward Phineas. "Delicious as always, Phin."

"Better than the Swinging Eel?" he asked, voice flush with mirth.

That got a laugh from Lisa. "You know I'd never betray your trust by patronizing them."

It was true. Of Habitat 2's two bars, the Swinging Eel was by far the seedier one, and especially dangerous for a Darkstream Security operative. Lisa far preferred to drink here at the Dusty Bucket, even if Bob O'Toole did seem to cling permanently to his customary stool like an unpleasant growth.

I wonder if anyone would dare sit on that stool, if he ever got up from it. I bet it's filthy. The thought made her grin wider. *Maybe a newcomer would.* Habitat 2 didn't get many of those.

Settling onto her own stool, Lisa cast her mind back over the day she'd had, which had involved busting two in-progress drug deals. Those were getting more frequent, lately, and they'd already been pretty bad. Her entire job seemed to boil down to arresting people whose crimes had something to do with drugs—smuggling them, selling them, buying them, or stealing enough credits to buy them.

It never ends.

Andy Miller entered the bar, nodding at Phineas before noticing Lisa.

"Seaman Apprentice," she said, with a slight nod.

"Seaman," Andy said, smirking.

Andy was a fellow Darkstream employee, and so he had a rank, like her. The company had given its hired military operatives naval ranks soon after deciding to colonize this solar system, to increase their perceived legitimacy as the closest thing the system had to a military.

Lisa had heard that Darkstream wasn't quite as finicky about ranks as the UHF had been back in the Milky Way, but the command structure was still taken seriously.

Lisa had gone on a couple of dates with Andy a few months ago, but suddenly he'd stopped messaging her, and so she'd stopped messaging him. Now, he treated her with a mixture of ridicule and disdain whenever they saw each other. She wasn't a fan of that at all.

"Just getting back from a run, Andy?" Phineas asked, sliding over a pint of stout.

Andy nodded. "Brought a big shipment back from the elevator, too."

Phineas grunted. "Thing makes me nervous. I don't care how far away they put it. I hear that thing is over twenty thousand miles high, and if something ever went wrong with it and it fell over the wrong way..."

A sharp laugh from Andy. "It'll never fall over, Phin. The physics are as dependable as your beer is good."

"Ah. Well, they must be pretty dependable, then." Still, Phineas sniffed sharply. "How's the weather out on Alex?"

"Could be a lot worse."

Alexandria was one of the two planets Darkstream's employees and former employees had colonized after arriving in this system, which company execs had christened the Steele System. It was a bit of a mouthful to say "Alexandria" all the time, though, so everyone shortened the planet's name to "Alex."

Andy shrugged. "The biggest dangers are inside Habitat 2. 'Hell is other people.' Someone said that once. Back in the, uh..."

"Yeah," Phineas said with a nod.

"Pansies," Bob O'Toole said around a belch. Lisa had no idea why Phineas let the man stick around when he constantly insulted him like that. On the other hand, Bob O'Toole could very well be keeping the Bucket afloat, with all his drinking, so maybe it made sense after all.

"What are you talking about, Bob?" Andy said.

"Just saying," O'Toole said, enunciating everything in that sarcastic way he had. "Grown men, whining about every little thing—sounds like you need yourselves a safe space to go cry in. Hmm? Why don't you go back to the Milky Way, if that's how you feel? Back where they give everybody a medal, including the losers, so that even a pansy like Captain Leonard Keyes could come to get respect."

"Keyes is a great man," Phineas said quietly.

That twisted O'Toole's face into a sneer. "Great man? Ha!" For a second, Lisa thought the jerk was about to spit, but he seemed to know that really would get him kicked out. "*Dead* man, probably," he said instead. "Everyone in the Milky Way's dead by now, I'd wager. Nineteen years is more than enough time for the Ixa to wipe out every last one of them. And soon enough, they'll come for us."

"Cut it out, Bob," Tessa Notaras said, voice icy, white hair swinging as she turned to glare at him once more.

Bob did cut it out. He always heeded Tessa. Most people did.

Lisa's com, which the company had set to permanent speaker-mode, squawked: "Attention all combat units. There has been a shooting at the southern collection node. Converge there immediately. Code red. I repeat, code red."

The message repeated once, and Lisa found herself exchanging bewildered glances with Andy.

"You're probably the closest soldier to there," he said.

Oh, God. Lisa's hand strayed toward her pistol unconsciously, but she caught herself. *I'm not ready for this.*

Her only training had been running combat sims while lucid. She'd never faced off with an actual person holding an actual gun. Her heart pounded, and she hadn't even left yet.

"You okay?" Andy said. "You're kinda pale."

"Yeah, I'm fine," she snapped.

"You're on foot, right? I doubt you'll get there in time, traveling that way. I can give you a ride on my bike."

"Sure. Yeah. Okay." Lisa took a deep breath. "Let's go."

CHAPTER 3

Gabriel Roach

Gabriel Roach woke up with a splitting headache and a mysterious sense of guilt. He normally felt guilty, actually, but this guilt was new, about something else.

For a few moments after waking, everything was a mystery. It took a moment for him to piece together where he was and what he'd done last night.

Then the pieces started falling into place. He was very hungover. The reason: last night, he'd downed way too many vodka cranberries at the summer festival, which this year had been hosted by Northshire, the village he'd been contracted out by Darkstream to protect.

And lying in bed beside him was Mayor Sweeney's daughter, Jess.

Ah, yes.

That was where the guilt came from.

Memory flooded back, from after they'd stumbled into his private quarters at the end of his unit's barracks, which he enjoyed because of his position as Captain of the Guard.

He remembered what they'd done together, in and out of lucid.

He wanted to vomit. There'd be a record of the lucid parts, if anyone cared to review his history. That was something new to worry about, for the rest of his career.

What he'd done last night was unprofessional, self-indulgent, and not to mention—

"Gabe?" Jess said sleepily, pushing herself up on one elbow, a strand of auburn hair falling across her face.

His hand sprang forward of its own accord, yanking the blanket up before it could fall any farther. "Keep yourself covered," he snapped, too harshly.

—not to mention, at twenty-one, Jess was eighteen years younger than him.

He began a frantic search of the floor, hunting down each article of clothing and tossing it in her direction without looking directly at the bed.

"What's wrong with you?" Jess was sitting up now, and clutching the comforter's edge to her chin, thankfully.

"This was a mistake," Gabe said, his fingers landing on a shirt, which went sailing over his shoulder.

"That's not what you said last night."

"I was ossified last night."

"I've seen the way you look at me when you're stone-sober."

"You're imagining things." She wasn't, of course. Gabe had definitely looked at her. And unlike most of the other women he'd ever looked at, the crazy thing was, he thought he might actually be catching feelings for Jess. She was so quirky and un-bridled, such a distillation of youth, so—

Listen to yourself, Gabe. You're a walking stereotype.
"You're twenty-one, Jess."

"So what? I'm a grown woman and I'm perfectly capable of making up my mind about what I want. I want you."

"You can't have me. I'll lose my job, for one."

"We won't tell anyone, then."

"That's not going to work. Darkstream can basically read my thoughts before I think them. It would be just a matter of time before it comes out that I'm sleeping with the daughter of the mayor whose village I'm assigned to protect!"

Gabe began to pace back and forth across the tiny bedroom, shooting glances through the kitchenette whenever he passed it. The window out there featured a view of the walk up to the barracks, and he wanted to spot anyone approaching long before they reached him.

The time on the wall caught his eye, which clued him in to the fact that he had to go on patrol in fifteen minutes. Cursing, he ran to the locker near the door, dragging out his fatigues and pulling them on article by article.

Behind the clothes, a rack held his SL-17, and he unclipped it, checking the action and the magazine before turning once more to Jess.

"I have to go on patrol. Keep the door locked and don't open it for anyone. Stay away from the windows. I'll figure something out."

"Gabe—"

But he was out the door, slamming it behind him and strolling down the path toward the village proper, trying not to look as ruined as he felt. Eresos' mildew smell invaded his nostrils at once. You couldn't get away from that odor, no matter how far you cut back the forest.

Gabe had been the very first person to step foot on Planet Eresos, and he *still* wasn't used to the stench.

As was typical behavior for the universe, Mayor Sweeney was the first villager he encountered.

"You look like hell," the mayor said.

"I look worse than I feel," Gabe said. "I call it being ugly."

Sweeney barked a laugh. "You're far from that. Not judging from the way the village girls look at you, anyhow."

Gabe forced a strained chuckle. "I'm sure that's not true," he choked out.

"Sure it is. Anyway, we're all at least a little hungover. I won't tell Darkstream if you won't. Listen, have you seen Jess?"

For a brief second, Gabe froze. Then he unglued himself from his terror enough to say something: "Jess? No. Why, is she missing?"

"Ah, I'm sure it's nothing. It's not like the Quatro have been active lately. Her and her friends probably decided to take the party into the woods again, after us adults went to bed."

Jess is an adult too, he wanted to say, for various reasons. But it didn't seem wise. "I'm going on patrol, but if I see her I'll send her your way, all right?"

"Thanks, Gabe. I can always count on you."

"Sure can," he said, flashing a grin, trying not to make it awkward-looking. He turned and marched on.

"Hey, Gabe?"

He froze. "Yeah?"

"I wanted to ask you something. About Jess."

Slowly, Gabe turned again, sure he could actually *feel* the blood draining from his face. "Yes? What is it?"

"You don't...you don't think Jess is a liberal, do you?"

Gabe blinked. Then he brayed laughter, so forceful the spit flew from his lips. "Jess? No. No way she is. Jess knows which side her bread is buttered on."

Mayor Sweeney shared in his laughter. "You're right, you're right. And she does the buttering by herself!" The mayor's grin threatened to crack his face clean in half.

"Uh, yeah! Exactly." He suspected the butter metaphor had gone astray at some point, but it was good that Sweeney was laughing. *Instead of smashing my face in with a plank.* "Anyway. I'd better start my rounds."

"You do that. Talk to you later, Gabe."

Continuing on, Gabe scanned Northshire, looking for anything out of the ordinary. Problem was, after the once-annual festival, *everything* seemed out of the ordinary.

Toby Horton lay sprawled in the middle of the village green, snoring like a bandsaw. Wrappers and drink containers littered the ground. Speeders from other villages were parked in a haphazard circle all around the settlement, their sleek contours glimmering in the morning light. The vehicles were modeled after stolen Winger tech, which rumor said that Darkstream had gotten by spying on the species using micro-wormholes.

Back when we used micro-wormholes.

Anything could be hiding behind those speeders.

Focus on what matters. What would Darkstream most want you to protect?

That was easy. The collection facility, first, which the company had provided in exchange for sixty percent of all resources collected. *That looks fine.* Second, the farming equipment Darkstream leased to the villagers in exchange for sixty percent of whatever food they produced. Third, the self-erecting structures, and the machines the villagers had used to expand their town with wooden buildings.

And finally, Darkstream's military operatives, plus the weaponry they carried. Gabe decided to check on them next. The current shift would be at their usual outposts, and he'd have to make a wide loop around the village to get them all.

On his way, he heard a grinding sound coming from behind one of the speeders, which was slowly inching forward. Gripping his assault rifle, Gabe jogged over, raising the gun to sight down the barrel at whatever was pushing the vehicle.

His gun barrel dipped the instant he saw it, and he suppressed the urge to scream in frustration. Then he dashed back toward where he'd last seen the mayor, forcing his aching legs to move as fast as they were able.

Gabe found Sweeney in front of the door to his residence, hunting through a set of keys. The mayor turned when Gabe shouted his name.

"What's going on?" Sweeney asked.

"Some idiot parked in the middle of a Gatherer route. Right now, their speeder's getting shredded."

"Let me see."

Gabe used his implant to summon footage of the incident, then flicked it over to Sweeney's.

The mayor frowned. "That's Randy Bradshaw's. Damn idiot was probably drunk when he got here." Stuffing the keys back into his pocket, the mayor jogged back into Northshire. "Let's track him down."

They found Bradshaw snoozing in one of the vegetable gardens. The robot in charge of planting, watering, and weeding was gently jabbing him in the abdomen over and over, its servomotors whining and beginning to smoke as its entire frame shuddered. Bradshaw showed no sign of registering the machine's efforts.

Without a word, Gabe walked over and grabbed Bradshaw by both arms, dragging him through the garden between two furrows and throwing him against the fence that ran around the perimeter. That done, he proceeded to slap Bradshaw's fleshy face until he began to blink and sputter.

"Wha? *Whaa!*"

Gabe grabbed the man by the front of his beige jacket and shook him. "Your speeder's obstructing one of the Gatherers, jackass!"

"My speeder?"

"It's getting totaled. You need to move it, now!"

Bradshaw began to panic, patting his pockets and shaking out his pant legs. "Can't find my v-lenses!" he moaned.

The mayor picked up a pair of glasses from the spot where they'd found Bradshaw sprawled. Dirt tumbled from the v-lenses to the ground.

"You'd better hope these still work," Sweeney growled. He tossed them toward Bradshaw.

Gabe caught them, certain the whining cretin lacked the motor skills to do so. Then he slapped them onto Bradshaw's face, who began to wave his hands in the air, tapping an invisible interface and then moving his open palm as though guiding something.

"Okay," Bradshaw said. "Okay. I got the path cleared."

Resisting the urge to punch the man in the gut, Gabe turned to the mayor. "We'd better go confirm."

Sweeney nodded, shooting Bradshaw one last glare before turning to leave the garden.

They passed the collection facility just as the automated bay door was admitting the Gatherer, which looked undamaged after its tussle with Bradshaw's speeder. That was to be expected. The speeder, on the other hand, would almost certainly have to be written off.

The Gatherers morphed into whatever shape best suited a given task, their gleaming exteriors a fluid surface of blades that spun, shifted, retracted, and jutted, depending on what the situation called for. They could become an impenetrable, seamless shell, or they could turn into a lance capable of running a person through.

They weren't weapons, though, and they used their diverse abilities only to gather Eresos' many resources and bring them to preprogrammed deposit sites, which was where the colonists had originally set up their villages.

The Gatherers' behavior was highly predictable. They mined the planet's various ores and minerals, bringing them to preset destinations, where vast underground chambers waited to receive the payloads. And when you put a speeder in front of one of them, that speeder got wrecked.

The Gatherers were well beyond humanity's ability to manufacture. No one knew who'd built them, and no species had ever returned to claim the resources they'd collected—not in the two decades since Darkstream had arrived.

The only certain thing was that without the Gatherers, the Steele System's economy would not have ramped up nearly as fast as it had.

After double checking to make sure Bradshaw's speeder was truly out of the Gatherer route, Sweeney exchanged glances with Gabe. "I'll have a talk with Bradshaw. Tell him if he wants to attend future events in Northshire, he'll have to get with the program."

"Sounds good."

"Hey, Pioneer!" a voice shouted.

Gabe turned. "Pioneer" was the nickname the others in his unit had given him.

Seaman Sawyer dashed toward them across the village green. It always seemed odd to Gabe, using the "Seaman" rank when basically all their contracts took them planetside. But Darkstream had decided to use naval ranks across the board.

"What is it, Horse?"

"It's Allendale, sir. Word just came in that they were attacked overnight."

"Attacked? By who? Quatro?"

"No. An Ambler."

"What the hell." Amblers were two-legged war machines, ten meters tall, and clearly made by whoever had made the Gatherers. They patrolled the Gatherer routes, meaning you had to watch out for them whenever you left a village in a speeder. But they never came near the deposit sites. Not till now, apparently.

"Is there anything left of the village?" Gabe asked.

"The Darkstream unit stationed there managed to drive it off before it could wipe out Allendale completely. That's Chief Banks's unit, right? Most of Allendale's residents were here during the attack, thank God. But there's no guarantee the Ambler won't come back to finish the job. It must be malfunctioning."

Gabe nodded, swallowing. "We need to put it down." He'd only fought an Ambler once, and the price paid in human life had been heavy. Since then, no one had taken down another one, mostly because Darkstream judged it was not worth the damage to company assets. Such as its employees.

Until now, probably.

"What do the higher-ups want?" Gabe said. "Have we heard from them yet?"

Sawyer nodded. "They want us to deal with it."

"Figures. Tell most of the boys to gear up. You stay here with Robinson and guard Northshire, all right?"

"Got it."

Gabe exchanged looks once more with Mayor Sweeney. "Good luck, Gabe," the man said.

"Thanks," he said, turning toward the barracks, to figure out a credible story for Jess to tell her father about where she'd been. That done, he'd have to successfully smuggle her out, before heading out to Allendale. "I'm going to need it."

CHAPTER 4

The Crazy Part

Habitat 2 raced past them as Andy gunned the hoverbike's engines, the ground falling farther away as the bike's energy cycle spiked.

Lisa's head crept toward the overhead parallelogram lights, designed to simulate sunlight shining through skylights, and she subvocalized to Andy using her implant.

"I didn't know hoverbikes could do these kind of speeds."

"They can't. Technically. I modded mine, for situations like this."

"Responding to shootings?"

"Uh...yeah. Stuff like that."

"I see." Lisa knew that before today, it was unlikely Andy had ever had a job urgent enough to warrant the mods. But she had no desire to use the knowledge to put him down. *That's something like he would do.*

Habitat 2 was a network of passages through sealed-off dwellings, shops, and storage units. Each structure's walls stretched from floor to roof, but if you peeled off the ceiling and studied Habitat 2 from above you'd see a giant honeycomb of passages and closed-in spaces.

It was in those spaces that crime took shape, spilling out into the passages like so much toxic sludge.

Lisa had been lucky, so far. She'd only had to deal with petty thugs who didn't put up much of a fight when faced with a Darkstream soldier.

Clearly, her luck was about to turn.

They arrived outside the collection node, and Andy engaged the forward propulsor to slow them. The bike whipped around in a wild arc, and Lisa's heart leapt into her throat. Instinctively, she clutched Andy tighter.

But he clearly had the bike under control, as he'd activated the rear propulsor the moment they'd spun. He turned to grin back at her once they came to a stop.

"Jerk," she said, sliding off the bike and drawing her pistol, willing it not to shake in her grasp.

A technician waited for them outside the collection node, his eyes slightly wide at the sight of Lisa's drawn gun. Clearing her throat, she put it away.

"Is the shooter gone?" she asked, trying to sound authoritative.

The technician nodded. Lisa's implant had automatically booted up its facial recognition function, identifying the man as Ned Stevens, one of four Darkstream employees in charge of the southern collection node. His shift had ended nearly two hours ago, but he'd received the same alert she had, requiring him to come back and ensure resource collection continued smoothly.

"Is there footage of the murder, Stevens?"

"It's fried, ma'am," the man mumbled.

"Fried? Fried how?"

"Just fried."

"Show me."

The man nodded and fumbled a pair of v-lenses from his breast pocket. He put them on, and following a couple sweeping gestures he flicked the footage over to her implant.

Fried is about right. First, the murdered woman, who Lisa's implant identified as Colleen Jensen, was shown approaching a Gatherer after it finished struggling against the thick titanium wall designed to prevent its entry into Habitat 2. Then the picture went snowy for several minutes.

Once it cleared up, Jensen lay dead on the collection chamber's floor, her blood speckling the metal. The Gatherer had already departed through the airlock.

"Someone got to the footage. How could that happen? Who would have access?"

Stevens shrugged.

"I need your help, here, Stevens. There's been a murder, and right now you're the closest thing we have to a witness. Who has access to the vid stream?"

"I dunno." Stevens stared at the ground and refused to look up. "You'll have to ask Darkstream."

Lisa squinted at him. She was sure the man was being intentionally obtuse. Why wouldn't he give her what she needed?

A doctor pulled up on a hoverbike, with a long, rectangular container in tow. That would be the cooler, for transporting Jensen's body.

"Doctor Yetman," Lisa said, sticking out her hand once her implant had IDed him. They shook, brief and perfunctory. Glancing at Stevens, she turned back to the doctor and said, "Give me a moment to take a pano. Then we'll help you load the body aboard."

"By all means," Yetman said.

She peeled her spherical pano-camera from her belt and then had Stevens let her into the collection chamber. When the heavy door rose into the wall, Lisa tossed the camera into the room. It flashed once, near the chamber's center, before clattering against the far wall.

As she crossed to collect it, she gave quiet thanks that the Gatherer had long since departed. The things gave her the creeps, and she'd always found it weird how everyone just accepted their presence. Just because their efforts had become so important to the system's economy didn't mean they should escape closer scrutiny. Who had built the Gatherers? Why had they abandoned them here? And what would happen once their creators found out humanity had been stealing the fruits of their labor for almost twenty years?

"All right," she subvocalized to Andy as she retrieved the camera. "Get the doctor in here."

They loaded Jensen's body into the cooler-trailer, and then they used Andy's hoverbike to follow Yetman deeper into Habitat 2, until they reached a structure no bigger than a shed.

"This is the autopsy room I share with two other doctors. They both have Q-level security clearances from Darkstream, so there should be no issue with bringing Jensen here. If you'll help me carry her body inside, I'll begin my examination."

"Not you," Lisa said as Andy positioned himself near the trailer's rear. "You only have K-level clearance."

Andy bristled, clearly not thrilled to be reminded his clearance was lower than hers. "I have things to do, anyway."

"Sure. Thanks for your help, Andy."

"Yeah." He climbed onto his hoverbike and sped off.

"All right, doctor. Let's do this."

Yetman keyed open the entrance, and together they slid Jensen's body out of the trailer, carried it inside, and laid it on a sterile metal table.

Before today, the only dead person Lisa had ever touched had been her grandmother. Somehow, this wasn't as bad as that. Kissing her grandmother's powdered, ice-cold forehead had made her sick to her stomach, but she found herself feeling fairly clinical about handling Jensen.

The doctor began inspecting the corpse. First, he studied the bullet's exit wound, through Jensen's face, and then he had Lisa help him flip the body over so he could scrutinize the entry point for several long moments.

"This has premeditated written all over it," Yetman said at last. "With a spontaneous crime of passion, committed by a jealous lover or unhinged coworker for example, you'd typically see several gunshots. But Jensen was shot once. This killing was efficient. Professional, almost."

"Professional," Lisa said, the word twisting her mouth. "The only professionals who use violence work for Darkstream. I sort of doubt any of our soldiers would do this."

"The murderer is clearly very familiar with firearms. That's all I can say."

Lisa shook her head slowly. "If this wasn't a crime of passion...what could the reason possibly be for killing Jensen? She was a low-ranking Darkstream employee. She only operated a collection node."

"The nodes are fairly important, when you think about it," Yetman said quietly. "One might say they form the basis of our entire society."

"Sure, but I checked the records, and nothing was taken from the zinc shipment that Gatherer brought in. We received exactly the expected amount."

Yetman cleared his throat. "Perhaps you're missing something about the shipments themselves."

"I've already said we aren't missing any zinc."

"Yes, but clearly someone considered that shipment important enough to murder someone over. It likely wasn't about the zinc itself."

Lisa stared at Yetman, blinking. The doctor was clearly getting at something, but Lisa was drawing a complete blank.

"Listen," Yetman said. "What's the main source of crime, around here? What do Darkstream's constables mostly find themselves policing inside Habitat 2?"

"Drugs."

"Exactly."

Lisa glanced to the side, then back to Yetman. She shrugged. "And?"

"Where do you think the drugs come from?"

"They have to be made in a lab. But we've never been able to find one."

"Which is unusual, isn't it? Considering that every square inch of Habitat 2 is accounted for."

"Yeah..."

"Darkstream knows what every chamber is used for. They also know where every kilowatt of energy goes."

Lisa nodded, continuing to stare at Yetman, trying to encourage him to go on. When he didn't, she said, "You're going somewhere with this."

Yetman squinted. "You seriously aren't putting this together?"

"I wasn't trained as a detective."

"Neither was I."

She sniffed. "Fair point."

"The labs must be *outside* of Habitat 2," Yetman said. "And their operators must have figured out a way to smuggle the drugs into Habitat 2 using the Gatherers."

"Yes," Lisa said nodding. "That makes, uh, a lot of sense. Thank you." She grinned, feeling thoroughly sheepish.

"Sure."

"I'd better go, um, continue investigating things. If you find anything else, or come up with—"

"I'll IM you."

"Good. Thanks. Thanks again."

Lisa left the autopsy room, immediately opening a channel with her direct superior, Chief Lannon. As she walked toward her dwelling, she subvocalized a full report.

"Thanks, Sato," he said once she was done. "I'll take it from here."

"All right. What do you plan to do, though? Someone's obviously messing with the Gatherers. That's really worrying."

"I agree. I intend to handle it."

"How, though? Do you see a lead we should follow first?"

"Just leave it to me, okay?"

"I can help, sir."

"Sato, you're in way over your head. What I need you to do is keep your nose clean and leave this alone. All right?"

"Y-yes, sir."

"Good. Lannon out."

Lisa stopped walking, staring into space. A crazy thought had just dawned on her. She had absolutely nothing to base it on, other than a feeling of certainty seated deep in her gut. *Lannon knows something about the murder.*

But there was something else, and this was the crazy part:

Lisa felt sure her boss had been involved with the crime somehow. Which was deeply unsettling, considering Lannon was head of all security for Habitat 2.

CHAPTER 5

Clearly a War Machine

As Peter inspected the mech, running his gloved hands over its ridged surface, his mind mostly drifted to Hub, where his wife and daughter lived.

Hub was the largest settlement out in the Belt. It consisted of several comets strung together with super-strong nanotethers, and its inhabitants hopped between those comets at will, using craft much smaller than the one he and Jake had spent so many months aboard.

The mech put him in mind of the machines Darkstream employees had first encountered on Eresos, and then on Alexandria—the two planets capable of accommodating colonists of any stripe. Those machines had the same scale-like skins of overlapping metal.

Except, internal energy sources animated the machines on the two colony planets, keeping them constantly moving. Peter had been afraid the mech would start to move once they freed it of its icy prison, but it remained inert.

He'd unburied the mech despite that concern and fear for his wife and daughter had made him do it.

What if the Belt holds others mechs? Who knew what they might be capable of, or when they might decide to activate and turn on humanity?

He'd needed to know. So he'd ordered Jake to remain inside the comet hopper, ready to flee at the first sign of danger. And he'd used the excavating equipment they leased from Darkstream to dig up the hulking machine.

Now that he knew there was no apparent danger, Jake stood outside with him, both of them in pressure suits, all but gaping at what they'd uncovered.

The question of where the mech came from ate at him, too. Everyone knew the surrounding stars showed signs of harboring life, though no one spoke of it. Life could easily mean intelligent, hostile life. Had another species been the ones to plant the mech here, and if so, why? Peter didn't trust anything about this situation.

When he'd contacted a Darkstream executive about the mech, she'd ordered him to immediately cease using company equipment to develop the comet until employees arrived to inspect the strange discovery for themselves. But Peter and Jake had kept plenty busy unearthing the thing—or un-icing it, more accurately.

Now that they were finished, they kept themselves occupied by brushing away the remaining flecks of ice, and studying the mech. A process that mostly amounted to staring.

The soft beep of an alert made Peter glance at his HUD's information window, and he saw that the *Javelin*, Bob Bronson's destroyer, had arrived at last.

"They're here," Jake said over a two-way.

Bronson's voice broke into Peter's helmet a second later. "Hi, Peter, Jake. I see you there, next to the mech. I've ordered my Nav officer to trail your comet in heliocentric orbit, and I'm coming over there via shuttle. Peter, I'd ask you to join me aboard the *Javelin* to discuss how we'll proceed."

"What about me?" Jake's voice cut in.

"This is a conversation for your father and I to have, son. I'd ask you to remain inside your comet hopper, well away from the mech, if you please. That'll be enough poking and prodding it."

"It's our mech," Jake said. "We found it. I don't want to wait inside the *Whale*, and I don't have to."

"*Jake*," Peter rebuked his son harshly over the wide channel.

That was enough. Gloved hands balled, Jake stomped across the comet's surface toward their ship's airlock.

Peter waited out on the ice. It took fewer than twenty minutes for Bronson to arrive in what was once a UHF combat shuttle. Now, it belonged to Darkstream. They'd stolen it, essentially.

"Why can't we have our discussion right here?" Peter said once he was aboard, dispensing with formalities. He settled into a crash seat across from Bronson and looked the man in the eye.

Bronson shrugged, the interior lighting playing across his shiny bald head. "We can, if you want. I thought you might prefer the comfort of the *Javelin*'s lounge."

"This is fine. Right here."

"All right, then." Bronson cleared his throat. "Darkstream intends to take the mech, Peter."

"Is that right? What if I won't allow it? The company's entitled to sixty percent of whatever I find. That was the deal when they leased me the equipment. The rest is ours to keep."

"Well, we can hardly take sixty percent of a mech, can we? Not without rendering it useless to either of us. Besides, what use will you have for what is clearly a war machine, Peter? Do you plan to wage a war against someone? You and your son?" Bronson laughed. "Darkstream, though...we can use this. If we can learn its secrets, it could help us protect people from the Quatro. It could save lives, Peter."

Now, it was Peter's turn to laugh—much more bitterly than Bronson. "Darkstream's suddenly become so noble. Fine. You can have the mech. But I expect to be reimbursed for my forty percent."

It's hard enough to make a profit, with the insane portion they take. Both Ingress and Plenitos, Eresos' major cities, had plenty of homeless and starving people as a testament to that fact. Unless you were well-off enough to operate on a medium-to-large scale, it was difficult to prosper when you could only benefit from forty percent of what you produced.

Raising a hand to his stubbled chin, Bronson scratched. "Reimbursing you could prove difficult. When you think about it, the mech is priceless. Considering its value for system security, it's impossible for anyone to calculate its true value. Tell me, are you always this hard-nosed when lives hang in the balance?"

"Cut the crap, Bronson. Hearing a Darkstream executive trying to tell a sob story is like watching a mortician attempt vaudeville. "

"All right, all right. You can't blame me for giving it a shot. Tell you what. I've been authorized to offer you up to two billions credits, and I'm putting the entire amount on the table right now. You can use it to grow your comet development business exponentially, maybe someday buy the equipment you need outright. Then you wouldn't have to give Darkstream their cut. The board has just one condition, though—you have to let me talk to Jake. One-on-one."

"Out of the question." Peter stood from the crash seat, glaring down at Bronson. He was about to leave.

"Now, hear me out, Peter. We know you've been filtering out the recruitment material from Jake's feed. And we've never said anything about that, because it's your prerogative. But I know what this is really about. We consider it unfortunate, what happened to you on Eresos. What you went through. But just because you went through a thing like that doesn't mean Jake will. I only want the opportunity to offer *him* the opportunity of a lifetime. Your son tops the system leaderboards in three different divisions of lucid wargaming. Darkstream has had its eye on him for a long time. I only want the chance to talk with him."

"He's too young, Bronson, not to mention too headstrong to follow orders. And he has too much life to live. He's not ready to have his innocence stripped away by the likes of you."

"Don't be so dramatic, Peter." Bronson sighed, and he actually looked regretful—as though every emotion he'd ever displayed hadn't been an act. Then, he sighed. "All right. If that's the way it's going to be, then we take the mech. No reimbursement. There are clauses in our contract that could easily be interpreted to entitle us to it, anyway. We don't have to interpret them that way, but if you won't play ball, the mech's too important to system security to just leave it languishing on this ice ball."

Peter's fists tightened. He continued to glare at Bronson, saying nothing, because he knew more would be coming. Darkstream always had another play. Always.

"It's too bad, really," Bronson went on. "I understand your daughter is very, very sick. Sue Anne, isn't it? I know she's the reason you do what you do out here, alone in the cold. Two billion could have made sure she got the treatment she needs."

At last, Peter's shoulders slumped. He hadn't meant for them to, but his energy had suddenly bottomed out; his resolve vanished. "I haven't been alone, out here," he muttered, staring at the shuttle's deck. "I've had Jake."

"And you won't be alone going forward. You'll be able to hire a proper crew." Bronson smiled, and when he looked up, Peter saw a glint of victory amidst all the feigned sympathy. "I only want one chance. No one will be forced to do anything. If he doesn't want to join, he doesn't want to join, and you'll still get your money. Even if he says no."

But Peter knew there was zero chance of Jake saying no. He was effectively signing over his son to save his daughter. But maybe, just maybe, Jake would be okay in the Darkstream military.

He didn't really believe that. But perhaps telling himself it would help him sleep at night.

"All right," he said.

CHAPTER 6

Mind on the Mission

Chief Banks gave Gabe command of most of Allendale's garrison, as well as full access to her arsenal. Plus an old tank, which would likely prove next to useless in the forest terrain.

Banks clearly didn't like giving him all that, but she didn't have much choice. Darkstream wanted that Ambler put down.

The giant machine wasn't hard to track. Their usual routes were well-known. They followed Gatherer paths, and Gabe could call those up on his HUD at will.

Of course, that wouldn't do him much good today, because the Ambler had clearly deviated from its programming. Much better to simply use the eyes God had given him, to look at the swath of felled trees that stretched into the distance. They followed that.

Amblers were still as much a mystery to Darkstream as the Gatherers were, along with whoever had made them. When the company's nerds had heard about Gabe and his unit felling one, so many years ago, they'd gotten pretty excited—until they'd learned that Gabe hadn't left much of the thing to study.

What bits of intact circuitry they'd been able to extract had remained inscrutable to them, as far as he knew. Of course, Darkstream wasn't in the business of trumpeting its discoveries. Knowledge was power, and by sharing knowledge, you gave up some power. The company had known that for a long time, and they'd gotten an especially harsh lesson in the truism right before coming to this galaxy.

Either way, Gabe felt fairly confident that Darkstream hadn't figured out how to reproduce the Amblers' lasers. Humanity had been using lasers in space for years to great effect, but hadn't quite figured out how to make them work inside a planet's atmosphere, where a phenomenon called thermal blooming heated the air and caused the laser beam to spread out, neutering its destructive potential.

When it reached the woods, the tank was able to progress a few meters into the trees, but no farther. That didn't come as a surprise.

The trees knocked down by the Ambler had likely posed little problem to *it*—the metal colossus could simply step right over the fallen trunks. Not so, the tank.

Gabe ordered the vehicle back to Allendale while he and his team clambered under and over the weird trees, heads and guns swinging to and fro, HUDs on full-alert.

The trees *still* seemed weird to him. Their cascading waves of bare branches like gnarly fingers, all pointing down at the ground. At the Quatro dens far below, maybe.

And that mildew smell. You couldn't get away from it, not even when you cut the trees back a mile—which every village did, as part of basic defense—not even when you went indoors.

I guess it's better than living on Alex. Small consolation, but it was something.

Sometimes, he missed the Milky Way, though he'd never admit it to anyone. That was not a thing you advertised in the Steele System. Not if you didn't want to become a total pariah.

That said, on occasion, becoming a pariah seemed like kind of an attractive idea.

"Hey," a young seaman apprentice said as he emerged from underneath a canopy of branches nearby. "Do you ever think about the day you set foot on Eresos? Kind of crazy, isn't it, to think you were the first one to—"

Gabe shoved the kid, sending him reeling back a step and nearly causing him to tip backward into the foliage.

"Keep your mind on the mission," Gabe barked. "Chief Banks didn't mention she was sending any morons along with me. If any of the rest of you happen to *be* morons, I recommend you conceal that fact by keeping your stupid mouths shut."

"S-sorry, sir," the seaman apprentice said, gripping his SL-17 tighter and keeping his eyes locked on the path ahead.

After that, Gabe didn't have to put up with any more of that fanboy crap. *Thank God.*

From the Allendale arsenal, Gabe had distributed among his team three rocket launchers, two SAWs, two sniper rifles, a plethora of grenades, thirteen assault rifles, and one heavy machine gun complete with tripod. It turned out they didn't need any of it.

Five miles from the village the Ambler had attacked, they found it sprawled on the ground, surrounded by nearly three dozen Quatro.

Larger than draft horses from Old Earth, most Quatro had royal purple coats, with long, powerful tails and eyes with colors never seen in humans—orange, purple, pink, black. Their bodies had the rough shape of bears, though with longer legs, and their heads resembled panthers.

The autonomous mech had certainly taken out a lot of the aliens, but the fact that the Quatro had won at all spoke to their size, ferocity, and strength. It likely would have taken hundreds of humans to accomplish the same feat without any weapons—if they could have accomplished it at all.

The Quatro's tenacity and power went a long way toward explaining why they were so feared. But it didn't fully explain it. Folks also found their primal nature disturbing. Most people assumed the aliens to be of much lower intelligence than humans, though not without a low cunning.

"That's weird," said the seaman apprentice from before, apparently having found the courage to use his stupid mouth again. Somehow, idiots always did. "Why would the Quatro bother taking on an Ambler? It's not like the machines are going to attack them in their dens. Wouldn't fit through the tunnels."

"Maybe the Ambler attacked *them*," said another Darkstream soldier.

"Yeah, but what were they doing aboveground in such numbers in the first place ?"

"Planning an assault, possibly," Gabe said, and heads swiveled toward him. His words ended the chatter.

"We need to secure the perimeter," he continued. "This is only the second Ambler that's ever been taken down, that I know of, and it's in much better shape than the first. Darkstream will want it for study. Move, people."

CHAPTER 7

Trying Not to Kill

If Chief Lannon had been corrupted somehow, then Lisa wasn't likely to get any help in investigating Jensen's death. Not unless she contacted someone higher-up in Darkstream, and if she did that, her boss would learn about it.

No, the company was now depending on her to find out exactly what was going on in Habitat 2, whether it knew it or not.

Time to go undercover.

She never wore caps, so the baseball hat she put on in front of a mirror in her tiny dwelling worked wonders, in her eyes.

This makes it much less likely I'll get recognized. I'm definitely not a hat person, so...

To make the disguise even better, she let her midnight hair loose, which she never did in public anymore—she always kept it pinned up. Now, it spilled down to brush her shoulders. She'd always liked the way it looked like this, but Darkstream required that long hair be cut or pinned, and she believed in following the rules. She took her job seriously.

Finally, she donned plainclothes instead of her usual Darkstream uniform. Wearing overalls and a plain white tee, she expected to blend right in.

Her investigation would begin in the Swinging Eel. Of Habitat 2's two bars, the Eel was by far the more disreputable. It was also where anyone involved in the drug trade was likely to drink.

The moment she entered and the door swung shut behind her, returning the front room to its former dimness, silence began to wash over the bar, until no one was talking or drinking and everyone was looking at her.

She cleared her throat, offering a grin. *Not so wide,* she told herself, and shrunk the smile a little. Drug smugglers would not smile so big.

Crossing the room to the bar, behind which a woman seemed to be trying to peer into Lisa's soul, she said, "Can I have, um, a whiskey...on the rocks?" She'd been about to order her usual whiskey sour, but had caught herself at the last minute. The drink didn't seem to suit the atmosphere.

"If you have the credits, I have the whiskey," the wiry bartender said, her eyebrows raised.

Drink in hand, Lisa decided to stick to her original plan. She crossed the still-quiet room to a table in the back corner, feeling immensely awkward. It felt like every eye in the bar was following her, and she was pretty sure that feeling wasn't far from the truth.

Sitting with her back to the wall, she studiously avoided eye contact with everyone. Gradually, conversation resumed, though it didn't come anywhere near the dull roar that had preceded the sudden silence.

Someone approached her table, hands on hips. Lisa followed those hips to a stomach, then to a chest, and then to a face.

It was Tessa Notaras.

"Tessa?" she whispered. "*You* drink here?" Lisa felt betrayed, somehow, mostly on Phineas Gage's behalf. How could Tessa give any business to the Swinging Eel when the Dusty Bucket had always treated her so well?

Tessa took a seat right next to her, brushing her swinging white hair out of her face. She'd brought no drink with her. "Did you really consider that an adequate disguise?"

Even at three times Lisa's age at least, Tessa still had plenty of fire in her. Her eyes shone with anger and disbelief as they studied Lisa, who tried not to cower into her seat.

"Tessa...why are you here? Do you drink here a lot?"

"Forget about that. You need to leave, Lisa."

"Why?"

"You're making a lot of people very nervous. You need to get out of here and find somewhere safe to hide. Don't come out until it's all over."

Squinting, Lisa said, "Until *what's* all over?"

Several sharp reports sounded outside, in quick succession. *Gunfire.*

Lisa's hand fled to her pistol, fumbling at it, though she didn't draw. "What was that?" she asked, her voice low and shaky.

Tessa cursed, leaping to her feet. "The answer to your question." She made to run toward the door, but hesitated, glancing back. "Listen, Lisa. Stay here, and stay down. If you're lucky, the fighting won't reach you in here, but you need to stay low and hidden. You're in greater danger than anyone in Habitat 2 right now, okay?"

"Tessa, wait! I'll come with you!"

"Stay here," Tessa hissed, dashing across the room and drawing the twin pistols she kept slung low around her hips.

Lisa's hands trembled around her whiskey. She took a sip, but her mouth twisted, and she placed the drink back on the table, glass knocking against the wood with her shaking.

Less than a minute after Tessa's departure, two groups of people stood up and faced each other across the bar. For the first time, Lisa noticed that there was a distinct divide among the Swinging Eel's clientele. Most of the members of one group wore black armbands and bandannas, and most of the other had their heads shaved, each with a small tattoo somewhere near their right ear.

"Not in here, people," the wiry woman behind the bar yelled. "Please. If my service has meant anything..."

Most of the bar's customers filed outside, then, where the gunfire continued. The two groups kept their distance from each other as they left.

But instead of following the rest, two well-muscled men from the bandanna group broke away from their fellows and approached Lisa.

"You're coming with us," said the taller one on the right. He looked to be of Korean descent, like Lisa.

"No, I'm not." Now Lisa did draw her gun, pointing it at the one who'd spoken and willing it not to tremble.

Gales of laughter burst from both men. Neither had drawn their own guns, though both wore shotguns across their backs.

"Please," said the one on the left, who looked Mexican. "We have no time for comedy. Your colleagues are being taken as we speak. We're trying not to kill Darkstream employees, but we will if we're pressed. We saw Tessa talking to you, but that only gets you so far."

"Tessa? What does she have to do with it?" Lisa knew this was far from the time to ask, but she was suddenly burning with curiosity about the older woman.

The Korean ignored the question, nodding at Lisa's pistol instead. "That's not a toy. Put it down and come quietly so that no one gets hurt who doesn't need to be."

Lisa shook her head, her fear having stolen her ability to speak.

The Mexican stepped forward, wrapped his hand around the gun's barrel, and yanked it from Lisa's grasp. He held it in front of her face, lips curling into a smile. "That was easy."

Why didn't you fire? Lisa demanded of herself. *You were within your rights to fire!*

But she hadn't fired, and she felt completely useless because of that. The idea that she'd been somehow important to the security of Habitat 2 was melting away, and from behind it, the ugly truth was staring her in the face.

The men bracketed her, gripping her firmly by her upper arms. Then they escorted her through the bar and out of a rear exit.

CHAPTER 8

Toe-to-Toe with Beasts

"What do you think?" Bronson asked Jake as they left one of the destroyer's corridors and entered a large room filled with comfortable-looking leather chairs that circled low mahogany tables. A gleaming bar stood at either end of the room.

"What do I think of what?"

Bronson's smile twitched. "My lounge. I had it installed six years ago." The smile widened again, and the destroyer captain continued. "I figured, since Darkstream keeps whittling down my crew for postings elsewhere in the system, why not make the most of it? So I had Engineering study whether this was feasible. Obviously it turned out to be, and I had them come up with a design. Then, I had Maintenance knock out the walls between twelve crew cabins. This was the result. The Starlight Lounge."

"It's cool," Jake said, nodding.

"Thanks." Bronson led Jake toward the bar on the right, and the captain went behind it, selecting a tall, dark bottle and splashing some of its contents into a tumbler. "What can I get for you, Jake? Juice? I assume your father doesn't allow you to drink."

"Yeah. He doesn't."

Bronson's smile took on a mischievous cast. "Well, would you like a drink anyway? He doesn't have to know."

Jake shrugged. "All right."

Splashing some amber liquid into a glass for Jake, Bronson held up his own. It took a second for Jake to figure out what he wanted. He clinked his class against Bronson's, and they both took a swallow.

"Ugh," Jake said, screwing up his face. "Gross."

"You'll get used to it. How old are you, Jake?"

"Seventeen."

"I had my first drink when I was younger. Of course, back where I come from, that was against the law."

"Yeah. I know."

Bronson's eyebrows jacked up a couple notches. "Your father told you about the Milky Way, then?"

"He told me a lot. Told me about Captain Keyes, and the rest."

The captain's tumbler hit the bartop with a *thunk*. "*Did* he?" he said, clearly trying to sound casual, though his voice was strained.

"Yeah. Did you know Captain Keyes?"

The smile grew brittle. "He and I go way back. But let's talk about something else. Let's talk about the reason *you're* here."

Jake held his breath. He thought he knew the reason Bronson had brought him here, and he also knew how he felt about it. But he wasn't certain it was right for him to feel that way.

"How would you like to be a Darkstream soldier, Jake?"

"I'd love to," Jake blurted out. "But...but I don't want to leave my dad alone out here."

"Well, we're planning to buy that mech from your father. Soon enough, he'll be able to hire a whole team. So either way, he won't be alone."

"Yeah. I know. But the reason we're out here is to help Sue Anne, my sister. She has stage four adenosarcoma, and she needs lots of medicine. A lot."

"I'm aware. But after our conversation, I think you'll find that working for Darkstream will be the best thing for your sister, too. You'll be paid handsomely, Jake, and you can do whatever you like with the credits we'll give you. That includes paying for top-tier procedures for Sue Ellen."

"Sue Anne."

"Right. Sorry. Sue Anne."

Jake sighed heavily. His dreams were pulling him one way, while his sense of duty tugged him in the opposite direction. What Bronson said made sense, but his dad had always criticized Darkstream, and Peter also said that what they were doing out in the Belt was best for Sue Anne.

"I just don't know, sir."

"I'll tell you what," Bronson said. "Why don't you take a seat in that recliner just over there." The destroyer captain reached under the bar, producing lucid sleepgear that was sleeker and much less dorky-looking than Jake's. "We have a special simulation that we only use for certain recruits. I want you to try it out. Go lucid for just ten minutes. At the end of it, I'll wake you, and I won't say anything else. I think you'll have enough to make your decision, then."

Jake took a seat, and Bronson slipped the headgear over his skull, positioning the electrodes so that they were spaced more or less evenly across his scalp.

He was too excited to get to sleep, so Bronson handed him a light sedative. That did it. He slipped into lucid and found himself piloting a powerful mech.

The machine conformed to his movements, offering just enough resistance to make the controls intuitive and realistic. Jake's strength was amplified a hundredfold at least, and the HUD exceeded anything his v-lenses were capable of. It showed Ixa piloting mechs of their own, fighting in an urban landscape populated by towering buildings and looming warehouses.

He'd run similar simulations in lucid before, but nothing this detailed, and nothing with such an advanced, intuitive interface.

Jake led a team of fellow mech pilots, and together they rampaged through the city, saving the populace from the mechanized Ixa.

The most memorable moments included punching an Ixan mech in what would have been its sternum, sending it hurtling from a seven-story building, and corralling an enemy grouping of three mechs using rockets alone, which bought enough time for some nearby civilian office workers to reach safety.

Historically, the Ixa had never had mechs, but as always happened in lucid, Jake's brain accepted the simulation as total reality. That was the strength of using dreams to run sims. The fear was real, and so was the sense of victory when Jake and his mechanized companions smashed unit after enemy unit until they were slag.

Ten minutes of lucid felt like hours, subjectively, and when Bronson finally removed the headgear, bringing Jake back to reality, he felt like he'd had a good run with the new tech. Of course, he also felt ready to go back for hours more.

But he didn't say so. He wanted to keep his cool in front of the destroyer captain.

"What did you think?"

"It was awesome!" Jake blurted. *So much for keeping my cool.* He coughed. "I loved the thermal lances for breaching bay doors, and the HUD was out of this world, but..."

"But?"

"Well, why did the sim only have me piloting mechs? I would have expected a sim designed for Darkstream recruits to be more well-rounded than that."

"I told you. This is designed for certain recruits only. Recruits with the skills to become mech pilots, namely."

"But Darkstream doesn't have any mechs."

"That's true, we don't. Yet." Bronson drew a long breath, his shoulders rising and falling. Jake got the sense that the old man felt almost as excited as he did. "Can you keep a secret, Jake?"

"Yes, sir."

"Good. Because what I'm about to tell you is classified. Darkstream has long had a program to develop viable mechs. They would be the perfect weapon against the Quatro, who currently overpower us. Yes, enough bullets will take them down, but they're remarkably resilient, and if one of them reaches you, well...it's lights out, isn't it? And we can't very well bomb the Quatro from orbit, because we'd risk damaging the planet that's best-suited for human colonization. We'd risk damaging the Gatherers, who have become so important to our industrial base. No, what we really need is a brand new war machine that can go down to the planet's surface and stand toe-to-toe with the beasts."

"Mechs."

"Yes. We need to win this fight on the ground, and mechs may be our only way to do it. You and your father finding this mech, way out here—it was an amazing stroke of luck. It's almost as important a discovery as the Gatherers. We haven't been able to create a viable mech, for multiple reasons, but now that we've found one, we know it's truly possible. By studying it, we can improve our own designs, and hopefully, before long, we can start producing them. The reason that sim put you in a mech the entire time is because your lucid scores are high enough that if you make it through Darkstream's training, you could conceivably pilot a mech. How does *that* sound, Jake?"

Jake's breath came much heavier, now. He tried to sort out his thoughts, tried to identify the right thing to do. But it was no clearer than before.

It didn't matter. One thing was clear: there was no way he could say no to the chance to drive a real-life mech. It was the ultimate incarnation of his lifelong dream to join Darkstream's military. Saying no simply wasn't an option anymore.

"I'm in," Jake said. "I'm in."

CHAPTER 9

Confession

The goons dragged Lisa through Habitat 2, avoiding streets with fighting. They both had their guns drawn now, and they seemed to pay more attention to the city's dark places—its smaller streets, its shadowy canopies, its alleys—than they did to Lisa.

That made sense to her, now that she knew she posed no threat to them whatsoever. Even if she'd still had her gun, they probably would have disarmed her just as easily as before.

I'm a total failure. A fraud.

If her captors noticed her dejection, they didn't remark on it. Instead, they brought her into a low building, whose door opened onto two short rows of poorly made cots. A kitchen followed, and then a set of stairs, and then Lisa was in a squat storage basement, with narrow, street-level windows filled with thick glass.

She had the presence of mind to wait a few minutes after her kidnappers' departure before seeking a way out.

She threw herself against the door they'd left through, but it didn't budge, and trying the handle produced no results.

A cursory glance at the horizontal slits the room had for windows showed that even if she could shatter their glass, there was no way she would squeeze through them. Knocking on them generated only a dull *thud*—no one outside would hear, especially not over the shooting, which continued still.

A man ran by with two children in tow, and Lisa waved at them frantically, but they took no notice of her or even of the building that was her prison. For all she knew, the windows were one-way.

Before long, she gave up, sitting on a long crate and taking stock of her surroundings.

Nothing that shouted criminality drew her attention. There were a few guns, but none of them had any ammo. Besides, anyone was allowed to carry pretty much any firearm, wherever they wanted in the Steele System.

That gave her hope. If the criminal element was taking over Habitat 2, then maybe its residents would find the strength to fight back.

She tried to imagine Phineas Gage holding a gun. Or worse, Bob O'Toole. Her shoulders slumped once more.

Dragging together some empty sacks to make a bed, she fell into them, awaiting her fate. Hopefully the men who'd brought her here weren't killed. That would be even worse than facing them again: starving to death down here, alone, forgotten.

Memories of her family came flooding back to her. They were in Kuiper Belt 2, or the Belt, as most of its residents called it. She'd been born in Hub, the de facto capital of the Belt, and she'd hated the close quarters there. The closed-in world, the ability to look directly up and see what your upside-down neighbors were doing...

Now, she wished she'd never left.

The door opened, and Lisa leapt to her feet instinctively.

This is it. She was ready to fight, this time. *I won't stay down here any longer.* If she had to take down several muscled goons, she didn't care. She'd do it. She would.

Tessa Notaras descended the stairs into the basement, clutching a pistol in each hand. When she saw Lisa, she came to a halt.

"Tessa," Lisa said. "What's going on?"

Glancing behind her, the white-haired woman motioned with one of the guns. "Come on. We have to go."

"I'm not going anywhere. Not until you tell me what the *hell* is happening to Habitat 2." Lisa wanted to stamp her foot, but it seemed like it might come off as childish. A real soldier would rely on the authority of her commanding voice alone.

But am I a real soldier? She didn't think so. Not anymore.

"Fine." Tessa turned around and ascended the stairs.

"Wait," Lisa said. "Okay. I'll come!"

The sound of the door clicking shut reached her ears, and Tessa reappeared. "Calm down. I was just securing the door." She reached the basement and crossed the room, placing her pistols on the crate Lisa had first sat on and taking a seat beside them. "Are you okay?"

"Yes. I'm fine. Are...are you?"

"Yeah. I guess." Tessa sniffed. "I need to make this quick, because we're very short on time. Listen carefully, okay?"

"Okay."

"The drug trade in Habitat 2 is controlled by two rival gangs. One gang just went to war with the other, and the worst of the two won. That gang, called Daybreak, now control Habitat 2. Their leader is Quentin Cooper, and he's a ruthless bastard. If we stay here long enough, he'll find us."

"How do you know all that?"

"Because I work for Three Points, Lisa. The gang that lost this fight."

Lisa studied Tessa's lined face. "You're serious, aren't you?" She shook her head. "How could you, Tessa?"

"Because the gangs are the only meaningful opposition Darkstream faces on Alex. And I have a lot of hangups when it comes to my old employer. Listen, why do any of us do what we do? I needed the credits, for one. But that doesn't matter right now."

"It matters a lot, actually. Darkstream will send troops soon to liberate the town, and when they do, it's my job to report your confession, Tessa." Lisa sighed. She really liked Tessa. Even despite what she'd just learned about her. Maybe there was some way to get some leniency for her. "If you cooperate, it's possible they'll reduce your punishment."

Tessa chuckled. "You're cute, Lisa. I wouldn't hold your breath on Darkstream liberating anyone. The company's negotiating with Daybreak right now."

"Negotiating what?"

"The terms of their occupation. That's been Daybreak's plan from the start. Take over Habitat 2, make themselves rich, and keep Darkstream happy by giving them an even bigger cut of the resources collected than they were getting before. If Habitat 2's residents become slaves, their standard of living can go down. It'll no longer matter whether they're happy—just that they have whatever scraps are necessary for survival. Meaning more resources, for the gang and for Darkstream."

"That's ridiculous. Darkstream would never allow that to happen. It would destroy their public image."

"They'll play it off like they had no choice. Maybe say something about the gang threatening to blow up the habitat if they tried to intervene. Something like that."

"I won't believe it."

"Believe it, honey. It's happening."

Lisa stood. "We have to do something. Darkstream will come soon, but we're no use to them in captivity, or dead. Maybe...maybe we could make it to Habitat 1. Recruit some reinforcements, to come back and help my colleagues retake this Habitat once they arrive."

Joining her in standing, Tessa said, "Leaving certainly seems like a good idea. For us both. They'll kill me if they find me, and they may kill you, if your employer doesn't bother to negotiate for your release."

Shaking her head, Lisa marveled at how brainwashed Tessa was. She'd had no idea that the old woman had drunk so deeply from the anti-corporate lemonade.

"Andy Miller does supply runs between here and the space elevator all the time," Lisa said. "If we can reach him, convince him to help—"

"Oh, we'll convince him," Tessa said, scooping up her pistols in one fluid motion. "One way or another." She grinned. "Grab some weapons and let's go. There should be ammo upstairs."

For their part, the guards busied themselves with removing Warren's handcuffs and settling him into the chair, which they strapped him to. A remote control dangling from the chair's side lowered it, until Warren lay perfectly horizontal.

Nanite injection was said to be the most humane method of executing someone ever invented. Tens of thousands of microscopic robots swarmed throughout your body, coating your vital organs. Then, at a command, they burrowed down—into your stomach, into your heart, into your brain. Death in an instant.

But could any method of killing truly be called humane? Other than the fact of the killing itself, there was no way to know how it actually felt to die from a legion of tiny robots shredding your organs. Not until it happened to you, and you couldn't exactly describe the experience afterward.

Caine took Husher's hand as the needle sunk into Warren's arm and the technician depressed the plunger. A mere ten seconds later, the technician produced a tablet, which she tapped twice.

Warren Husher's entire body surged upward against the restraints—once. Then he fell still, and Husher's father was no more.

CHAPTER 10

White and Scarlet

Gabe watched the woods roll by as the armored personnel carrier trundled along the Gatherer path, much slower than the speeders most civilians used. For vehicles this size, it was much more efficient to use old-fashioned wheels than to try to make it hover. But it sure made for a slower trip.

So did having to delay their departure from Allendale, because of an Ambler patrolling the path between there and Northshire.

Luckily, this one was functioning properly, and it didn't go on a rampage. Instead, it turned onto a connecting Gatherer path, following the same circuitous route it had followed since Darkstream had first mapped this planet and documented the predictable behavior of its high-tech inhabitants.

Once the Ambler left the route between Northshire and Allendale, it was finally safe for Gabe and the others from the Northshire garrison to head back toward their original posting.

Part of him was anxious to get back, to see Jess, and part of him was extremely hesitant—to face Jess's father, Mayor

Sweeney. Had she successfully hidden their encounter from him? And did Gabe really want her to?

Over the years, there'd been no shortage of young women throwing themselves at him. Probably because of his fame as the first man to set foot on Eresos, and also his role in carving out a foothold for humanity on the planet, though no one fully knew what he'd had to do to accomplish that.

Mostly, he'd rebuffed their advances, but sometimes not. He led a lonely life. Most professional soldiers did; there was no hiding that fact. And sometimes the urge roared louder than his willpower.

But even the ones he'd lain with had amounted to nothing but a flash in the pan, and he doubted they'd been any more upset about his eventual departure than he was.

Jess, on the other hand...Jess was different. He couldn't quite say why, but no one had ever set his heart to racing like she did. She made bizarre thoughts parade through his head. Thoughts of trying to change, of quitting Darkstream, of settling down.

He'd done some awful things, in this galaxy and the one he'd left behind. Could there be redemption for a man like him? Was there such a thing as cleaning a blood-covered slate?

Suddenly, his implant HUD washed red. Considering they'd dialed them back from full-alert mode, the fact that this notification was getting through meant that it was serious, and also that it directly pertained to them.

Sure enough: "QUATRO ATTACKING NORTHSHIRE. REPAIR TO POSTING IMMEDIATELY."

His heart tried to crawl up his throat and out of his mouth. "We only left Robinson and Sawyer there," he choked out. "They'll be completely overwhelmed."

The driver, Seaman Morrissey, cursed softly.

"Don't just sit there, you idiot!" Gabe yelled. "Step on it!"

Morrissey did, and the personnel carrier lurched forward, doubling its speed. That still wasn't very fast.

Gabe felt like he could get out and *run* quicker than this. He knew that wasn't true, but watching those weird trees crawl by, it sure felt like it!

"*Faster!*" Gabe barked.

"Sir, this vehicle was not designed to go any faster than this on an uneven dirt surface. To avoid tipping over, I strongly recommend—"

"I don't give a shit what you recommend, Morrissey. I'm ordering you to go faster!"

The seaman accelerated, and the vehicle didn't tip. Eresos' strange forests sped by faster, and with Gabe's constant urging, they began to blur.

At last, Northshire drew into sight.

By then, of course, it was far too late.

The personnel carrier barreled past burning buildings on the village's perimeter. Nearer the village green, the Darkstream self-erecting structures had fared better.

Not so, the people of Northshire. Bodies were strewn everywhere—all over the green, between buildings, on doorsteps. Gabe saw Toby Horton draped over a fence surrounding a garden. His blue overalls were soaked red.

The personnel carried ground to a halt, and Gabe threw open the door, not bothering to close it behind him. He ran through the village toward the mayor's residence, SL-17 at the ready, legs pumping as hard as he could force them to. Blood surged through his veins like molten lava.

A white shape caught his eye, and he came to an abrupt halt. The white of a summer dress. Stained with the scarlet smear of blood.

He dropped to his knees roughly five meters from the body of Jess Sweeney. His assault rifle tumbled to the grass.

He had no idea how long he remained there, staring at Jess's corpse.

The blast of a gunshot brought him back to his senses. It had come from inside the Sweeney residence.

Gabe forced himself to move. Just inside the house, he found what remained of Mayor Sweeney, sitting in a plain, wooden chair. He'd lodged the barrel of a shotgun under his chin and pulled the trigger with his toe. His face was gone.

Stumbling out of the house. Stumbling through the village, past pock-marked metal structures, past burning wooden ones.

Unsure where he was going.

He came to a halt again, hands on knees, and his breakfast of eggs with hot sauce came steaming up his throat and onto the neatly clipped grass. Then came the retching. And the tears.

"Pioneer," someone croaked.

It was Seaman Sawyer. Horse. Lying sprawled near the bay doors where Gatherers entered and exited the collection facility. His torso mangled.

Gabe went to him.

"They had guns, Pioneer. Guns."

"What? How'd they hold them? How'd they pull the trigger?" Quatro had only paws, with no opposable thumbs.

This makes absolutely zero sense. The aliens weren't known to possess technology of any level. Just their sheer size, brute strength, and low cunning. And yet...

"The guns were strapped—mounted, like—on their backs," Sawyer said. "As for how they fired them..." Horse shook his head, which looked like it took more effort than it needed to.

"I'm going to get you help, Horse. Don't move."

Gabe pushed a hand through his short hair as he jogged away. None of this made any sense.

But in the end, it didn't matter. Guns or no guns, technology or none, it didn't matter.

He intended to make the Quatro pay.

CHAPTER 11

Pockets of Resistance

The gang that had taken over Habitat 2 still hadn't secured their hold over it. Pockets of resistance remained, with bullets being traded intermittently.

The city's artificial night was falling, which coincided with Alex's actual night. That made Lisa's and Tessa's job easier, as they crept from doorway to dumpster to alley, waiting for the way to clear before moving ahead to stop again and wait.

Residents were still getting dragged violently from their homes. Sometimes, that was the source of the gunfire.

Lisa clamped a hand to her mouth as she watched a bandanna-clad Daybreak goon forcing a man to his knees in front of his home. Casually, the thug drew his pistol and put a bullet in the back of his victim's head. He walked away, leaving the body to cool in the street.

As Lisa and Tessa passed the dead man, Lisa glanced down and recognized him. He was Jordan Lee, a councilman. It seemed the gangsters were executing anyone important to Habitat 2's civil power structure.

"They'll face big consequences for this," she subvocalized to Tessa.

"Maybe. Cooper's the kind of man who'll call any bluff, whether it's actually a bluff or not. He's willing to reach for anything he wants, and he leaves it to his adversaries to try and stop him. Normally, they don't dare."

Lisa sent Andy an IM ahead of time, and when they reached him he was ready, opening his door to admit them and closing it just as quickly once they were inside.

He wore a grim expression as he eyed their weapons briefly, then turned back to the bags he was in the process of stuffing full of clothes and other personal effects.

"I see you have the same idea we do," Tessa said, watching the vid feed that showed the street in front of the residence.

"You got that right," he said. "Somehow, I doubt I'd keep my position in the new order. I don't think the gangsters will trust me to do supply runs for them."

Lisa scrutinized his expression. "Would you work for them even if they did trust you?"

Andy paused his packing to meet her gaze, frowning slightly. "Of course not, Lisa." He continued packing.

"It's still possible Darkstream will negotiate with Daybreak for their employees back," Tessa said, never taking her eyes off the street outside.

"I'd say it's likely," Andy said.

"Exactly," Lisa put in. "Because it's the right thing to do."

"No," he said with a chuckle. "Because if it gets out that they abandoned their employees to live as slaves, they'll suddenly find the labor market much less accommodating to their needs. Even so, I'm not willing to take any chances. I'm leaving within the hour."

"Darkstream will come for their employees, Andy. They will. They'll do right by us."

"Don't be naive, Lisa."

"Screw you."

That brought another chuckle. "Spitey as always."

"Cut the squabbling, children," Tessa said, her tone flat. "Andy, how likely are we to secure a beetle?"

"How good are you with those pistols?"

"Good enough."

"I hope so. Because I'm sure the beetle bays were the first thing Daybreak locked down."

Andy finished packing, then slung the enormous, overstuffed duffel bag over his shoulder.

"The definition of stealth," Lisa said, quirking an eyebrow at him.

"Oh, I'm sure *you'll* keep me safe," he said, his voice dripping with sarcasm.

Somehow, they managed to make it to the western beetle bay without drawing unwanted attention. Maybe the gangsters figured no one would be brazen enough to attempt stealing a beetle.

Tessa drew up beside Lisa. "Can you patch the bay's vid feed through to my implant?"

"Uh...yeah. Sure." The idea of using her Darkstream security clearance to help a confessed criminal didn't appeal to her very much, but Lisa couldn't see an alternative.

After a few seconds of studying the feed, Tessa nodded. "Okay. Open it up, Lisa, and stay out here with Andy."

"Are you serious? I can help!" She hefted the SL-17 she'd taken from the basement where Tessa had found her, to help make her point.

Tessa locked eyes with her. "Stay here with Andy."

"Fine," she said, her voice coming out more sullen than she'd wanted. But she wasn't about to oppose Tessa when she gave her that look. In fact, she didn't know of anyone who ever did. Not anyone who'd made it through the experience unharmed, anyway.

Lisa opened the entrance to the beetle bay, which disappeared upward into its casing. Producing a flashbang, Tessa tossed it inside, then pressed her back to the wall near the entrance.

Lisa took cover herself, looking away, but she still saw the bright flash of light, and the loud *crack* reached her ears, amplified by the hollow of the bay. When she looked again, Tessa was already inside, her pistols firing in tandem.

Five gunshots later, the white-haired former Darkstream soldier emerged, nodding at Lisa and Andy. "Clear."

They both followed Tessa into the beetle bay, where four of the awkward-looking vehicles awaited them in a neat grid. There were also five bandanna-wearing thugs sprawled on the ground, each sporting a bullet hole in their skulls.

"Wow," Andy said. "Good work."

"Just do your job, beetle jockey. Take your pick of these wrecks."

"Yes, ma'am. I pick the wreck closest to the exit."

"Good choice."

Andy had sufficiently high security clearance to open the beetle's rear hatch, which lowered to become an entrance ramp.

They strode up it, and Lisa used her clearance to open the wide portal into the airlock.

CHAPTER 12

Accelerate Vengeance

Gabe hoisted the thermobaric grenade launcher onto his shoulder and dropped to one knee, lining up the arc of his shot with care. He really didn't want to mess this up. Not with Darkstream troops milling all around the area, making sure no Quatro escaped.

"Careful, son," Commander Bob Bronson said, behind him and somewhere to the left. "That's a fuel-air explosive you're about to deploy."

"Yes, sir. I've fired them many times before, back in the Bastion Sector. I know the risks."

"Good. We want to set the air *they're* breathing on fire, not ours," Bronson said with a chuckle. "Are you ready?"

I think so. "Yes, sir."

"Then fire."

Gabe did, angling the launcher upward, bracing for the kickback, and pulling the trigger. The grenade left the launcher's tube with a *whoosh.* He watched it arc toward the mouth of the cave system where this group of Quatro had made their home.

"Right on the money," Bronson said. "Hit them again."

Without warning, everything shifted, and Gabe was inside the caves themselves, among the Quatro.

He heard the first grenade quietly skitter across the rocks near the cave mouth. Several giant Quatro heads swung toward the sound, gazing warily into the darkness.

Then came the explosion, rapidly converting the world into flame and death.

A fiery shockwave tore through cave after cave. Those Quatro closest to the bomb were simply incinerated, while those farther in caught fire, their burning fur reeking.

The bomb consumed the air for its fuel, in an explosion that never seemed to end.

Even those farthest from the explosion would suffer countless internal injuries—concussions, burst ear drums, ruptured lungs. Blindness. If any of the Quatro or their pups managed to escape the endless barrage, they would limp away with maladies they'd likely carry for the rest of their lives.

Gabe bolted upright amidst sweaty, tangled blankets.

Another nightmare. As it receded, he recalled that his life had also become a nightmare, of sorts.

Jess. The thought of her made him want to stay inside and weep. But there was work to do.

The smell of perfume still clung to the sheets he'd shared with her just two nights before. Trying his best to ignore it, he pulled himself out of bed and started getting dressed.

Yesterday had been a day of searching for survivors and burying the dead. Today would be one for figuring out exactly what had happened during the Quatro attack on Northshire.

And why.

To that end, Darkstream was sending a team of analysts down from Valhalla. If Gabe were to guess, he'd say the team would likely focus on the fact that the Quatro had shown up with *guns*, when it had always seemed like a given that the aliens couldn't possibly operate technology of any kind, due to the simple facts of their anatomy. Their paws weren't evolved to grasp anything—case closed. At least, it should have been closed.

Gabe felt like his skin concealed a vast well of emptiness inside him. Only bitterness could fill that void, if he let it. But he couldn't. Not yet.

However they did it, the Quatro have shown their true nature. We haven't touched them for years, and then they did this to us. Slaughtered the people of Northshire. Took Jess from me forever.

He'd gotten one night with her. Just one. After months of glances stolen across the oaken dining table, at meals with the mayor and his family. Months of chance meetings on the village green, paired with sly winks and wry remarks from Jess, which had always left him blinking, baffled.

More importantly, it had left him *feeling* something. That had always been a rarity, for Gabe. But Jess had managed it.

No more.

He'd been such a coward. Their difference in age should have meant nothing to him. He should have cast aside his career the moment they'd met, spirited her away to...somewhere. Anywhere. It shouldn't have mattered. But it had. And now she was gone.

Cursing quietly, he left his private quarters and headed down the path into the village, the one he'd walked every day during happier times. Hopefully, he wouldn't have to walk it for much longer. He wanted to leave Northshire behind and never return.

At the village green, he found the team of company analysts had already arrived and were inspecting everything there was to inspect.

"Anything I can do to help?" he asked after walking up to one of them.

"Secure the perimeter. And try to do a better job of it, this time."

It took everything Gabe had not to knock the little weasel to the ground. "I was ordered away," he growled. "Darkstream ordered me away."

"Whatever."

Gabe stalked off, his chest rising and falling rapidly with rage. Almost, he turned around to attack the cretin who'd tried to lay Jess's death at his feet.

This wasn't Gabe's fault. It was the Quatro. It was the Ambler's who'd attacked Allendale. But it wasn't his.

Or is it? a tiny voice asked.

He decided to check on Seaman Sawyer, who had managed to survive his injuries and was recovering in the infirmary. Doctor

Poe even said he might be battleworthy again, after a few months.

But before Gabe reached the infirmary, a message came in over the system-net, glowing yellow in the upper-right corner of his HUD. He willed it to open, and it did.

Captain Bob Bronson's face appeared, hovering over reality. That gave Gabe a start, given how recently he'd seen that face, in his nightmare. And how long it had been since he'd seen it in real life.

"Roach," Bronson said. "I have a proposition for you. The company made a strange discovery, out in Kuiper Belt 2. We found a mech, and it's pretty clear that whoever built the Gatherers also built this thing. It means a huge leap forward in Darkstream's own attempts to build one, and we expect to have a working model soon. A unit's worth of them, shortly after that."

Bronson grinned. "We have a lot of viable candidates to pilot them, but they're mostly untrained scrubs who score highly on the relevant lucid leaderboards. We need somebody who can whip them into shape, fast. That somebody's you, Roach. We know you have the chops for it, and we also know you like being the first to do things. At least, if you're the same man I remember, you do. This is classified for now, but the public will learn about it soon enough, and we expect having your name attached to the project will make for decent PR.

"This goes without saying, but the mechs should give us a huge advantage against the Quatro. And it seems like we'll need that, given how feisty they've become. Take a day to think about it, if necessary, but no longer than that. I need to know your answer soon. Bronson out."

"Feisty," Gabe muttered. That was one word for what the Quatro had done.

He already knew his answer to Bronson's proposal. He would take the job.

Vengeance was all he had left, now, and it seemed likely this opportunity would accelerate that cause nicely.

That was all he needed.

CHAPTER 13

Beetle

A ndy tried to radio Habitat 1 for what seemed to Lisa like the twentieth time. Still no luck.

He sighed. "Either we're specifically being locked out of the com satellites, or the entire system-net is down."

That brought a grunt from Tessa, who sat in the seat opposite Lisa's. "I'm not sure which possibility is more alarming right now."

"Indeed."

Tessa returned to whatever she'd been doing on her implant—reading a book, probably. They'd been fleeing Habitat 2 for two days, but for Lisa, those days had felt like weeks.

It didn't help that it also felt like the beetle was crawling. Andy assured her that any pursuers would be traveling just as slowly. If they knew what they were doing, anyway.

The terrain of Alex would punish the unwary, Andy said, opening a ravine beneath their wheels when they least expected it, or upending them with rocks that looked as though they should have posed no problem.

Darkstream had plans to eventually terraform the planet, but currently they didn't have the extra resources to devote to the effort. So for now, Alex would remain as she was. Beautiful but forbidding. Harsh. Blue.

Everything natural on Alex was mostly the same sapphire hue, and so was the dust that kicked up and clogged suit valves and engines. Even travelers following the strictest protocols would eventually find everything they owned coated in a growing layer of blue dust.

The beetle boasted a number of tricks for navigating the treacherous landscape. Perhaps the most important feature was its individually articulated wheels, which allowed it to "walk" over rocks that would otherwise impede it. Almost as crucial was the jointed arm mounted in front of the crew cabin, for rolling rocks out of the way.

They were headed for Habitat 1, which was one of only four permanent habitats Darkstream had established on Alex. It had taxed the system's economy and industrial base to get just those four up and running, but they more than paid for themselves, now. They had the endlessly toiling Gatherers to thank for that.

Lisa felt embarrassed at the realization that she'd never taken enough of an interest in the geography of Alex to figure out how far away Habitat 1 was. She vaguely knew that 3 and 4 were well out of reach, and separated from the first two by a gargantuan canyon that stretched across half the planet and was basically impassable.

But she didn't have a good idea of how far 1 was from 2. Ever since she'd been assigned to provide security for the businesses and inhabitants of Habitat 2, she'd focused on the particulars of the job, not on the planet that existed outside it.

Eventually, as much as she hated to admit her ignorance to Andy, she decided to just ask. "How long will it take for us to reach Habitat 1?"

Andy seemed too focused on navigation to bring his usual snark to bear, thankfully. "I've never made the trip. I've only gone to the space elevator and back, and that's roughly equidistant between the two Habitats."

"How long does that trip take, then?"

"Three months, if you're going at a sane speed. Which we will be."

"I'm guessing by 'sane' you mean slow as hell."

"If you consider our current speed to be slow as hell, then yes. And we can assume the rest of the trip to Habitat 1 will take about as long again."

Shaking her head, Lisa said, "Why did they put the elevator so far away?"

Tessa snorted. "Well, the official explanation for that is the company could only afford to build two of them on Alex, so they put them equidistant between each pair of habitats. But that's bull. The real reason is so the habitat residents can't easily mount an offensive on the elevator, should they ever become disgruntled enough with their lot."

That brought a short, awkward silence, and Lisa wondered whether Andy found Tessa's conspiracy theories as off-putting as she did.

She decided not to engage with Tessa's paranoia. "Why don't we just go as far as the elevator?" she asked instead. "We can take that up to orbit and ask Darkstream for help."

That made Andy glance back at her. "You seriously don't know?"

Lisa suppressed the urge to frown. It wasn't hard to see that she was about to feel stupid again.

"What?" she said, her voice small.

"Darkstream maintains a minimal security presence on the orbital station at the top of the elevator. Definitely not enough to retake Habitat 2, if that's what you're hoping. The company only uses it as a pickup point for the resources we produce and a drop-off point for supplies. Us beetle drivers do the dirty work of hauling both back and forth."

"So..."

"So, if we're going anywhere, it's all the way to Habitat 1, across the most treacherous terrain humanity has ever willingly subjected itself to. Buckle up."

CHAPTER 14

Your Favorite Video Game Character

Captain Bronson invited Jake to the CIC to watch their approach to Valhalla Station. He even let Jake sit in the Captain's Chair, while Bronson stood off to one side of the main viewscreen, hands curled at his sides.

Jake accepted both offers, though he kind of felt like he was being treated like a giddy little kid.

It surprised him that Bronson would let him inside the CIC at all. Overall, protocol seemed fairly lax aboard the *Javelin.*

I guess that's what comes of not having any enemy ships to fight for almost twenty years.

Those thoughts fled Jake's mind the moment Bronson ordered his sensors operator to magnify their view of Valhalla Station. His breath caught in his throat, then.

The structure dwarfed any warship he'd ever seen in vids or heard about, including even the *Providence,* the last supercarrier humanity had ever built—at least, as far as anyone in the Steele System knew.

Valhalla had four main sections that spread out from a central core, like two sets of wings. The orbital station was all sweeping curves and no edges. It maintained a geosynchronous orbit over Eresos, and the planet's single space elevator extended down from Valhalla's center, until it became a near-invisible ribbon that vanished beneath a pillowy cloud cover.

"It's massive," Jake said.

Bronson turned to him. "You've never left Kuiper Belt 2, have you?"

"Huh? Oh. No, I've been in the Belt ever since I was born."

"Well, lucky for you, you'll experience exactly the same gravity here as you did there, thanks to the healthy Ocharium stores we brought with us when we first traveled to the Steele System."

"That's good," Jake said.

Bronson nodded. "Enjoy it while it lasts. Soon, we'll be injecting you with extra Ocharium nanites, to get you accustomed to the heavier gravity of Eresos."

"Yes, sir."

The more Ocharium nanites his body had, the more it would attract the fermion matrix that infused every ship's deck, as well as all of Valhalla's flooring. Jake didn't look forward to the experience of having more weight to carry around.

Using Ocharium and fermions to simulate gravity was an example of dark tech, which also permitted the generation of wormholes—that was how Darkstream had reached the Steele System in the first place.

Back in the Milky Way, Darkstream had learned that humanity's use of dark tech was actually unraveling the fabric of the universe, and so since arriving here they'd wound down their use of dark tech by a lot. They'd scrapped the wormholes, along with the micronet that had once enabled instantaneous communication.

That said, they still used it for gravity, figuring that since theirs was a relatively small fraction of humanity, that should result in minimal danger. In the short- and medium-term, at least.

It's possible that we're not *a fraction of humanity, of course. If the Ixa won the war, we might now be* all *of humanity. And if it's true that the nearby stars could also hold powerful adversaries...*

Jake decided to abandon that line of thought. Bronson's Coms officer communicated with a space traffic controller on Valhalla, who informed them that Landing Bay Theta was ready to receive them.

Fewer than thirty minutes later, Bronson and Jake were exiting a shuttle's airlock inside the designated landing bay.

A tall man with a hard face met them outside the airlock. Short black hair stood at attention above a creased brow, which overshadowed a hooked nose.

Jake cursed, drawing a sharp look from Bronson. "Sorry, sir. B-but that's...that's Gabriel Roach!"

"Ah. Yes. I take it you're a fan?"

Since leaving his father's comet hopper to journey into the inner system aboard the *Javelin*, Jake had attempted to display the proper deference toward officers, which he knew would be expected of him at all times once he enlisted. But he often slipped, and now was no different.

Ignoring Bronson's question, Jake stepped toward Roach, his entire body vibrating. "E-excuse me, sir, but...could I have your autograph?"

Eyes widening and mouth twisting, Roach surged forward to grab Jake by the lapels, driving him backward until his back collided with the side of the shuttle. Pain shot through his torso, and he winced.

Bronson observed the ordeal impassively, hands folded behind his back.

"What's your name, boy?" Roach said softly, his voice dripping with menace.

"J-Jake Price, sir."

"Listen to me, Price. You will never ask me for anything again, least of all my *autograph.* I'm not your favorite video game character, nor am I your favorite movie star. From this day forward, I am *merely* your instructor and your superior officer, and you will *merely* follow every order I give you without question. Is that clear?"

"Yes, sir." Jake was still shaking, but with an entirely different emotion, now.

"Perfect." Roach released him, and Jake slumped against the shuttle. He quickly righted himself, his cheeks burning.

Roach stood with his back to him now, facing Bronson.

"You didn't have to be so hard on him right off the bat," the destroyer captain said, in a tone one might use to inform a server that he'd brought the wrong type of cheesecake.

"Sir, I can be hard on him now or the Quatro can tear him limb from limb upon their first encounter."

"That seems a bit dramatic."

"I'm sure it does seem dramatic, to a man who watches people bleed and die for him from space."

Bronson blinked, but offered no other reaction. Even so, Jake got the sense that Roach would pay for the disrespect he'd shown today.

Roach paused to speak to a man standing at attention nearby, who Jake hadn't noticed until now.

"Wipe the kid's nose for him and then show him his quarters. If he already wants to run back to his mother, send him out on the next shuttle."

"Yes, sir."

With that, Gabriel Roach left Landing Bay Theta.

CHAPTER 15

Burpee

Andy claimed that he was capable of simultaneously finding the safest path over Alex's surface, attempting to establish communications with Habitat 1, and keeping an eye on satellite images of the surrounding area. Even so, he delegated the latter two tasks to Lisa most of the time.

"I can do the multitasking, but it'll be better for all of us if I don't have to," he said.

As for why Andy could access satellite imagery but not the system-net, well, that was another mystery.

Occasionally, usually toward the end of the day, Lisa wondered whether Andy was screwing with them. She accused him of it once, and he brought the beetle to a halt, getting up from the driver's seat and gesturing toward it.

"Go ahead, Lisa. See if *you* can raise Habitat 1."

And she'd tried. For a few minutes.

Nothing. They had access to satellite photos of Alex, but not to communication with the rest of the Steele System.

"Sorry," she said, returning to her seat in the back.

The beetle's crew cabin wasn't designed for sleep—almost every inch of it was taken up with vital instruments, and there was certainly no room for the seats to recline. Luckily, it did have an inflatable habitat, which Andy deployed out of the rear of the vehicle each night.

The habitat even had its own airlock, which accordioned out. Stowing the thing each morning was a pain, but it was better than attempting to sleep in the cramped beetle, or worse, inside their pressure suits on the rocky surface of Alex.

One morning, Tessa said something Lisa found fairly insulting. It came after Lisa asked whether they could be sure their oxygen supplies would last until Habitat 1, and as usual, Andy's answer dripped with sarcasm.

"Wow," he said. "Okay. Think about this for a second, Lisa. Have you ever heard of Habitat 2 ever getting any oxygen shipments?"

"Um, no."

"That's because it has multiple large zirconia electrolyzers, all around the roof, constantly breaking down carbon dioxide for its oxygen and venting it into the city. The beetle has a smaller electrolyzer. We'll have oxygen for as long as that's functioning."

"Thank you for informing me, Andy," Lisa said stiffly. Her father had always told her never to feel ashamed of admitting ignorance by asking a question. She'd always lived by that principle, but Andy sure was testing it.

Then came Tessa's remark. "What sort of training did Darkstream give you, anyway, Lisa?"

That cracked Lisa's emotional dam, and her temper came steaming out.

"Well, they never trained me on any zirconia electrolyzer, Tessa. Maybe back in your day the company doled out training that had nothing to do with an employee's job, but they've become a bit more efficient since then."

Tessa chuckled, which only made Lisa angrier.

"I passed every course I did take with flying colors, for your information," she added.

"That's interesting," Tessa said. "Considering how useless you were back in Habitat 2."

"Excuse me?"

Shrugging, Tessa shifted in her seat, leaning against the beetle's inside wall and facing Lisa. "Your disguise back at the Swinging Eel was laughable. And you crumbled when faced with just two low-level criminals. What did you actually *do* back in Habitat 2, other than the handful of arrests you made for possession?"

"I can handle myself, Tessa. You can see for yourself, if you like. Why not fight me in lucid?"

"Lucid," Tessa said, chuckling again. "Of course it's lucid. All right, girl. I'll see you in lucid. You choose the terrain."

"Done." Lisa popped a sedative designed to boost REM sleep and tried her best to get comfortable in the beetle seat.

Soon, she stood in one of her favorite levels: a vast warehouse with "islands" of freight that formed narrow corridors between them. She knew of paths that led to the top of three different islands, and if you were stealthy and patient, it was possible to get the drop on even the most formidable opponent.

Lisa crept to the top of a central island that consisted of stacked shipping containers. She relished her ability to leap from surface to surface silently, like a cat.

From her chosen vantage point, she scanned the three pathways in her line of sight, taking full advantage of her assault rifle's scope.

A flicker of movement caught her eye. *There.*

Tracking her opponent's anticipated trajectory, she was rewarded with another flicker of dark clothing, and she fired a short burst.

Tessa cried out, spinning out of sight once more, and Lisa allowed herself a moment of silent celebration. She was sure she'd gotten Tessa in the shoulder.

In the dream, Tessa's fear would be real, as well as her pain. This wouldn't take long. *I told you I could fight, Tessa.*

Remaining in this position was not wise, now that she'd given it up by firing on her adversary. Instead, she crept across the top of this freight island and leapt over to the next, which was the only way you could access it.

Time to find another spot to lie in wait for my prey.

This second island consisted mostly of wide crates, stacked in towers, all of which rested on a bed of pallets that sat flush with one another. Lisa knew of another excellent vantage point up here, which would give her a line of sight on two well-trafficked ground-level paths.

Just before she reached her chosen spot, a blur of black surged toward her from behind a nearby crate.

Tessa struck Lisa's gun hand, sending her assault rifle flying.

Raising her hands to defend herself, she deflected the first blow, but a hammerhand got her in the temple, followed by a roundhouse to the ribs.

Lisa staggered dangerously close to the edge before regaining her balance. Then, she charged at Tessa.

The old woman seized her as though she was a rag doll, tossing her against the crate from behind which Tessa had emerged.

Lisa's assailant followed along, landing a jab on her jaw, and then a hook that found her eye.

Railing against the blinding pain, stumbling toward Tessa in an attempt to tackle her, Lisa yelled in frustration. Somehow, Tessa's foot connected with her buttocks, sending her staggering toward the edge once again.

Tessa followed, tripping Lisa. She fell, her body colliding with the wood of the crate beneath her, sending the air out of her lungs.

Then Tessa was on top of her, clutching the hair on the back of her head, making tears spring to Lisa's eyes. The dizzying drop stretched below her.

"Take a good look," the old woman said, and then she sent Lisa hurtling over the edge. The concrete floor of the warehouse rushed up to meet her.

The dream ended, and Lisa jolted awake in her seat, heart hammering in her chest.

She looked at Tessa. "How—how did you—?"

"Beat you?" Tessa looked fully alert, as though she'd never been asleep at all. "Easy. I've had *actual* military training, not this lucid crap Darkstream uses to puff up its new recruits. I trained in the UHF, girl. Whereas you've let yourself be convinced by fictions. You're used to dreaming that you're stronger and braver than you actually are."

"What are you talking about? Lucid has been an important part of the Darkstream recruitment process for almost a decade."

"And it's a useful tool—if you use it correctly. Darkstream doesn't. You passed their tests while you still lived out in the Belt, right?"

"Yes..."

"Well, those tests are essentially useless, unless you have an experienced soldier who's used to training recruits and who's able to *physically* test you. Not in the dream—in real life. Yes, the implants can lend structure to our dreams, but there's still plenty of room for the subconscious to influence an improperly calibrated sim. You need a real-live person who can test your actual abilities and your fear responses, in real life, and who can then calibrate your implant to simulate them properly. You, Lisa—I hate to tell you—you're strong-spirited but you aren't much else. The problem's rather pronounced in your case, because you're good at convincing yourself that you're great. But you're not. You're a weak, incapable soldier."

Lisa's eyes strung, but she refused to give in to tears. Her gaze drifted to Andy, to see how he was reacting to Tessa's commentary, but for once he knew not to speak. He kept his eyes glued to the terrain before the beetle.

"Well, thanks," Lisa said, her voice a little shaky. "Thanks for that."

"There's a reason I'm being this harsh, girl," Tessa said, her voice just a jot more tender than before. "I wouldn't be so candid with you if I wasn't willing to train you."

"You said I need UHF training," Lisa said flatly. "Not this 'Darkstream lucid crap.'"

Tessa nodded. "You do indeed. Your training should involve the mental, physical, and emotional rigors of actual military training. And you're in luck. The UHF may be in another galaxy, but you have me. I trained soldiers for the UHF before I went to work for Darkstream."

Slowly, Lisa nodded. "All right. Fine. When do we begin?"

"Right now." Tessa moved from her seat to the empty one next to Andy. "Do you know what a burpee is?" she asked Lisa without looking at her.

"Yes."

"Good. There should be enough room in the aisle. For the push-up part, you can spread your arms out between the seats. Now get to it. And don't forget to compensate for the beetle's movement. No need to have you bouncing around the cabin and bothering the rest of us."

"How many do you want me to do?"

"I haven't decided yet. Maybe I'll let you know once I do. Maybe."

CHAPTER 16

Firing a Real Gun

It turned out Tessa wanted her to do as many burpees as it took for her arms to become limp noodles and for her to collapse on the beetle floor in a sweaty, panting heap.

When they stopped for the night, as Andy inflated their portable habitat, Tessa set up some virtual targets on a cliff face a few dozen meters away from their campsite. She sent them to Lisa's implant, which painted them maroon, right over the blue rock.

"Why can't we just do this in lucid?" Lisa asked.

"Because there's no replacement for firing a real gun, girl."

An hour of shooting told Tessa that Lisa's accuracy needed a lot of work, which she announced over a wide channel as they were stripping off their suits inside the habitat airlock and using the built-in vacuum to catch as much of the blue dust as they could before entering their temporary home.

The inflatable habitat consisted of a central area with four private "bedroom" bubbles leading out of it. The portals to the bedrooms also sealed tight, so that if there was a leak in one section, it wouldn't affect them all.

It was just one of many safety precautions, of course: an alarm was supposed to sound in the event of a leak, allowing them to repair it in plenty of time.

Hopefully.

It depended on the size of the leak.

"I'm heading to bed," Lisa said. "I'm wiped."

"No, you're not," Tessa said.

"Huh? Yes I am. I'm exhausted."

"You can address me as ma'am," Tessa said. "And I wasn't disagreeing that you're tired. I'm disagreeing that you're going to bed. I want fifty shock push-ups, right now, and that's just to start."

"What's a shock push-up?"

Tessa demonstrated, performing a regular push-up on the way down but throwing herself into the air with her hands and clapping before catching herself and lowering into another rep. "Got it?"

"Yes, ma'am," Lisa said wearily, and got into position herself.

"Keep your back straight, Seaman," Tessa barked. "You're letting it droop."

"Yes, ma'am," Lisa grunted.

Andy sat on one of the air-filled seats that projected from the inner wall of the habitat, looking on, wearing a blank expression. He seemed to be lost in thought.

Not Tessa. She stood in the space between two of the seats, berating Lisa for her poor form.

"I don't think you're taking this seriously, Seaman!" Tessa yelled. "I see you letting your back droop again. If you don't straighten it right now, and *keep* it straight, I'm going to sit on it. Then I'm going to want twenty more shock push-ups, with me riding shotgun. So straighten up."

Ninety minutes later, Tessa said, "Okay. That'll do for tonight."

Lisa allowed herself to fall back from the leg raise she'd been performing, her chest heaving, her eyes wandering across the ceiling of the habitat.

"I'm heading to bed," Tessa said. "You're welcome to do that as well, girl, if you can make it there." Opening the portal to her bedroom bubble, Tessa disappeared inside it, sealing it shut behind her.

"Go ahead," Lisa said to Andy, her breath still ragged. "Say something snarky."

"You look good."

"What? Really?"

Andy nodded, saying nothing else. Gradually, Lisa's breathing slowed, and she managed to heave herself onto one of the seats, where she sat with her elbows on her knees and her head hanging. Her raven hair had become loose, and now it spilled down toward the floor.

"Why'd you stop returning my calls, Andy?" Lisa asked. The words just came out, surprising even her. Maybe the intense PT had dislodged them.

"Oh. I...I just...I don't think I could be happy with you. Sorry, Lisa. I should have said something, but...it was just easier to fall out of touch."

And to act like a jerk whenever you ran into me at the Dusty Bucket, Lisa would have added. But she didn't. "Why'd you think you wouldn't be happy with me?"

He shrugged. "Too many options."

"Huh? Options?"

"Yeah. You know. If I'd gone with you, there would have always been a prettier girl to distract me and cause trouble."

"A prettier girl."

"Yeah."

"I see," she said, and the words sounded icy even to her ears. She was glad. She dragged herself to her feet and trudged to the portal that led into her own bedroom. "Good night, Andy."

"Good night," he said, his expression unreadable.

What a jerk. Lisa vowed never to engage Andy again, on anything other than topics that pertained directly to their jobs.

CHAPTER 17

Living Hell

Darkstream had devoted an entire section of the Omega Quadrant to training and housing its security forces, with several floors filled with equipment, gyms, obstacle courses, Olympic-size swimming pools, barracks, a shooting range, an arsenal, an infirmary, a mess, and so on.

Jake filed into the largest gym Darkstream trainees and soldiers had exclusive access to, along with hundreds of other recruits. As they passed through the enormous double doors, they were told to gather in a central, circular expanse, which was the only one devoid of equipment.

Instructor Gabriel Roach awaited them there.

"I have limited time to get you battle-ready," he told them the instant they'd all assembled, his low tone making them all shut up and lean forward so they didn't miss anything.

"The Quatro aren't waiting. Ever since they razed Northshire, they've been ramping up their aggression against human settlements all across Eresos. So far, they've mostly been focusing their attention on villages that can't afford Darkstream protection, and they've been having a lot of success with that approach. But the board expects them to strike more vital targets soon."

Roach paused to let that sink in, and as it did, the recruits around Jake shifted their weight, some of them murmuring to each other.

"Shut up," Roach said, and without having to raise his voice, utter silence swept across the gathered trainees. "As I said, we don't have much time. Darkstream needs a full mech team, staffed only by the best and meant for deployment wherever we're needed most. And they need it *now.* Which means that those of you who aren't already seventy percent of the way to where I need you are going to wash out." He grinned. "Right now, each of you is telling yourself that it won't be you. But it will be. I can almost guarantee that it *will* be you. I do invite you to prove me wrong."

Jake felt the corners of his mouth curl backward as his jaw set, teeth grinding together.

It won't *be me.* But that was exactly what Roach had just predicted he'd be thinking. *I don't care. It's not going to be me.*

"There are hundreds of you standing in front of me, gaping like you just walked off a farm. In a sense, a lot of you did, though not in the way humanity's traditionally conceived of farms." Roach chuckled. "Sorry. I don't mean to overtax your brains. Instantly forget any big words I happen to let slip, and remember that of the hundreds of you here today, most of you *will* wash out. Hell, it's possible that every one of you will. Even if some of you don't—even if some of you really are seventy percent to where I need you—the process of digging deep and finding that extra thirty percent is going to basically kill you. That's a promise.

"The training will be grueling, children. Darkstream needs fresh recruits to pilot the mechs they're developing, and they need them soon. Unfortunately, the only place to get individuals suited for the job is the system's lucid leaderboards. To succeed there, you need to have the exquisite reflexes and situational awareness it takes to pilot mechs. Many of the games you played in lucid involved mechs. This is because Darkstream has been developing them for a while, and it anticipated the need for pilots a long time ago."

Roach shook his head, smiling widely at them, his forehead bunched in ever-increasing amusement. "I'm sure what I just said went straight to your heads. Suddenly, you think you're a bunch of hotshots, don't you? I tore you down and then I built you back up, right?" Terse laughter. "Wrong. Just because you're good at Darkstream's video games does *not* mean you're going to make it through what I'm planning to subject you to. It's my job to find among you individuals who can be molded into soldiers who won't choke at the first taste of battle. To do that, I intend to kick your asses around and around this station. I intend to make your lives a living hell. And that's just to start."

CHAPTER 18

We're All Starting to Hate

Chief Gabriel Roach was a man of his word.

By the end of the first day, Jake felt like someone really had kicked his ass.

By the end of the first week, he felt like he was going to die.

He'd always considered himself fairly fit. Developing comets with his father, using just the equipment Darkstream leased to them—it involved a lot of physical labor.

Sometimes, during rare visits to Hub to see his mother and Sue-Anne, or more frequent supply stops at various outposts in the Belt, Jake would challenge other guys his age to arm wrestle, or just straight up wrestle. He'd rarely lost, though he'd always been a pretty good sport about winning, in his opinion.

Roach's version of PT involved moving from exercise to strenuous exercise without stopping. At the beginning of each day, he laid out their training schedule, and it was always daunting, but Jake quickly learned that it never encompassed everything they would do that day.

For Roach, everything that happened was an excuse to pile on extra PT.

If someone faltered, he assigned the entire group more PT. If someone complained, that was at least sixty minutes of added PT. Once, Roach said that one of the recruits looked funny, and as a result, the entire group earned two hours of extra PT.

Jogging ten miles, jogging backwards ten miles, push-ups, burpees, pistol squats—Roach prided himself on constantly hitting them with new exercises that none of them had heard of before. He wasn't happy until someone collapsed.

When someone did, that meant more PT.

In class, they were taught tactics and strategy, insertion and evacuation techniques, weapon use and maintenance, explosives, unit formation, Quatro anatomy and strategy—such as it was. They spent a fair bit of time on the shooting range, as well, with Roach ridiculing them whenever they missed.

They were also shown vids of every Quatro attack that had ever occurred.

When he was shown the first vid, of the recent attack on Northshire, Jake was struck by the savagery of the aliens, as well as their complete lack of mercy.

The aliens chased down men, women, children, the elderly, the infirm, the disabled. It didn't seem to matter to the Quatro, who rent their victims with scythe-like claws and tore at them with teeth like knives, or simply tossed them into buildings using powerful jaws.

During that first vid, he happened to glance at Roach, standing on the side of the classroom.

Even with the lights dimmed, Jake could see how Roach's eyes burned, and the way his jaw protruded with tension. Roach hated the Quatro; that much was clear.

Jake was coming to hate them, too. He'd never hated anything or anyone in his life—not really. Not true hatred. But after watching those vids, he hated the Quatro.

Then, suddenly, something began to bother him. Other than the Northshire attack, there really wasn't very much footage of Quatro attacking human settlements. Roach just rotated the same four or five, showing them in different orders, cycling them again and again.

But what really stoked animosity toward the aliens were the lucid sims Roach had them run, where the Quatro were consistently the enemy.

Their mission was always to defend a helpless village from the Quatro, or to stop a Quatro attack already in progress, or to rescue a group of children the Quatro had captured, or to contend with some other atrocity the aliens had committed.

The sims had the greatest effect—even greater than the vids. While lucid, Jake had to watch the Quatro tear his fellow recruits apart again and again.

Several times, he experienced a Quatro savaging *him*, tearing at his guns, jaws coming away with glistening intestines dangling.

And because the human brain consistently mistook dreams for reality, the fear was always real. And the pain.

And the hatred.

During lunch, halfway through his third week of training, Jake commented on it to those sitting around him in the Recruits' Mess.

"We're all starting to hate the Quatro, but it's mostly because of what they do to us in lucid, right? I hate them. I can't help it, because of what they've done to me and what I've seen them do to my friends. But the hatred is coming from simulated events. They didn't actually happen, not any of it. Does that bother anyone else?"

"There are vids, too," said Ash, a trainee around his age. She had a thin nose, blue eyes, and short, wheat-colored hair. "The way they act in the sims is what they're really like. We know that because of the vids."

"But there are only five vids, tops," Jake said. "How many times have humans attacked Quatro dens? We haven't seen any vids of us attacking them. I mean, if they want me to fight an enemy, fine, but are these tricks really necessary?"

Ash shook her head, and started to speak, but she trailed off, her gaze fixed on a point over Jake's head.

He turned to see Gabriel Roach standing behind him, arms crossed, eyes ablaze.

Jake felt certain he could actually *feel* the color draining from his face. But Roach didn't say a thing. He just stood there, for at least a minute, until at last he walked away without a single word.

"I'd watch your back," Ash told Jake, eyebrows hiked up her forehead. "That looked like a death glare to me."

The first couple of weeks had seen only a trickle of washouts, but there was something about that third week. Seventy trainees quit that week, over twenty percent of the total.

On the evening of Jake's conversation with Ash in the Recruits' Mess, Roach suddenly announced that he wanted to test how far their conditioning had come. He brought them to the gym and told them to line up in ranks, fists locked at their sides.

"Tighten your abdominals," Roach told the first recruit he came across, giving him only a second to do so before striking him in the gut.

The recruit grunted, falling back a step.

"Needs work," Roach said. "A lot of work." He moved to the next recruit. "Tighten your abdominals." Then came the blow.

Roach worked his way down the first line, and then the next. Jake wasn't totally clear on how this tested their conditioning. He supposed having a strong core was part of it, but the regular PT should have already given the chief a much better idea of their conditioning overall.

When Roach reached Jake, he saw the glint in the officer's eye, and suddenly he knew what this was really about.

"Tighten your abdominals," Roach said softly, and Jake did, praying silently.

Roach's fist felt like a rocket launched straight into his guts. The chief put his full weight into it, sending Jake reeling backward into the recruit behind him, who caught him by the arms.

"Let him fall," Roach said, and Jake's fellow recruit immediately let him drop to the floor.

The chief walked over, looming over Jake for several seconds, glaring down at him as he gasped for air. For a second, Jake expected Roach to drive his foot down into his stomach.

But he didn't. Instead, he shouted: "Training's over for the day. Retire to your quarters and lick your wounds." His lips curled into a tight smile, which he directed at Jake, and then he stalked out of the gym.

Most of the recruits left without ever having to tighten their abdominals.

Somehow, the fact that Roach hadn't assigned more PT after Jake collapsed was even more humiliating than getting knocked to the floor.

Going down is supposed to mean more PT. But not this time.

The other recruits followed their chief as Jake lay on the floor, still gasping. All but one of them.

Ash Sweeney walked over and offered him her hand. He took it, wincing as she dragged him to his feet.

"Told you it was a death glare," she said.

Jake nodded. "You had the right of it."

"I heard a rumor that Roach lost someone to the Quatro. That's why he hates them so much. Maybe that's why he didn't like you defending them."

"I wasn't defending them. I was just saying."

"Yeah. Well, if the rumor's true, then I know how Roach feels. I lost my sister in the attack on Northshire. My father, too."

"God. I'm sorry."

"Thanks. You wanna fight each other in lucid?"

"Yeah. Okay."
They left the gym together.

CHAPTER 19

Plenty to Worry About

When Tessa wasn't running Lisa into the ground, she exchanged increasingly lewd jokes with Andy, with whom she appeared to be holding a contest to see who could be the raunchiest.

That bothered Lisa, for some reason.

Maybe it was because, with Tessa as her mentor, and with Lisa's vow to mostly ignore Andy, she had no one she could really talk to.

Either way, she'd never been a prude, but being forced to hear Andy and Tessa swapping off-color jokes all day got really old, really fast.

Even though there's nothing else to do.

They still had access to satellite imagery, though they'd grown less concerned about checking it regularly. Before, they'd taken turns getting up throughout the night in order to search the latest photos for plumes of blue dust that might indicate pursuers.

They were two months out from Habitat 2, however, and Andy figured that anyone wondering about the missing beetle had probably given up looking for it by now.

On the second day of training, Tessa had calibrated Lisa's implant to properly simulate her actual strength—physical, psychological, and emotional. And though she'd been skeptical, Lisa had to admit that the white-haired woman had been right. Now that she could no longer dream herself into a superwoman, lucid combat had become much harder.

During the times Tessa wasn't putting her through another round of endless PT, or handing her her butt in lucid battles, Lisa stared out the crew cabin's silicon nitride windows at the unchanging terrain.

When they'd first left Habitat 2, she'd cherished the planet's sapphire color. It made her think she hadn't spent nearly enough time out on the surface, before. But now, she wanted to retreat inside a habitat, any habitat, and never leave it again.

Constant defeat had stolen her joy for going lucid. Now, staring at the terrain was the only thing she had any interest in doing. Not that she had very much interest in that, either.

On the bright side, as the weeks crawled by, she could feel herself growing stronger, more proficient. Much more.

Tessa called those "beginner gains," but whatever. It didn't make them any less real. Lisa was making progress.

One morning, she woke to getting shaken roughly. She opened her eyes to find Andy standing over her inflated bed.

"What are you doing in my room?" she asked, her voice dripping with venom.

"Lisa, you need to get up. I just had a glance at the latest satellite photos. I think there's something coming. Three somethings."

Leaping out of bed, trying not to think about the fact that she wore only a bra and underwear, Lisa pulled on her uniform and ran out into the habitat's common area.

"Where's Tessa?" She glanced back at Andy. "You woke me first?"

He shrugged. "You're my colleague, not her."

"Get her up."

"Sure thing." Andy went to the portal leading into Tessa's bubble and opened it.

Soon, they were all standing around the common area, studying a pair of photos Andy had forwarded to their implants.

"These were taken an hour apart, and judging by the distance those dust plumes covered, our pursuers are traveling faster than it's safe to. The beetles may have been named to encourage slowness, but they're capable of pretty high speeds. Whoever's driving those beetles, they're obviously not afraid to take advantage of their full power."

Although Lisa was the ranking Darkstream official, and the beetle was Darkstream property, Tessa had already taken command. "I'll help Lisa deflate the habitat and stuff it into the beetle. Andy, you get the beetle's systems up and running. Be ready to floor it as soon as we climb in."

"Sure thing."

"How much time do we have?"

"Enough, probably, if we stop wasting it this second and hustle."

Tessa nodded. "Let's get moving, then."

They barely spoke as they rushed to put everything away, deflate the habitat, and collapse the airlock. Using the habitat's venting system, they were able to deflate it and pack it into the beetle's undercarriage compartment in under thirty minutes. Then they clambered aboard, and Andy gunned the engine.

Just in time. The rear viewscreen showed the pursuing beetles cresting the horizon and barreling toward them, rapidly closing the distance.

"Andy, now is not the time to observe proper safety protocol," Lisa said. "You need to go faster."

"I'm on it," he said, his voice tight.

"What kind of artillery do beetles have?" she yelled, her voice shaking as the beetle went over a shallow ridge. Glancing behind her, she saw that one of the chasing beetles had nearly reached them.

"None."

"Then we have nothing to worry about, right?"

At that moment, the lead beetle caught up to them.

It slammed into the side of their vehicle, forcing Andy to veer toward a gaping canyon. At the last minute, he jerked the wheel to the right and accelerated, clearing the front of the pursuing beetle by what seemed like inches.

Their pursuers had been trying to ram them, and now they barely managed to rein in their speed before careening into the canyon themselves.

Andy glanced back at Lisa. "Traveling at high speeds over dangerous terrain, with three beetles trying to do *that* to us? I'd say we have plenty to worry about, Lisa."

CHAPTER 20

Test Run

Darkstream's Department of Military Research and Development was located in Alpha Quadrant, on the opposite side of Valhalla Station from Omega Quadrant, where Gabe's recruits lived and sweated and washed out.

Gabe stood at an observation window, flanked by two of the company's nerds. Six more nerds sat behind them at two rows of consoles, poring over various data readouts.

Below, in a large, titanium-reinforced chamber, Chief Zimmerman took another step toward the alien mech that Peter Price and his son had discovered inside a comet on the edge of Darkstream-occupied space. The mech reacted as it always did—by doing absolutely nothing.

Gabe had fought alongside Peter Price, during the first missions on Eresos. Together, they and other company operatives had cleared out enough Quatro to make room for humanity to set up shop.

Of course, Price had processed those missions differently than Gabe. They'd taken a heavier toll on Price, who'd been honorably discharged after his psyche broke down for a time.

Following that, he'd fled to the Belt, found a wife, and never returned to the inner system.

Price was a good man. Gabe hadn't gotten along very well with him, but he could still recognize that the guy was a good person.

That didn't mean he'd go easy on his cocky upstart of a son.

The nerd on Gabe's right tapped a console projecting from the bulkhead underneath the window. It had the effect of projecting his voice into the reinforced room. "Are you ready, Chief Zimmerman?"

Zimmerman nodded. "Ready as I'll ever be."

"Please approach the mech."

One of the major roadblocks R&D faced in building a functioning mech of their own involved an inability to figure out a working control interface.

So far, nothing they'd tried afforded the minute level of control required for combat. If the mech didn't react the instant you reacted, you'd be as good as dead, in a lot of cases.

They'd already learned much from studying the alien mech, and had improved their own design dramatically. But given Darkstream's inability to grasp the code with which the alien mech was programmed—or whether it was programmed at all—the only way to learn about its controls was to send someone with an implant inside it so that their sensory data and brain waves could be recorded and analyzed.

Zimmerman reached the mech and laid his palm over its left "calf." Instantly, the guts of the mech distended, forming a ramp for Zimmerman to mount. Gabe had heard somewhere that they'd learned how to open the thing shortly after bringing it here.

Presumably, that mechanism won't work if there's someone already inside it. If it did, it would make the thing vulnerable to any enemy that could play tag.

Zimmerman appeared to take a deep breath, and then he climbed up inside the mech. The ramp folded seamlessly back into the machine, making it so that there was no sign of an opening there at all.

The war machine took a step toward the observation window, and instantly, Gabe lost any doubt he'd had that the thing had been created by whoever made the Gatherers and the Amblers.

It had the same fluid metal surface, comprised of overlapping plates like scales, which shifted as it moved.

When Zimmerman had first climbed inside, the feed from his implant had shown a smooth, man-shaped shell waiting to envelop him. Gabe suspected that the mech likely had the same level of versatility as the Gatherers, maybe more—which would make it a weapon of immense power.

He realized something else: no matter how impressive the mechs Darkstream ended up producing, none of them would ever come close to touching the machine he looked at now.

The mech's right arm jerked toward the observation window, rapidly morphing into what looked like a cannon. Both nerds ducked as the mech fired.

Gabe remained standing, knowing nothing could pierce that window, short of a nuclear blast.

When the glass began to splinter, he gasped, taking a step back.

"Zimmerman!" one of the nerds shouted. "Chief Zimmerman, come in!"

"He's attempting to regain control!" another shouted.

The cannon-arm zigzagged down, then back up again. The mech took a stuttering step backward.

"Chief Zimmerman, exit the machine if you can!"

Clearly, he can't.

As Gabe looked on, transfixed, the mech's entire torso morphed, folding inward, and he knew that Zimmerman was dead.

Indeed, seconds later, the thing's guts flexed outward, a thousand jagged spikes protruding every which way. A pulpy, red substance began to leak to the floor in streams.

Having turned Zimmerman into paste, the mech stood motionless once more.

CHAPTER 21

Beetle Chase

Even amidst the chaos of the chase, Lisa found a moment to feel some sympathy for Andy. He'd only ever been trained as a driver, not as combat personnel. This was probably the first time he'd ever had other human lives depending on him.

At least he's recognized the importance of speed.

Their beetle now raced just ahead of its pursuers, though Andy was still taking too much time to scrutinize the approaching terrain, even going so far as to glance at recent satellite images.

If he'd been trained as a soldier, he would know that sometimes, taking on immense risk was the only way of having a shot at survival.

The pursuing beetles, which Lisa felt sure had been tracking them all the way from Habitat 2, were clearly no strangers to risk. They capitalized on every opportunity to close the distance, whether it included accelerating over rough terrain or gathering enough speed to sail over pits of unknown depths.

Still, Andy's skill as a driver went a long way, and though he'd almost certainly never had to drive so defensively, Lisa noticed him experimenting on the fly, and starting to capitalize on opportunities to throw off those chasing them.

"I'm going to try for that narrow canyon, there," he said, his voice shaky. "I'm pretty sure it's big enough for the beetle."

"You can do it, Andy," Lisa said, going so far as to reach forward to place a reassuring hand on his shoulder.

"Thanks," he said, actually sounding grateful.

The beetle picked up speed, and behind them, the others rearranged their formation, probably angling to cut Andy off, if it turned out his run at the canyon was a bluff.

But Andy wasn't bluffing. He roared between the sheer cliffs of blue rocks, and two of the pursuing beetles did the same.

One of them didn't make it. The sound of its collision with the rock face reached them even inside the crew cabin.

"One down," Andy said. "Hopefully."

They screamed out of the other end of the canyon, the remaining two beetles in close pursuit.

Andy jerked the wheel to the right, and the beetle banked suddenly, sending a spray of blue dirt flying out into empty air—out over the cliff he'd narrowly avoided taking them over.

Behind them, their remaining two pursuers also completed the turn successfully.

"Damn," Andy said. "I thought that would do it."

"Any other ideas?" Tessa asked.

"One. If I remember right, there's another cliff dead ahead, which is easy to drive straight over if you don't know it's there.

That's fine, because there's a wide shelf just underneath it, which you can catch yourself on if you aren't going too fast and you know what you're doing. But if they follow us over it, there's a good chance they'll fly right over the second cliff, and there's no shelf to save them beneath that one."

Andy glanced back at them, wearing an adrenaline-fueled grin. "Make sure you're strapped in nice and tight, ladies."

The beetle barreled forward, and the knowledge that they were speeding toward a cliff, combined with her ignorance of exactly where that cliff was—it made Lisa's toes curl inside her boots.

Their pursuers were coming on even faster, which was probably good, but it did nothing to slow her racing heart.

Andy slammed on the brakes, the beetle skidded forward, and suddenly the ground fell away from beneath them.

Lisa's stomach somersaulted toward her mouth as the vehicle plummeted, and she braced for impact.

The force of the beetle slamming into the hard-packed regolith of the shelf felt like it would dislodge her teeth from her skull.

At last, the tumult subsided, just as one of the beetles soared overhead, toward the second cliff.

Miraculously, it managed to catch itself on the lip, with one of its wheels dangling in midair. Then it began to reverse, and Lisa saw what had saved it: a rock outcropping it had chanced to get lodged on.

"Andy, drive!" Lisa shouted.

He did, gunning the engine and accelerating straight for the other beetle.

The entire frame of their beetle shuddered as the two vehicles collided, and Lisa heard a cracking sound.

Dutifully, the other beetle's wheel "stepped" over the rock that had saved it, allowing Andy to nudge it the rest of the way over the cliff. It tumbled forward, its rear facing directly upward, and then it was gone. A few seconds later, they heard it collide with Alex far below.

A fracture now stretched from the bottom-left corner of their main forward window to the top-right. It didn't do much to obscure visibility, but its presence was alarming.

"Is that going to hold?" Tessa asked.

"It should," Andy said. "Silicon nitride windows are almost impossible to shatter. You'd need a hell of a lot more force than that."

Lisa took the liberty of angling their rear camera upward, so that the viewscreen showed the cliff they'd just driven over. The third beetle from Habitat 2 was parked up there, watching them. After another minute, it drove away.

"I guess they're giving up," Andy said.

"Hopefully," Tessa said. "But I wouldn't count on it."

CHAPTER 22

For Our Sisters

Jake flicked the air in front of his face, using his v-lenses to scroll through his messages.

A lot of them were from his gaming friends, most of whom he'd never met in-person. He'd barely met them in-game, actually. Because of how long it took signals to traverse the system, out in the Belt he could only ever compete for the highest score, without ever actually fighting other players in real-time.

That was perhaps his favorite thing about being on Valhalla Station—the ability to fight living, breathing opponents in lucid.

And today was the very first day Roach had given the recruits off from training, so Jake finally had the opportunity to seek out people he wanted to face. Some of his gaming friends even lived on Valhalla.

Yet here he was, lying on his bunk, scrolling through page after page of messages. Because as fun as lucid combat was, he needed to check for messages from his family.

I can't wait till they give me an implant. His control over the digital interface would be much more intuitive, then, and directed by his thoughts, not by goofy gestures in midair.

At last, he found a message from his father, and opened it.

Peter Price was brief, as always. He hadn't shaved in a while, which was unusual for him, and there were bags under his eyes, but his news was good: "Jake. I hope you're well. We've almost finished developing the comet where we found the mech. We've been able to include a lot of little extras because of the money we made from selling that thing. Well, the payment hasn't been processed yet, but I took out a loan, knowing it'll come soon. I should be able to get a much better price for this comet than usual. I've only hired on one guy so far, but I'm screening new applicants all the time. No one can replace you, of course. Message me back soon. I miss you."

"Miss you, Dad," Jake whispered. But he'd message him back later.

Next, he found a message from his mother. She looked tired, too, and her hair, as red as Jake's, bracketed her face in loose disarray.

Everyone's tired. Just like me.

Brianne Price had less good news.

"Hi, love. Your sister wanted to record a message, but she's still not feeling well enough. She isn't responding as well as we'd hoped to the radiation, but the doctor says there are alternatives, which we should be able to try as soon as the payment from Darkstream is processed. And your father's business is growing, so that will help, too. Thank you for doing your part for that, Jake. I hope you're staying safe. Love you."

"Love you, Mom," Jake said, and suddenly he wanted to cry. Roach hadn't been able to make him do that, but lying here on his bunk, alone while the others enjoyed Valhalla Station, missing his family...he almost cried.

But he didn't. He forced himself to get up and leave the bunkroom. It was about time he "Experience Valhalla," as the well-known slogan went.

The company had poured a lot of money into this place, which explained why it was such a popular destination, even for people down on Eresos, which was the only place in the Steele System where you could actually go outdoors without wearing a pressure suit.

Valhalla doesn't have Quatro. So I guess that's a fair trade.

The station also did a decent job of mimicking the outdoors. The ceiling, far too high to touch, was one giant, seamless viewscreen, which offered a convincing illusion of blue sky, dotted with just a few wispy clouds.

Of course, that was only in the common spaces. Businesses could make their ceiling screens show whatever they wanted, and they used that to great effect.

Jake had heard there was a theater where live actors performed only Shakespearean plays, and they used the ceiling there to show the storms that inevitably turned up in those scripts. For indoor scenes, they showed the ceiling of whatever structure those were set in, whether it was a witch's hovel or a royal palace.

Valhalla was also dotted with green spaces, and Jake walked through one of those now. Here, anyone rich enough to live on Valhalla could enjoy actual nature, or at least as close to nature as you could get aboard a space station. The flowers and grass and bushes and trees were all Earth-based species, which had been taken off of humanity's homeworld—before its degradation was complete—and cultivated through the generations.

He found Ash Sweeney sitting with her back against a giant oak, whose branches stretched way up toward the artificial sky. Jake wondered briefly whether the entire tree was real, or whether it became simulated at some point along the way up. He wasn't sure how that would work, but he also wouldn't put anything past Darkstream.

"Hey," he said to Ash, who hadn't noticed him yet.

She looked up, and he saw the sadness in her eyes before she managed to mask her emotions, just like adults were supposed to do. Especially adults trying to make it as mech pilots.

"Hello."

"You all right?" He took a seat beside her, though as soon as he did it occurred to him that he probably should have asked to join her first. *Oh well.*

"I'm, uh..." Ash sighed. "I'm thinking about my sister. Missing her."

"That's a coincidence. Here I am, thinking about mine."

"You lost your sister, too?"

"I probably will soon. She has stage-four adenosarcoma. That's partly why I want this so bad. A mech pilot's pay will go a long way toward getting her the treatment she needs, not to mention paying the debts my family have already racked up trying to make her better."

"I'm sorry, Jake."

"Don't be. Not yet. It might be time for that, soon, but not yet."

"Okay."

"But forget about all that. It's our first day off. Is it crazy that I can't stop thinking about going back to training tomorrow? And wondering what it'll be like to actually pilot a mech?"

Ash laughed. "If that's crazy, then I'm right there with you. Mechs are *so* freaking cool." She swept a hand through her short, straw-colored hair. "I've been telling my mother since I was a girl that I wanted to drive a mech. She always said it was crazy, and I knew she was right. I figured it probably wouldn't be hundreds of years before humanity built them, if ever, and I'd only ever get to pilot one in lucid. And yet...here I am."

"Here you are," Jake said. "One of just three-hundred remaining recruits, all competing for the exact same thing."

"Yeah."

"Did your, uh...did your mom survive the attack on Northshire?"

Ash nodded. "Yes. She made it. Still recovering, but...she made it."

"I'm glad."

"Me too." She paused, for a long time. Then: "You think I'm going to wash out, don't you?"

Jake met her eyes, which were the same color as Planet Alexandria. "Well, Roach seems to be just as hard as you as he is on me, for whatever reason. But no, actually. I don't think you're going to wash out. I think we're both going to make it."

"Why do you say that?"

"Because we're both doing this for the right reason. For our sisters."

"My sister's gone already."

"Doesn't mean you can't do this for her."

"You mean, like avenge her?"

"Sure."

"While you save yours."

"Hopefully."

"One to avenge, one to save. Kind of epic, when you think about it."

"It is."

Ash held out her hand. "For our sisters."

Jake gripped her forearm, and she gripped his. "For our sisters."

CHAPTER 23

Do Not Flinch

"We're not moving fast enough," Roach told the two hundred and sixty-nine remaining recruits.

He'd let them rest for an hour after getting into their bunks. Jake had fallen directly asleep, exhausted from a day packed full of PT, only to be jolted awake by his fellows, who'd been warned that Roach would go harder on them the longer this took.

After cutting their sleep woefully short, Roach had made them double-time across Valhalla, to the Epsilon Quadrant, which housed the Endless Beach—a vast ring of sand that circled a wave pool, whose behavior mimicked that of the ocean. Mist hung perpetually along its center, obscuring the opposite side and preserving the illusion that this was a real beach, and not a construct built by humans aboard a gigantic metal space station.

By day, the Endless Beach was endlessly populated by the families of Darkstream's hardworking executives. But now, it was empty. Closed to the public.

Either Roach had connections, or he was violating station protocol. Neither would surprise Jake.

"We need to move faster," Roach said. "The Quatro are getting more aggressive. And none of you are close to ready."

Jake's mouth moved faster than his thoughts, and he called out, "R&D hasn't even developed a working mech yet."

"Who said that?"

"I did, sir." Jake's emotions had caught up with him, and he was afraid, now. But that didn't mean he wouldn't own up to his actions. He stepped to the front of the group.

Roach approached until he towered over Jake, his muscles taut in the artificial sunlight. "Since when do you have access to information about R&D?"

"It's all over the station, sir. Rumors."

"Is that right? What else does rumor have to say?"

Roach's face was as hard and stern as it ever got, and it took everything Jake had not to quake in his boots. "Rumor says that they haven't even figured out the control interface, and a guy died."

"Hmm." Sweeping the other recruits with a glare, Roach said, "Did everyone hear what this cocky brat just said? Did you hear the hearsay he's trying to pass along to his fellow recruits as indisputable fact?"

"Sir, yes, sir!" the recruits called in unison.

Roach lowered his face closer to Jake's. Then he screamed: "You just made this ten times worse on yourself and your fellow trainees, Recruit. Now, run. All of you, run! Run!"

They ran, and so did Roach, right at the heels of the last trainee. He taunted them if they stumbled, and he especially made fun of the person in last, shaming them into running faster, until there was a new last place.

Rinse, repeat, until gradually the entire group ran faster. And faster.

"I haven't even begun to break a sweat," Roach boasted. "Have you? Tell me the truth, Recruits!"

"Sir, yes, sir!"

"That doesn't bode well for you, Recruits! Because the night has just begun, and you're not going to stop until the first Darkstream exec comes to soak his fat heels. If you do stop, even for a second, you're done. Washed out. If you make it till morning, you can stay."

Jake's heart raced, faster than the running alone should have caused. *He's going to make us run the entire night, after doing PT the entire day?* This was insanity. It was abuse.

When Roach shouted, he was somehow able to project his voice enough for everyone to hear while he kept pace. He hadn't even begun to breathe heavily.

Of course, he hasn't been going through PT hell all day.

"I know what you're thinking," Roach said. "You're thinking this isn't fair. You've been doing PT since morning, while I'm fresh as a daisy. Well guess what? My training in the UHF was *tougher* than this. You babies are coddled in this system. They say the Milky Way was the safe space, but not the part I came from. The way I see it, you babies have lived in a safe space your whole lives, and I'm the first one to rip you out of it and show you what life is really like. *Move,* Recruits!"

When they completed their first lap, Roach made a pit stop at the case he'd carried with him from Omega Quadrant. He tore it open and produced what looked like a gun, though it wasn't like any gun Jake had encountered before, and he knew guns pretty well.

"Keep running, Recruits. Keep running, if you want to pilot mechs." Roach sprinted to the front of the group and then he turned around, running backward, the gun's stock cradled between his elbow and side, its long, thin barrel sticking straight up. "About now, you're probably thinking about washing out. Maybe you're wondering if *any of you* are going to make it through the night."

From near the front of the pack, Jake could see that, incredibly, Roach *still* hadn't broken a sweat.

"Let me tell you something," the chief went on. "It's very possible that none of you will make it to the morning. But if any of you do, it'll mean I've successfully culled the weaklings from the group. And we need to do that, quickly. Eresos needs us."

Roach brought the gun up to his eye, sighting along the barrel—straight at Jake. "*Do not flinch,*" he yelled, and pulled the trigger.

Something smacked into Jake's cheek at high speed, splashing liquid across his face. Some of it got in his right eye, setting it on fire, and he stumbled, trying to wipe it out. It stung like hell.

"Stop and you're out, Price!" Roach called, sounding like he was enjoying himself a lot. "Stop, and you're out of my program on the spot."

Somehow, Jake kept moving, though his eye continued to sting. He fingered his cheek, and could already feel a welt forming there.

Think of Sue Anne, he told himself. *You're better than this, Jake. You're going to beat this. You're better than everyone here.*

"Paintballs," Roach said. "Filled with good old-fashioned lemon juice. Who else wants some? No volunteers? How about you, Sweeney?"

Roach sighted along the barrel once again. "*Don't flinch!*"

The paintball zipped toward Ash, who cried out, stumbling, just as Jake had.

Come on, Ash. For your sister.

And Ash managed to keep running, too.

"Flinch, and you might lose an eye, people. My aim is good. If you lose an eye, it's no one's fault but your own. Feel free to wash out at any time."

Roach took aim at another recruit and fired. Another.

By morning, of the two hundred and sixty-nine recruits who'd come to the beach, only fifty remained.

Their faces were covered with black and purple welts, and their heads all drooped toward the ground as they ran, along with their arms. Everyone's skin was ashen, and their clothes were soaked through.

But Jake and Ash were among them. When the first patron walked onto the beach, and it was finally over, they limped toward each other, embracing, tears and snot and blood streaming down their faces.

Jake wasn't even sure this was worth it, anymore. He was unconvinced that *anything* was worth this.

The thought of Sue Anne's gaunt face was the only thing that had kept his legs moving.

CHAPTER 24

Dangerous for Basically Everyone

Gabe sat with his right foot atop his left knee, hands resting on his thighs. He peered across a mammoth, mahogany desk at Captain Bob Bronson.

He knew what this was about, but it wasn't Bronson's style to go straight to the heart of any matter. Instead, he had to bring up other bits and pieces first, after which he would cut suddenly to the chase, as though it was a surprise to anyone.

Maybe that sort of tactic did surprise others. But Gabe had been serving under Bronson for too long to be caught off-guard.

"R&D have put together some pretty compelling composites from the brain scans they pulled from Zimmerman's implant," Bronson said. "It was intact, you know. They found it on the floor beneath the mech."

"Unlike Zimmerman."

"Yes." Bronson sniffed. "Anyway, it seems the mech was taking commands directly from his mind, via the implant itself. He willed it to move its leg forward, and it did. Somehow, it managed to access the data from the implant and take its directives from it."

"Did Zimmerman will it to fire on us, then? Did he will it to kill him?"

"Possibly. Probably not intentionally, but it is possible. The prevailing theory is that his death was caused by a simple break in concentration. A stray thought, which the mech interpreted in a way that was...counterproductive."

Gabe barked a bitter laugh. "You have quite a way of putting things."

"Mm." Bronson ran a hand over his bare scalp. "It could mean that piloting the alien mech is very dangerous for anyone unable to maintain perfect focus at all times. In other words, it's dangerous for basically everyone."

"Yeah." Gabe had already put all of this together for himself, and he even had some theories of his own, which he'd been working over in his mind. But he let Bronson ramble, as he knew the man needed to.

"Our geeks also put together aural data from Zimmerman's scans, and something emerged that was somewhat unsettling. Spoken words. English."

"English?"

"Yes. It's possible the mech is advanced enough to have learned basic English just by analyzing the data from Zimmerman's brain. Or maybe it's been listening to us all along, somehow."

"What did it say?"

"A question: 'Is our union that which nullifies?' Does that make any sense to you?"

"Not much. It's creepy."

"Yes. That it is. I wanted to speak to you about something else, as well, Roach."

Ah, yes. Here it is.

Gabe uncrossed his legs, switching them so that his left foot rested on his right knee. He wanted to get comfortable for this.

"I have no choice but to reprimand you for being as hard as you have on the recruits," Bronson said. "Dropping from two hundred and sixty-nine to *fifty* in a single day, it's simply—"

"Night."

"Excuse me?"

"They dropped from two hundred and sixty-nine to fifty during the night."

"Right. Listen, Roach, the higher-ups are worried you're going to scare away potential future recruits by being so hard on your current ones, especially Price and Sweeney. If we become the company that crucifies anyone who tries to work for it, we're going to have a real problem."

Even though he'd seen this coming, Gabe felt no less angry about it. The fact that Bronson was mentioning Ash Sweeney didn't help.

Jess's sister. Gabe knew he was extra hard on her, partly because she reminded him of Jess. Part of him he wanted her to wash out, so that the Quatro couldn't do to Ash what they'd done to her sister.

Another part of him knew that Ash was too good, too determined, to wash out, and that if she managed to endure the extra pressure he piled on her, she would become an even better soldier as a result. She had no idea about Gabe's connection with Jess, of course, and he intended to keep it that way.

To Bronson, he said, "What are you worried about, *sir?* It's not like there's another private military firm around to apply to. What I'm subjecting these recruits to is no worse than the training I went through to join UHF special forces. In some ways, it's easier. These kids have no real military experience, unlike nearly all the Darkstream soldiers who were with the company when we first came to this system. And we're expecting them to pilot mechs in combat. It's time for a reality check, sir. We need to make sure they're ready, and this is the only way we can come close."

Bronson spread his hands, adopting a faux helpless expression. "I'm just passing on to you what the higher-ups are telling me. They say the military landscape has changed since we left the Milky Way. System security means a healthy private sector, and that means Darkstream must follow its profit imperative. Which means actually retaining its employees."

"A healthy private sector also usually means competition, and Darkstream doesn't have any of that." Gabe stood, staring down at Bronson. "If you want to retain all the recruits that wash out, you can feel free to stick them into whatever flabby, coddled unit you can find for them. But if I'm taking these kids into battle driving *mechs,* then I'm going to do my best to drive them into the ground first. If there any are of them left standing once

I'm finished, then maybe, just maybe, they'll be worthy of the responsibility involved in piloting a four-ton war machine the likes of which humanity has only dreamed of till now. Are we finished, sir?"

Bronson sighed. "Well, no one can say I didn't try." He gestured with the back of his hand toward the hatch. "Dismissed."

Storming out, Roach slapped the panel to close the hatch behind him. Bronson had a way of getting under his skin every time, no matter how prepared Roach thought he was for the man's tactics. He was sure the captain made a game of it. *He's sick.*

On his way out of Alpha Quadrant, which was where Bronson's office was located, Gabe passed Darkstream R&D. He paused in the middle of an intersection of corridors, suddenly thoughtful.

To keep going would mean heading back to his quarters in Omega Quadrant. To turn left, through several sets of double doors, and increasing security measures...

"Screw it," he spat, and pushed through the doors. The next set required he demonstrate his V-level security clearance, and so did the next, and the next.

He wasn't sure whether his clearance would get him all the way to the titanium-reinforced room that held the alien mech, but he was pleasantly surprised when it did.

Time to test my theory.

The mech still stood inert in the center of the chamber, Zimmerman's dried blood caked onto its surface and the floor.

Taking a deep breath, Roach walked up to it and put his palm on the thing's calf.

The mech opened for him, but before climbing inside it, Gabe popped a fast-acting, lucid-inducing sedative. After waiting a few seconds, he pulled himself into the mech's guts.

He cleared his mind, in one of the many exercises frequent lucid users used to clear their minds of thought before sleep. Before long, he was inside the dream.

It took him a moment to realize he was standing in the titanium-reinforced chamber. But something was different. In the dream, he was taller than usual; a lot taller.

Gabe dreamed that he lifted his arms toward the observation window, and as they rose, those arms became twin cannons.

The cannons fired, and from the readouts that overlaid his vision, Gabe could see that the rounds traveled faster than any ammunition humans had ever designed. Within seconds, the unbreakable glass shattered into a million pieces.

Gabe dreamed that the cannons became long, scaled bayonets, and then he dreamed that he plunged the blades into the reinforced wall, gradually shredding it with titanic strength.

Gabe dreamed he *was* the mech.

CHAPTER 25

War Never Asks

After the excitement of the beetle chase, the tedium and strain of the daily training routine was punctuated.

During the day, while Andy drove, Tessa either taught Lisa the principles of combat and warfare or made her do what exercises she could within the cramped confines of the beetle, typically wedged between the two back seats.

At night, while Andy inflated their habitat, they worked on Lisa's shooting, alternating between her own SL-17 and Tessa's pistols to fire at virtual targets painted on whatever surfaces were handy.

Once they were inside the habitat, Tessa subjected her to yet more PT. Her only rest came in the very early morning. "I'm not a morning person," Tessa said simply, and so during those times Lisa was left to stare out the window as the barren wilderness rolled by.

Even more than she felt tired, she felt lonely. As her mentor, Tessa remained cold and distant, with none of the friendliness she'd shown over their years of drinking together in Habitat 2.

Andy seemed to be making a point to ignore her, probably because she ignored him. The reason didn't make it any less unpleasant.

Sometimes, Lisa even wondered whether Andy and Tessa might be flirting with each other. It seemed ridiculous, given the age gap, but there it was.

Maybe he's trying to make me jealous.

One night, they camped in sight of the space elevator, though Andy announced he intended to give it a wide berth. "It has nothing for us, and anyway, we don't know how far Daybreak's reach extends. Their takeover may have involved units coordinating in multiple locations."

That gave Lisa pause. "Do you think they might have taken over Habitat 1, too?"

Andy shrugged. "Anything's possible."

That wasn't comforting, and it threw off Lisa's aim that evening. She couldn't keep her mind off the possibility that they could be driving toward the same horrific mess they'd left behind.

"Get your head in the game, girl," Tessa said.

Lisa lowered her gun, glancing back at the older woman in her pressure suit. "I'm not in the mood for this right now. Ma'am."

"So? War never asks whether you're in the mood. It comes either way, ready or not. It's better to be ready."

"War isn't out here. *Nothing's* out here."

"Would you like to wash out, then?"

"Huh?"

"Wash out. Quit. It's what quitters do."

Lisa gestured at the surrounding blue landscape. "This isn't some UHF boot camp. It's the middle of nowhere."

"You're right. And I'm not really your superior officer. I only have the power you choose to give me. You're welcome to quit anytime."

"I don't want to quit. I just want to knock off for the night."

"You skip tonight, you quit. This is about making you battle-ready, girl. Battle doesn't give nights off. If you want me to continue training you, keep shooting. Or you can go inside that habitat and put your feet up. Completely up to you."

With a sigh that she chose not to broadcast over the two-way channel, Lisa turned back to the target and raised the rifle once again.

In the distance, Darkstream's space elevator stretched from horizon to sky, becoming hair-thin before disappearing out of view.

CHAPTER 26

Quatro

The news that Gabriel Roach had solved the mystery of the alien mech buoyed the remaining recruits.

It also made them fear him, though it was difficult for the terror Roach inspired in them to grow much greater.

For Jake, it made him respect Roach a bit more. The rumor mill, which was always churning on Valhalla Station, suggested that Roach had accessed the mech without direct authorization. Probably because Darkstream would have considered his attempt an unacceptable risk, given his importance to the mech program.

So Roach had gone ahead and done it without asking, risking his life for the advancement of humanity and, more immediately, of Darkstream.

The lesson seemed clear: the only time being insubordinate turned out positively was when the disobedient soldier achieved great results through his insubordination. Then, his superiors forgave him, and sometimes even lavished him with praise.

Jake would keep that in mind. Especially since he considered himself smarter, faster, and more skilled than many of the

Darkstream officers he'd met. Sometimes he wondered whether his superiors weren't outright incompetent. The fact that the mechs were only now nearing readiness was ridiculous.

There are lives depending on this!

That said, the news that those who made it through Roach's training would pilot their mechs using lucid—using dreams, essentially—did make Jake even more excited. The mechanism would allow the pilot to *become* the mech, in a very real sense, which Roach said would give them a proper appreciation for the danger involved and also underscore the need for self-preservation. It would dispense with the illusion that the pilot was somehow apart from the fighting because of the awesome machinery at his command. Instead, the level of immersion would be equal to that of a regular soldier in battle.

The training remained as harrowing as always, especially now that they were down to only fifty recruits. Days off were a thing of the past, and in the haze of PT and study and more PT and eating and PT and sleep, two words came to be repeated over and over again, in hushed, fearful tones: Final Evaluation.

It was coming, said the rumor mill, which Jake had now realized was his most reliable source of information on Valhalla. Roach liked to keep them in the dark about most things.

He did tell them three things:

First, R&D had eight mechs that would be outfitted with the interface they'd developed after Roach's breakthrough. Twenty-four other mechs were in various stages of construction and development, but they wouldn't be finished within a meaningful timeframe to fight the Quatro. So Roach had to cull forty-three more of the recruits, since he would pilot one of the eight mechs himself.

Second, the final eight to be cut would be in line to pilot the next batch of mechs, and they'd also act as backup pilots should anything happen to the first eight.

Third, graduates from Roach's training program would belong to a brand new special forces division, the name of which was yet to be determined. The mechs themselves would be called MIMAS, after a giant from Greek mythology.

Of course, they'd learned a few days ago that all fifty of them would have jobs with Darkstream's security forces if they wanted them. Should they fail to make it as mech pilots, they'd be assigned to units based on their individual skill sets.

Which was great, but Jake didn't think it actually comforted anyone. They all wanted to pilot mechs, and they wanted it badly.

If they hadn't, they would never have put up with Roach's unending abuse. Achieving anything less would leave a bitter taste.

Still, when the board authorized all fifty of them to receive implants, on the understanding that they'd work at least a five-year contract with the company, everyone accepted the terms.

Partly because undergoing the procedure to have the implants surgically installed inside their skulls was the closest they'd come to a day off in over a month.

The night after receiving his implant, Jake decided not to go lucid. The implant didn't actually confer an improved lucid experience over the headgear—the main benefits included not having to wear v-lenses and make those stupid gestures all the time.

Besides, he wanted to dream natural dreams, tonight. About piloting a MIMAS mech into battle.

The idea didn't occur to him that, this very night, his childhood dream might get snatched away from him right before he achieved it.

"*Code Scarlet,*" a panicked voice yelled over the intercom. "*Valhalla Station is under attack. Code Scarlet.*"

Jake bolted out of bed, his heart thumping in his chest as he fumbled at the drawer underneath his bed for his jumpsuit.

In the time it took him to get dressed, two other trainees bumped into him, the second one almost knocking him back into bed. The bunkroom was chaos.

"Under attack by *who?*" he heard someone mutter.

But Jake had only one thought running through his head, and he doubted he was alone in that.

It was the same thing feared on some level by every inhabitant of the Steele System: the Ixa. Having finished with the rest of humanity, they'd finally found them, and now they'd come to finish the job.

Sure enough, the word "Ixa" was soon getting repeated over and over, all through the room.

"What do we do?"

"Should we find the chief?"

Cursing, Jake walked to the front of the room, stopping near the door. He placed two fingers over the light controls and tapped them rapidly, flickering the lights off and on. Then he put two fingers in his mouth and whistled, loud and shrill.

Everyone fell silent, turning toward him.

"Shut up," Jake said. "All of you. Obviously, there's no protocol for what we're supposed to do when the station's attacked, because no one expected that to happen. But if Valhalla falls, it's not going to be because the recruits in line to become Darkstream Special Ops cowered in their bunks like frightened little snowflakes. All right? We don't need Chief Roach to tell us what to do, because we *know* what to do. We're going to double-time it to the armory, arm ourselves, and then we're going to fight. I want everyone out in the corridor within two minutes. *Move!*"

Shaking his head, he made his way into the corridor himself, where Ash soon joined him.

"Good speech," she said. "Didn't know you were into making those."

"I'm not. But I like getting blown apart while Roach's finest students play guessing games even less."

"Right. Still, though. That was at least triple the amount of words I've ever heard you string together."

"Don't get used to it."

Soon, the fifty recruits were on their way to the armory, where they began to equip themselves.

"Don't be shy," Jake said. "Take what you can reasonably carry. We know how to use everything in here—Roach saw to that, if our lucid gaming hadn't already. We have to assume that whoever's attacking is looking to take over the station, not destroy it. Otherwise, we probably wouldn't be alive right now. If they're looking to occupy it, they probably don't want to damage it. That means they almost certainly came in through one of the four flight decks."

He divided the recruits into four squads—one to search each quadrant. The moment one squad spotted something, they'd fall back, using their implants to alert the others and broadcast footage of what they were dealing with. Then, they'd confront the enemy as a single, unified platoon.

As it happened, splitting up wasn't necessary. When they left Omega Quadrant, they found the station's Core had plunged into total chaos.

Right away, Jake spotted two shops on fire, and a nearby green space was littered with the bodies of civilians.

"Omega Squad, form up and follow behind me, squad file formation," he hollered. "Ash, you take Alpha Squad and check those shops for survivors. "Kincaid and Beth, take your squads in opposite directions and patrol likely avenues of attack. Let me know right away if you encounter anything."

With Omega Squad at his back, Jake trotted over to the green space to investigate the bodies there. He found their clothes and skin rent with deep gouges and massive bite marks. One man lay crumpled at the base of a tree, his skull caved in.

"Quatro," Jake muttered. "Quatro did this."

"How?" asked another recruit, named Marco. "How could they possible be here? Could they have taken over the space elevator?"

Jake shook his head. "I don't know. Maybe. Not sure how in hell they would have managed that, but now isn't the time to puzzle over it. We need to find and stop them before they hurt more people."

"Quatro in the Core!" It was Kincaid's voice, coming in over Jake's implant. "Jake, there are five Quatro here outside a clothes store. They've smashed out the windows and they're trying to get at the people inside!"

"Kincaid, do they see you?"

"No! My squad's crouched behind a low café wall."

"Good. Ash, you hearing this?"

"I'm hearing it."

"Beth's squad is too out-of-position to engage in time," Jake said, studying the real-time minimap his implant had superimposed near the top-left of his field of vision. "But if we make our way to the edge of the green space we're in, and you set up your squad behind the bank...Kincaid, you start shooting, then we flank them. Hopefully we can put them down before they reach you."

"Yeah, hopefully, eh?" A note of sarcasm had entered the other recruit's voice.

"Listen, I've never fought Quatro before, but it's just as possible they'll run toward my squad once we start firing. We're all in danger here, buddy. That's what battle means."

"Sorry, Jake. I'm just feeling a little tense."

"We all are. But there's no more time for chitchat. Move, everyone! And don't let your situational awareness falter for a second!"

Omega Squad trotted through the trees as quickly and as quietly as they could. Before long, Jake could hear the screams of those trapped inside the shop, and soon after that, he spotted the Quatro who were menacing it.

Subvocalizing to his squad, he directed them to find cover wherever they could. For his part, he nestled his body between two bushes, peering at the giant, purple aliens between a screen of branches, with only his assault rifle's muzzle sticking out.

"All right, Kincaid. Hit them."

No answer.

"Kincaid?"

Incredible. He couldn't wait any longer. Cursing under his breath, Jake leapt to his feet, tearing a grenade from his belt and lobbing it as hard as he could toward the Quatro.

"Take cover!" he yelled to those inside the shop. "Get deeper inside! Grenade!"

The Quatro turned toward the source of the yelling. Then they noticed the grenade, and they started to run. Toward Jake.

"Ash, hit them. Hit them!"

Unlike Kincaid, Ash obliged immediately. Her squad emerged from behind the bank where they'd concealed themselves, crossing the cobbled terrace in lockstep and firing on the Quatro hurtling toward Omega Squad.

The grenade blew, blowing the rear legs clean off one Quatro while the shockwave knocked down the next-closest. Jake and his squad opened fire on the leading three, who weaved and crouched as they ran, to make themselves harder to hit.

The recruits were all decent shots—if they hadn't been, they wouldn't be here. Several bullets hit home. But only one of the Quatro went down, with the front one limping and the third seemingly unaffected.

Jake turned to Marco, who carried a rocket launcher. "Fire that thing and retreat back into the trees. Everyone else, follow me!"

They did, and as they withdrew into the green space, Jake directed them to various hiding spots.

"Climb the trees if you can. Fire on the Quatro from above!"

Soon, seven of his twelve squad members were sitting on branches, and those who weren't lingered near the periphery of the green space, ready to run if a Quatro took an interest in them.

Marco appeared through the trees.

"How'd it go?" Jake subvocalized.

"Took out one," Marco said. "The one that was limping. But that other Quatro's a beast."

"No kidding. Come with me."

"What's the plan? What are we doing?"

"We're being bait."

They ran back toward the area where they'd first entered the green space. Behind them, Jake could hear the remaining Quatro crashing through the trees.

"Hold your fire," Jake told the rest of Omega Squad. "Wait till my mark."

The Quatro appeared through the foliage, pausing to sniff the air. Jake nodded at Marco, and they both raised their guns to fire on the alien.

That got its attention. It charged toward them, emitting loud *huffing* noises.

"Mark!" Jake said.

From various treetops and hiding places, Omega squad fired on the Quatro from multiple angles. But that didn't slow its charge.

Jake gave thanks for all that practice running backwards as he and Marco jogged in reverse, unloading clip after clip into the alien's muscular hide.

At last, the Quatro crashed to the ground before them, at a distance of just a few feet.

Jake and Marco exchanged twin looks of relief. Then, Jake started subvocalizing to the entire platoon: "Good work, Omega and Alpha squads. Kincaid, where the hell were you?"

"We, uh...we decided we were too exposed. Sorry, Jake. It didn't seem fair."

"I almost died. Is that fair?"

"I don't know. Listen, I had to look out for my squad."

Unbelievable. "Kincaid, you do what you want, okay? Go back and crawl into your bunk, if you like. The rest of us will go save Valhalla from the Quatro. You and your squad aren't invited. We clearly can't trust you to have our backs."

"Jake—"

"That's final, Kincaid. You're a liability. Do not follow us."

"Look out, Jake!" It was Ash. "Behind you!"

Jake turned to find a Quatro running at him and Marco. The beast must have come from behind the lucid arcade nearby.

He shoved Marco back toward the trees of the green space and turned to face the charging alien.

"*Run!*" he yelled to his fellow recruit as he switched his assault rifle to full-auto and opened fire.

Other Omega Squad members moved to support him, but it was far from enough. Jake jogged backward, continuing to fire, but the Quatro closed the distance rapidly.

Suddenly, it was on top of him, massive claws tearing open the front of his jumpsuit, gaping fangs descending to sink into his neck.

He woke in his bunk, staring with wide eyes at the gunmetal ceiling.

What the hell?

Then he noticed Chief Roach standing nearby, hands folded behind his back.

"Congratulations," Roach said. "You were the first to die."

Jake's innards went icy, and for a moment he felt even more afraid than he had with a Quatro about to run him down.

"That was the Final Evaluation, wasn't it? Does dying mean I wash out?"

"No one washes out anymore. You'll all get jobs with Darkstream Security."

"Sir, with all due respect, you know what I mean. Did I wash out? Did I fail the test to become a mech pilot?"

Roach frowned. "It's not a simple matter of survival. That's part of the evaluation, but death doesn't necessarily disqualify you. It's also about keeping a cool head. Demonstrating team-work. Demonstrating resourcefulness, leadership, and courage, not to mention tactical competence and facility with firearms."

"Did I make the cut, sir? Please. Just tell me."

"I can't tell you just yet, Price. Not for certain." Roach walked closer to Jake's bunk, where Jake sat with his arms propping him up, heart still racing. "I can say, however, that without your intervention at the start of the sim, *everyone* might have washed out. The confusion and ineptness your fellow recruits displayed then was frankly depressing, but you saved them from themselves. You rallied them, organized them, gave them a purpose. And then you sacrificed yourself for your fellow soldier." Roach sniffed. "For you *not* to make the cut, seven other recruits will have to impress me as much as you just did. I highly doubt that will happen. So I *can* say, somewhat provisionally: welcome to the team."

Drawing a relieved breath, Jake nodded. "Thank you, sir."

"Just don't whine about it if the others surprise me and you don't make the cut, all right?"

Roach grinned, turned around, and paced past the sleeping recruits, who were still deep in the throes of their lucid nightmare.

CHAPTER 27

No Warning

This time, those hunting them gave no warning.

Lisa jolted awake to the sound of gunfire, followed by a sharp hissing sound. "Andy," she subvocalized. "Andy. Come in."

"I'm here," he said, a tremor in his voice. "Suit up, Lisa, as fast as you can. I'll contact Tessa."

"No, I'll get Tessa. I spent my childhood in the Belt—I'm used to putting on pressure suits quickly. Focus on getting yours on."

"Okay."

"Move fast, Andy."

Positioning her suit so she could slip into it quickly, Lisa was about to try subvocalizing to Tessa when she contacted Lisa herself, just as more shots went off, followed by more hissing

"Seems like they found us," the older lady. said. "Are you all right?"

"Yes, ma'am. You?"

"I'm fine. Judging by that sound, we've lost the habitat. If we hang out in here much longer, we'll risk getting hit ourselves."

Lisa pulled on the suit's gloves and worked on joining them with the sleeves to create an airtight seal. "We can't go out the airlock—that's where they'll expect us to come out. They'll hit us for sure. Hold on, I'm switching to a wide channel." She sent her implant the mental command to include Andy in the conversation. "Andy, is there any way to tell which part of the habitat those bullets hit?"

"Yeah, hold on. I can access its sensors via my implant." A brief pause. "Looks like both tears are between my bubble and yours, Lisa."

"Okay, so with the airlock between your bubble and Tessa's, that means we should cut our way out between Tessa's and mine. That way, we won't be emerging into someone's line of fire." *Hopefully.*

"Right. I keep a diamond knife sharpened for that purpose—it's the only thing that will cut through the nanofabric."

Lisa grabbed her assault rifle from next to her bed, and after a cursory inspection, she joined Tessa and Andy in the habitat's common area.

"I'm going to miss this place," Andy said as he began cutting through the exterior with the knife he'd fetched from the central storage compartment.

"Me too," Lisa said, "especially if it means I have to spend all my time stuffed inside that beetle."

"I say we take *their* habitat," Tessa said, her voice grim.

The opening Andy made let them out near a rock face that ended just above their heads.

"Here." Tessa thrust one of her pistols into Andy's hands. "Stay behind the habitat for as long as you can. If you can get a clear shot at one of them, take it. I'm going around the right, to make sure they're not messing with our beetle. Lisa, can you climb onto this ledge?" She slapped the rock with a gloved hand.

Lisa nodded. "No problem."

"Circle around, fast as you can, and flank them. Stick to cover as much as possible. Be careful."

"You too. Let's move."

Behind his faceplate, Andy looked white, but he held the pistol steady, which was good.

Lisa clapped him on the shoulder before finding a foothold halfway up the short cliff and hoisting herself on top of it.

She saw the profile of one of their attackers right away, crouched behind a low rock outcropping. To take her shot now, out here in the open, would be suicide. Instead, she ran for a shallow in the ground to the northeast.

Her heart hammered in her chest as she went—she could feel each palpitation. Her eye twitched. This was her first real engagement. Unlike in lucid, if she was successful here, real people would die. And if she wasn't, then *she* would.

She made it to the hollow, nestled her SL-17 on the rock, lined up her shot, and took a deep breath, letting it out in an even *whoosh* to steady her aim. Then she fired.

The burst took her target in his neck and the side of his faceplate, which cracked but didn't shatter. Even so, the figure collapsed, clutching at his throat, and soon was still.

No one came for Lisa, so he must not have been able to speak to warn his fellows over the radio. Still, the realization that she'd just taken a human life—one that couldn't be restored by waking up from lucid—it hit her like a bus.

Can't think about that now.

She clambered out of the hollow, running to take up her target's position. More gunfire sounded from below, near Tessa's location, but she ignored it. Tessa had her job to do, and Lisa had hers.

Moving from cover to cover, keeping hidden, she took down two more enemies before coming up on what must have been their beetle, which seemed utterly abandoned.

That's odd. She would have expected them to keep a close eye on that.

As soon as she thought it, she heard the sound of another beetle start up and then begin to move. It was coming from the shallow valley where she, Tessa, and Andy had set up camp.

"Tessa?" she subvocalized. "What was that?"

"That was our beetle driving away," Tessa said, cursing. "I tried to stop them, but they had me pinned."

"They left theirs," Lisa said. "I'm looking right at it."

"Ten credits says there's something wrong with it," Andy said.

They approached it warily, but soon discovered it truly was abandoned. Once inside, they found that Andy was right.

Ten minutes later, he had the result of a diagnostic scan. "It's the front-left wheel as well as the front- and middle-right ones," he said. "We might get a day or two out of them, if we're lucky. But sooner than later, this beetle's going to break down."

"Can you fix it?" Tessa asked.

"I can switch the middle-right wheel with the front-left one. That's what may give us the day or two, since the middle-right one is in a bit better condition. But there's no fixing them. Grit got in through the seals, into the bearings, and then when they seized, the friction melted parts of them. After that, the whole mechanism started twisting into scrap, a process that will soon be complete."

Lisa was still grappling with her emotions after the engagement with the Daybreak goons. She was feeling somewhat shell-shocked, but Tessa was as sharp as ever: "Seems like there would be a failsafe of some kind, Andy. To prevent this from happening."

But Andy was vigorously shaking his head. "I told you, these beetles weren't meant to go as fast as we've been driving them over Alex's terrain. This is what happens. Yes, the feedback circuitry on the drive motor *should* have shut off the wheels when the current increased, but that's not what happened. Instead, the motor burned out too."

"That's why they kept chasing us," Tessa said. "They had no choice."

Andy nodded, his hands dancing over the instrument panel, checking a series of readings that he must have been feeding straight to his implant. "The electrolyzer's working fine, so we won't run out of oxygen. We can sit in here and breathe the air for as long as we like. Food, however...that's another issue. Either way, we're not making it to Habitat 1. We're not making it anywhere."

"What about the space elevator?" Lisa managed, struggling to snap herself out of the mental aftermath of the battle. "We could head for that."

"We passed it almost four weeks ago. This beetle's good for two days, tops. We're not going to make it there walking. We can't carry this beetle's habitat with us—it's too heavy—and so even if we tried to walk, we wouldn't be able to eat. Have to take off the pressure suits for that."

"Then we have to chase the beetle they stole from us. Take it back."

"They have no habitat," Tessa said. "Meaning we won't catch them outside of it, like they did to us. Getting it back will probably involve damaging it, maybe irreparably."

"We have to try," Lisa said. "They'll be heading back to Habitat 2, right? We can drive after them in that direction. And if we fail, at least we'll be closer to the elevator than we would have been, once this beetle breaks down. That'll make it more likely we get spotted and rescued."

Tessa nodded. "Lisa's right. It's our only shot. Get this thing moving, Andy."

"Yes, ma'am."

CHAPTER 28

Claustrophobia

When Jorge Delgado saw Ingress' gleaming metallic walls, he heaved a sigh of relief. Rumors had been flitting around the system net about Quatro sightings near the planet's second-largest city, but that was also where the only space elevator was located, and he had to continue his supply runs for Darkstream.

Bertha was on his back enough without him skipping out on his job because of the irrational fear that always got play on the net. And Jorge knew she was *right* to be on his back.

They had three little mouths to feed, and it was bad enough that he hadn't taken that job on Alex. He got claustrophobic, was all, and he hated the idea of living in cramped spaces for months at a time, maybe years. If he took the Alex job, who knew how often he'd be able to fly across the system to visit his family on Eresos?

Bertha didn't view the claustrophobia as a good excuse. That was why she kept on his back all the time.

And she's right to be, darn it. I know she is.

But he hated the idea of those small spaces.

The speeder jerked to the side, suddenly, as though something large had collided with the hover-trailer he towed along behind him. Looking in the side-mirror, he saw that was exactly what had happened.

A Quatro had charged his trailer, and it now ran alongside it, as though angling to do it again.

Suddenly, he felt claustrophobic, even inside his speeder, which he never had before. He was having trouble breathing, but he managed to keep his foot on the accelerator.

Whack. Another Quatro came from the right, barreling right into Jorge's speeder, which tipped sideways a little before leveling out.

"Oh, no," he moaned, maxing out the vehicle's speed, even though he knew the Quatro could keep up if they were motivated enough.

Turned out they were motivated. Not only that, a dozen more Quatro emerged from the trees and out into the Gatherer path ahead.

Looking in the mirror, he saw that maybe two dozen more were amassing in the path behind.

That was when he realized he wouldn't make it to Ingress today.

The Quatro charged, tipping over his speeder so that it was belly-up. They clawed at the door, which made terrible screeching sounds, and Jorge knew that they were smart enough to get inside, eventually.

I should have taken that job on Alex after all.

CHAPTER 29

Stranded

"Okay, what are we going to do, Andy? Seriously."

He glanced back at her from the beetle's driver seat, brow furrowed, then returned to his study of Alex's sapphire landscape. "What do you mean, seriously? Do you think I'm joking when I say we're out of options?"

"No, but it all seems kind of ridiculous, doesn't it? That there wouldn't be more safety precautions than this put in place? I mean, this is your job!"

"It is my job, and it's a dangerous one. I knew that going in. But we aren't supposed to get attacked by a drug lord's cronies, and the wheels aren't supposed to seize up, and we're supposed to be able to use the satellite link to call for help if we need it!"

"How can our specific signal still be blocked? Even after we switched beetles?"

Tessa chuckled. "I already told you that, girl. Who controls the satellites?"

"Darkstream would not intentionally strand us in the middle of nowhere. Uh, ma'am."

"They've done worse."

"Like what?"

But Tessa clammed up, like she always did whenever someone asked her that question.

"Isn't there *anything* we can do, Andy?" Lisa said. "Anything at all? To keep from dying out here?"

"There is, actually. We're going to keep driving until the beetle stops."

"I know that already. What do we do then?"

"We walk."

"But we can't carry nearly enough oxygen to get us to the space elevator."

"Well, we'll fill up what tanks we have from the electrolyzer, and then I'll put them in the detachable trolley. I was thinking...we can use the trolley to carry the inflatable habitat, too, so we can at least eat. And we'll see how far we get. See if someone picks us up."

"What if no one does?"

Andy sighed. "If it makes you feel any better, Darkstream provides flares we can fire off. See if that helps."

"Wow."

"Yeah," Tessa said. "We're kind of screwed, girl."

The training regimen had come to a halt after their beetle was stolen, since as Tessa had remarked, Lisa would need her energy for walking across Alex's craggy surface.

Still, she could sense that she was nowhere near the level of military prowess that would satisfy Tessa.

And I probably never will be. She didn't even know whether she was cut out to fight in another engagement. The first one had left her depressed and feeling hollow, in a way that their present misfortune didn't totally account for.

A whining sound began, loudly at first, but steadily growing softer.

Two minutes later, the beetle rumbled to a halt.

The trio exchanged wordless glances, then they set about gathering together the consumables they'd need to survive in the Alexandrian wilderness for as long as possible.

They left the beetle sitting alone in the blue dust, to become a relic in the middle of Alex's barren nowhere.

CHAPTER 30

Oneiri

Jake made the MIMAS pilots, and not only that, he would be among the first eight to ever pilot mechs in human history. Not counting Chief Zimmerman, that was, whose death had been declassified and painted as a tragic act of heroism in service to the advancement of humanity.

For their failure to back up Omega and Alpha squads when they needed them most, Kincaid and his entire squad washed out of the program.

In fact, they were unlikely to ever see combat, though they would have other jobs with the company if they wanted—such as maintenance and repair, supply runs, collecting payment from those Darkstream leased equipment to, or whatever.

Kincaid had complained, loudly, but Jake had no time for it, and neither did Roach or anyone else in Darkstream.

It's more than fair. If Kincaid had done what Jake had told him to, Jake might not have had to sacrifice himself in order to save Marco. It wasn't a big deal in the sim, but they'd thought it was real, meaning Kincaid would likely be just as unreliable in real life.

They couldn't have that. The MIMAS pilots couldn't have it. And the people of Eresos deserved better.

After graduation from Roach's program came several weeks of nonstop test runs with the mechs, during which Jake and the others learned the ins and outs of the mechs' controls along with exactly what they could do.

The extent of the MIMAS mechs' capabilities astounded even Jake, who'd assumed he'd seen it all during his years of running mech sims in lucid, where features were limited only by the game designers' imagination.

But he'd been wrong. From the impressive arsenal of the mechs—boasting twin rotary autocannons, a heavy machine gun, rockets launchers, twin flamethrowers with nozzles projecting from the wrists, grenade launchers, and thermal lances—to the ability to use its boosters to launch from a planet's surface and straight into low orbit, Jake was blown away by everything the mechs could do. He'd expected early models to be sort of underwhelming, but the fact that Darkstream had been working on developing them pretty much since arriving in Steele really shone through.

Flamethrowers had reentered the company's arsenal only recently. Back in the Milky Way, they had long been banned by widely agreed upon galactic conventions, but of course, Darkstream was no longer subject to those conventions, and the flamethrower was considered an effective tool against Quatro.

Part of Jake railed against the notion of using a weapon that most of his species considered inhumane. Somehow, however, that voice has been turned down to a soft murmur. He suspected that probably had something to do with the constant anti-Quatro messaging they'd been subjected to, and although he was aware of that, it rendered the messaging no less effective.

Ash Sweeney also made the first eight mech pilots, along with Marco Gonzalez, Beth Arkanian, Tommy Tomlinson, Henrietta Jin, Richaud Lafontaine, and Gabriel Roach himself.

"We need a team name," Roach had said, the day after graduation. "I don't have a creative bone in my body, but if you want to brainstorm it amongst yourselves and come up with a half-decent one, please do, before Darkstream labels us with something extra cheesy."

He'd stood up, then, and there'd been some more uncomfortable shifting and throat-clearing from the newly graduated mech pilots.

Looking around at them, Roach said, "You aren't my trainees anymore. I know I put you through absolute hell these last few months, and there's certain things you may never forgive me for. That's fine. In fact, I think it's as it should be. But you all met my standards. All seven of you. You all passed muster, in my eyes. I plan to maintain total authority, of course, but I never want you to forget that you belong on this team. Go into battle with pride, armed with that knowledge, and with everything you've learned. You earned this. You made it."

Battle, it seemed, was coming to them. They learned about the Quatro besieging Ingress a week before they were finished getting trained in on the **MIMAS** mechs. The aliens were attacking any speeder that attempted to approach the city, and no speeder dared to leave. Since Ingress had Eresos' only space elevator, and since the planet was the breadbasket of the Steele System, this was a big deal.

A week was also around how long it would take Darkstream to muster the force it deemed necessary to break the siege. So the mech pilots would finish with preparations just in time.

Jake was ready. While he remained skeptical about the way they'd been indoctrinated into hating the Quatro, the aliens were proving that indoctrination right more and more. They weren't content to live peacefully among themselves, or to leave humanity at peace. Even though there were plenty of resources to go around, the Quatro apparently resented the human's presence too much. So they'd struck.

Another shock came when the mech team was shown classified footage of the Quatro using guns to fire on Ingress' defenders, as well as on civilian speeders. Before, there'd only been jumbled rumors to that effect, but actually watching it happen, watching how the Quatro seemed to operate the guns without even touching them...it was unsettling, to say the least.

The day before they deployed, during one of a long string of tactical meetings, Ash suggested a team name.

"How about Oneiri?" she said. "Since we're going with the whole Greek mythology thing, with MIMAS...the Oneiri were gods that ruled over dreams and nightmares. It's especially fitting, considering the way we interface with—"

"It does fit," Gabe said. "And no one's come up with anything better. I'm good with it. Any objections?"

No one objected, so Oneiri Team it was.

And the following day, Oneiri would find out what it was really made of.

CHAPTER 31

Taken

With their limited oxygen, Andy only inflated the central area of their habitat, and all three of them spent the night in there, attempting to sleep on the cramped, air-filled seats.

Before they'd entered, he'd sent one of their ten flares into the sky. They'd all watched as the red beacon rose up, sparkling beautifully against Alex's darkening sky. Then it extinguished, and Lisa sighed.

They got up before dawn the next day—they tried to spend as little time inside the habitat as possible, to maximize their walking time.

It was laughable to think they could get anywhere near the space station. Laughable to think anyone would notice them, little specks that they were amidst the vast alien wilderness.

Andy sent up another flare as they got underway, and this time, no one bothered to watch it.

Eighteen years didn't seem long enough to get to spend in the universe. Sure, she knew some babies died during birth—pretty rare, these days, but it did happen.

Still, she felt like she'd gotten just a small taste of life, and now it was about to be snatched away, in what would probably be one of the most excruciating ways possible. Starvation or suffocation.

Take your pick.

The sun still hadn't risen, and Alex was freezing. Her HUD told her the air around her was very, very cold: thirty degrees Celsius below zero. They'd set their suits to the minimum requirements for survival, and Lisa's breath came out as fog.

"See that?" Andy said.

"What?"

"Something moved, on that ridge over there, to our left."

Out of the corner of her eye, Lisa saw Tessa unlimbering her pistols from their holsters. She followed the example, unslinging her assault rifle and holding it at the ready.

"Look to our right," the older woman said. "About two o'clock. Don't be obvious about it."

Lisa did. A dark shape stood against the sky, atop a second ridge. At first, she'd assumed their assailants from Habitat 2 had returned to finish the job, but that thought evaporated as quickly as it had taken shape.

This thing, it...it looked like a monster.

A powerful force seized her from behind, separating her gun from her hands at the same time. Amazed, she watched the SL-17 hover in midair, attached to nothing.

Then, whatever gripped her slowly turned her around, and she saw that nothing actually held her, either. An invisible force manipulated her, just as it did her rifle.

There *was* something standing behind her, however, and it was very visible. It was a quadruped, and it wore a sleek, form-fitting blue pressure suit.

Through its faceplate, its species was undeniable, though it made about as much sense as the force that held her.

This was a Quatro.

Quatro weren't supposed to be on Alex.

With that thought, everything went dark.

CHAPTER 32

Subterranean Ship

When Lisa woke, she was still being transported by the bizarre, unseen force, the toes of her boots scraping along the rocky ground.

Dim light came from a single incandescent strip that ran along the ceiling of what seemed to be a rocky underground tunnel.

The bluish hue of the poorly illuminated tunnel walls told her she was still on Alex, which didn't surprise her. Then again, after getting hoisted along by an unseen power, she wasn't sure she'd have been surprised by discovering she'd left the planet, either.

An oppressive sense of helplessness set in, and she began to breathe rapidly, black spots swimming in front of her eyes.

You're okay, she told herself. *You're not hurt. You're okay.* But she couldn't unclench her jaw.

Ahead, the backside of a pressure suit-clad Quatro filled most of her vision, but when the tunnel curved, Lisa glimpsed Tessa ahead of it, suspended in the air in a similar manner, her boots dragging on the tunnel floor.

Those boots moved, attempting to scrabble for purchase, but with the futility of a titmouse attempting to defend itself against a lion.

"Tessa," Lisa subvocalized.

"That's ma'am, to you," Tessa said.

When an implant user subvocalized, his or her voice was rendered in a neutral tone, though it usually came pretty close to how the speaker actually sounded. Even despite the supposed neutrality, Lisa knew that Tessa had meant her words to come across as clipped.

"Ma'am. Have they hurt you?"

"No. You?"

"I'm fine. Where's Andy?"

"He's being carried by the beast ahead of me."

A sigh escaped Lisa's lips, which she realized the subvocalization probably would have transmitted.

"That's good," she said, glad her tone would come across as somewhat disinterested to Tessa. "Have you ever heard of Quatro being on Alex before?"

"No. Never. It's as bizarre to me as the way they're managing to heave us along this tunnel like helpless babes. These aren't just any Quatro, apparently. They're mystical, magical Quatro."

"Somehow, I doubt that's an improvement."

"Me too. Though, we'll probably end up just as dead."

A comforting thought. "Did you pass out, too?"

"No. I gather you did, since you weren't answering me, earlier. Must have been from shock. If it was something they did to you, they'd have done it to me, too."

Their situation was doubly bizarre. As Lisa remembered an ancient author once writing, any sufficiently advanced technology was almost always indistinguishable from magic.

Of course, that was providing this unseen force *was* due to a technological advancement the Quatro had made, and not...something else.

What seemed even more mystical—and certainly not the exciting, fun 'mystical' of old fantasy novels—was how the hell the Quatro were here in the first place.

"The Quatro are supposed to be primitive. Aren't they?"

"That's what we've always assumed," Tessa said. "The ones on Eresos have never shown any sign of using even basic technology. The first Darkstream combatants that encountered them classified them as just highly advanced predators, with cognition on the level of dolphins. And look how the dolphin ended up."

Lisa vaguely remembered that losing the dolphins had been looked on as a great tragedy, and that it had also heralded the ultimate destruction of Earth.

Most people who'd come to Steele with Darkstream considered that sacrifice more or less worth it. Earth had been the price paid for humanity's mighty corporations to expand into the stars.

She took the fact that she was thinking about dolphins right now to mean she would do anything to distract herself from how terrifying it felt, to be this helpless.

The tunnel ended in what turned out to be an airlock installed right into the rock. It opened, and the Quatro brought them inside. Once the airlock finished oxygenating, it admitted them into what looked a lot like the interior of a spaceship.

Not any human spaceship, though. It was huge, for one—huge enough to accommodate the Quatro, who were larger than the largest horses of Old Earth. And whereas most ships built by the UHF and Darkstream had an austere, gunmetal aesthetic, vibrant colors filled this one. Yellow, red, green, blue, purple—the royal purple of Quatro—they all swirled together, or fit together in elaborate geometric patterns.

Even the floor provided a canvas for the art, and Lisa was calmed slightly by the fact that these Quatro, whatever their true nature, were capable of producing such beauty.

She soon came to suspect, however, that the art was not meant to impress them, or indeed meant for them at all.

The ship seemed fairly old, actually, and in a general state of disrepair, with intermittent flaky patches amidst the artwork, as well as worrying cracks in the bulkhead.

A hatch slid open at the Quatro's approach, squealing with age, and Lisa and her companions were deposited inside a chamber that was huge by human standards.

The same invisible force held them in place until the Quatro withdrew and the hatch closed, leaving no discernible avenue of escape. Only then did the force release them.

Their HUDs told them the air was breathable, and so the trio removed their helmets and took in their surroundings while they attempted to shake the blue dust of Alex out of every pocket, fold, and crevice of their pressure suits and persons.

"The furniture looks like it would be comfortable, if we were Quatro," Andy said.

It was true. Couch-like pieces lined the wall, except they curved into peaks and troughs, like waves—but waves designed to accommodate a quadruped at rest.

The trio performed a frenetic search of the room, but escape appeared totally out of the question. There was a grated vent near the ceiling, but Lisa had to get on Andy's shoulders to reach it, and it was firmly sealed. The hatch remained as impenetrable as before, and an ear pressed to its cold surface yielded no sound.

At the rear of the chamber, an enormous, hanging chair lined with a fine mesh turned out to be surprisingly accommodating, and Lisa climbed up into it, letting her back rest against the net of small, flexible wires.

She glanced at Tessa, suddenly wary that the white-haired woman was about to make her get up again, to begin a prolonged round of strenuous PT.

But even Tessa seemed dejected—too dejected to read, apparently, since she didn't seem to be doing anything with her implant, even though she'd taken advantage of every other spare moment since leaving Habitat 2 to read one of the thousands of books she had loaded onto the device.

Eventually, Lisa's eyes drifted closed. She floated away from her bizarre circumstances for a time, and nightmares soon took their place.

CHAPTER 33

Drop

The space elevator only made one run a day—down during the night, up during the day—and so it was built big; a wide, circular disk with dark-orange walls that bulged outward and a gunmetal ceiling that hung well over the mechs' heads.

The elevator climbed up a carbon nanotubes composite ribbon by way of a robotic lifter at its center. The ribbon looked way too thin to Jake, but nevertheless it had done the job of transporting the elevator up and down for the decade and a half since Darkstream had built it, along with the free-electron laser system located inside the depot at the elevator's bottom.

The ribbon was anchored by the depot in Ingress' center, and Valhalla Station, in its geosynchronous orbit, provided the elevator's counterweight.

Normally, the elevator went both ways packed full of cargo, stopping for a set period on either end, which was based on Darkstream's calculation of how long loading and offloading should take.

Tonight, its only cargo was one of Darkstream's reserve battalions. This one called itself the Force Multipliers, though Jake wasn't sure who had come up with that somewhat hokey name. It fit, he supposed—despite being a reserve force, they did have access to some of Darkstream's best training, hardware, and personnel. They were under the command of Commander Benjamin Clifford.

I shouldn't be too hard on them. They'll play their part. Just so happens we'll be ten times more effective, at least.

He expected so, anyway. The fact that Darkstream was sending both Oneiri and the Force Multipliers meant the company considered Ingress very important. Which made sense: not only was it their main gateway to the planet, given the elevator terminated there, but it was one of Eresos' two major human cities. Losing it would mean losing an essential foothold on the system's only planet with a breathable atmosphere.

Oneiri Team didn't intend to let that happen. And neither did the five armored personnel carriers, three tanks, two mortar teams, fifteen snipers, and four platoons of battle-hardened infantry that comprised the Force Multipliers.

None of the MIMAS pilots strayed far from their mechs to make small talk with the other soldiers. Probably because they coveted their new war machines, each feeling a certain sense of ownership over their respective mechs, which made sense, given how hard they'd worked to earn the right to pilot them.

For Jake's part, he just wanted some peace and quiet, to find focus before his first actual battle.

His eyes met Gabriel Roach's, who leaned against his mech's legs, arms crossed. They exchanged nods.

Jake had half-expected Roach to pilot the alien mech into battle, but it turned out Darkstream's board considered that way too dangerous. He'd already taken a tremendous risk by climbing into it in the first place, which they'd forgiven him for since it had led to such a breakthrough in the company's development of MIMAS mechs.

But actually taking the thing into battle—they weren't okay with that. They much preferred him to pilot *their* mech, whose designers had left out the feature where the mech folded inward to kill its occupant.

"Ingress will end up much deeper in debt to Darkstream after this," said Ash, stepping up beside Jake.

"You figure? Their current contract doesn't cover siege-busting?"

"I highly doubt it. I mean, look at the scale of this operation. Also, word is the Quatro have figured out how to disrupt the flow of Gatherers to the city."

"Wow, really? We haven't even been able to do that."

"I know. And if Darkstream can manage to fix the Gatherers after the battle...well, they're going to want expanded resource rights in return, aren't they? Hell, I'd say signing over those rights is the only way Ingress can afford to pay for all this. The city's already stretched as thin as it can go."

"How do you know all that?"

Ash met his eyes. "My father was mayor of Northshire. He had friends in almost all of Eresos' sitting councils."

Roach appeared to be subvocalizing with someone over his implant. He held a hand to his ear as he spoke, which a lot of the old-timers did, even though it wasn't necessary. When he was finished, he locked eyes with Jake.

"Everyone meet me next to Price's mech," Roach's voice said into his ear. "There's been an update. Double-time."

The rest of Oneiri jogged over. "What up?" Richaud said as he neared.

"Wait till everyone's here," Roach said.

Henrietta was last to arrive. "What's the word?" she asked. "Let me guess—the other soldiers have started asking for mechs of their own?"

Roach didn't even crack a smile. "The Quatro have started to tunnel."

"But Ingress' walls extend down almost two hundred meters, don't they?" said Marco. "We'll get down there in plenty of time to stop them."

"The Quatro are proficient diggers, and the tunnel entrance was only just spotted by satellite—we don't know how long they've been working on it. They could emerge inside of Ingress any minute. The higher-ups are worried. They don't think the elevator will make it in time."

"So...what's the solution?" Ash asked.

"We engage the elevator's emergency stop. Then Oneiri Team jumps, landing in the hills directly behind the Quatro force. We'll rain hell on them from the hilltops."

"That's insane," Jake said. "We haven't even tested the reentry tech."

Roach shrugged. "The physics check out, and the engineers seem confident in their design. We have our orders, Price. I've already sent the elevator operator the command to stop."

"I told you, Jake," Ash subvocalized over a two-way channel. "Ingress is too important to Darkstream. They probably see this as a calculated risk."

I wonder if the calculus would be different if it was their *lives on the line.*

The nanoribbon emitted a deep groan, then, and the elevator slowed to a stop.

"It's time," Roach said. "Everyone inside your MIMAS."

CHAPTER 34

Stars

The door sprang open without notice, slamming against what Lisa had come to think of as the bulkhead.

Starting from her sleep, Lisa gasped as the invisible force seized her once more, yanking her from her giant hanging basket and into the corridor.

As the Quatro spirited the trio through the underground vessel, she noticed something odd: none of the hatches they passed appeared to have opening mechanisms of any kind. That perplexed her for several seconds, distracting her momentarily from her panic, until the explanation dawned on her:

The Quatro used whatever strange force they wielded to manipulate their ship as well.

Something else about the ship had become quite apparent to all three of them as they attempted to rest: it was freezing. They were forced to keep their pressure suits on, for fear of hypothermia. It was even colder in here than it was on Alex's surface at night. Whenever Lisa's helmet was off, her breath fogged in front of her.

How can they live in such frigid conditions?

The Quatro did not seem interested in providing her with that information. Instead, they carried the mystified trio deeper into the ship, until they arrived at a chamber that was much less accommodating than the first one.

Lisa, Tessa, and Andy were thrust inside, and the hatch squealed shut, as though on rusty hinges.

"I guess they thought we were too comfortable," Tessa said, glancing around at their new room.

"You call that comfort?" Andy said with a terse laugh. "Maybe Lisa was comfortable, after claiming the only piece of furniture remotely hospitable to humans."

But Lisa barely registered the jab. Their new accommodations had her attention, and there was something even stranger about them than the rest of the ship.

"Check out that fountain," Andy said, pointing. "That Quatro looks ready to tear someone's head off."

Lisa followed his finger to the sound of burbling water. A metal sculpture of a Quatro spewed the liquid from its mouth, into a tiny hole, where it presumably got recycled.

"I guess they don't want us dying of thirst," Tessa said. "Although, what I really want is a slice of cheesecake."

"*Cheesecake?*" Andy said, looking at her strangely.

"What? It's just what I'm craving."

"Fair enough. I guess."

A strange basin projected from the bulkhead across the chamber, directly opposite the Quatro-head fountain. Drawing nearer, Lisa discovered that the bottom was uneven, with a convoluted pattern of dips and swirls. It wasn't attractive by any measure, and she was sure it had a purpose of some kind, though she couldn't sort it out.

Not far from the basin, what was unmistakably a computer console rested inside a hollow.

As with the rest of the ship, beautiful artwork covered every bulkhead of the room.

But what seemed most important, for some reason, was the fact that this room reminded her of going lucid.

She approached a panel in the bulkhead that appeared to depict an alien landscape. It had rolling hills that exhibited a strange symmetry, foreign to nature. Above, twin moons hung in place. The whole scene had a dreamlike, watery aesthetic.

Lisa knelt in front of the panel, pushing against it.

Nothing happened.

"Lisa?" Andy said. He'd ceased chattering with Tessa, and now they both studied her, wearing twin expressions of mild concern. "What are you doing?"

Lisa tried to slide the panel left, then right. Still nothing.

Then, she tried to slide it up. As she pressed upward against it with her palms, the panel rose an inch, but fell again when she lost her grip on the smooth surface.

"Help me lift this."

Tessa stepped forward, kneeling beside Lisa, and joining her in attempting to push it up. This time, the panel rose several inches before hitting a barrier inside the bulkhead with a *thunk.*

"Come and search underneath it, Andy," Lisa said, her voice a little strained with the effort of keeping the panel raised.

"What in Sol for?" Andy said.

"Get over here, boy," Tessa barked. It was the first time she'd called him that, though she'd called Lisa "girl" plenty.

When Tessa spoke like that, people moved, and Andy was no exception. He knelt between them.

"Don't drop that thing," he muttered as he ran his hand over the ledge they'd revealed, as well as over the bulkhead behind the panel. "There's nothing here."

"Try gripping the bottom of the panel and pulling it out," Lisa said.

With a sigh, Andy positioned his fingers on the bottom of the panel. "I can't—" he said, but then he found enough purchase, and the panel lifted away from the wall by barely an inch.

It was enough. When Lisa and Tessa lowered it, the panel slid from its casing, till Andy dropped it. It came to rest on the deck, still partially locked in the twin runners that held it in place.

Above, in the space that had been revealed, was a grid with symbols along the left and bottom sides, which corresponded with the various rows and columns. Lisa picked at the edge of the grid with her finger, and it peeled away from the wall with ease.

When it did, she saw that the grid's squares were transparent, and so were the symbols themselves. The horizontal and vertical lines, as well as the edges, were opaque and purple—the same shade as the Quatro.

"Congratulations," Andy said. "You found a stencil."

"It's not," Lisa said, her tone level. She poked her finger at one of the squares, and it encountered a barrier. "There's something there; it's just see-through."

Lisa walked around the room with her discovery, peering through it and ignoring Andy's ongoing commentary.

She stopped in front of a mural depicting a starry sky. It had the same dreamlike quality as the panel. "I think it goes with this."

Suddenly, five of the stars twinkled, which only strengthened her convictions. When she looked at them with her naked eye, they did nothing, but they twinkled when viewed through the grid.

"It's not a painting," she went on. "It's a mostly static display, but some of the stars twinkle when you use this."

A quick study of the floor revealed a faint black line, and she held the grid directly above it, squinting through it at the stars.

"Check that console across the room," she said over her shoulder. "See if the symbols are the same as the ones along this grid."

"Do it, boy," Tessa said, and Andy did. Then he returned to study the grid, recrossing the room once more to stare at the console.

"They're the same," he said at last. "I'm sure of it."

"All right. I figured out something, too. I'm pretty sure these symbols are supposed to be numbers. The same ones are in the same order going up as well as across." After another moment's study, she said, "There are five rows and five stars. I bet if I go up row by row, describing the symbol of the column each star falls, and you punch them into that console..."

"What?" Andy said. "We'll win a prize?"

"Something will happen. I'm sure of it."

Looking back, Lisa saw that Tessa was frowning. "As strange as Quatro on Alex is, this feels even stranger," the former Darkstream soldier said. "It's like they're making us play some weird game."

"*They're* not making us do anything," Andy said. "Lisa is. And you're making me follow her orders."

"I rank higher than you, anyway, Andy," Lisa said.

"What does that matter, anymore? We're prisoners."

"That's when it matters most. Now, are you ready to punch in these symbols? The first star falls in a column marked with a sort of crescent moon with a line through it."

Andy sighed. "All right. I see it. There." He punched a button. "What's next?"

Lisa continued to describe the symbols, one after another. Andy entered the fifth, and after a few suspenseful seconds, something happened: two slim metal drawers sprang open from the bulkhead next to the panel they'd moved. Both drawers were empty, but before long, Lisa discovered that the bottom one came all the way out.

She set it on the floor, and was able to reach her arm through the hollow the drawer had left behind, at the back of which she found a metal receptacle, like an extremely narrow drinking cup with a rim that was ridged unevenly all along its circumference.

Near the bottom, it was circled by a rubber-like black band covered in evenly spaced dots.

Together, they worked through puzzle after puzzle, almost all of which required plenty of cooperation and communication. The cup allowed them to transport water across the room to the strange basin, and when they filled it up, the water took the shape of three more symbols.

After several minutes of wondering over that, Andy discovered another panel that could be pulled away from the wall to reveal three concentric wheels covered in symbols. When they lined up the three symbols from the basin, another drawer sprang open nearby.

Twenty minutes later, after assembling an image from six pieces collected from various hidden compartments around the room, accessed by solving yet more puzzles, an entire wall lifted upward—the one that bore the stars from one of the first puzzles—revealing a long, dark tunnel.

Lisa looked at Andy, who looked at Tessa.

"We're not actually going down there, are we?" Andy said.

"What else can we do?" Lisa asked, shrugging. Then she took the first step into the tunnel.

The others followed. Her heart beating a tattoo in her chest, Lisa tried to focus on her exhilaration over her fear. What might their reward be for their work on the puzzles? Assuming there would be a reward, and not a punishment. Every lucid sim she'd ever played had trained her to expect the former, but this wasn't lucid, was it?

It would make a lot more sense if it was.

Without warning, the invisible force seized her once more, followed by three Quatro stepping out of the shadows, piercing lights clicking on behind them to blind her.

The Quatro dragged the three humans the rest of the way down the tunnel and into the brightness of the rest of the ship.

After whisking them through a series of corridors, the Quatro deposited them in the first room they'd stayed in—the one with the strange furniture.

The hatch screeched shut once more, closing with a *clang*.

Andy was shaking his head. "What just happened, exactly?"

"We were played for fools," Tessa said with a drawn-out sigh. "We just don't know what kind of fools yet."

CHAPTER 35

Miscalculation

Though he'd put on a brave face for his young team—or, possibly, an indifferent face—Gabe wasn't thrilled about dropping through a wide section of Eresos' atmosphere using untested technology.

Well, the tech itself is pretty old. It was using it to send mechs hundreds of kilometers to the ground without killing their occupants that was new.

The fact that, in order to interface with the mech, he would also technically be asleep...that didn't help his composure very much.

He felt a bead of sweat creeping down his forehead, but he refused to wipe it away. It wouldn't be good to let the team see that.

Before his stress could show through in other ways, he popped a sedative and placed his hand over the sensor pad on the mech's calf, long enough for it to read his biometrics. A section of the mech's backside folded down, becoming a ridged ramp for him to climb.

The designers had seen an opportunity in the fact that each pilot would go lucid for the entire time they spent inside their mech. In other vehicles meant for battle, it was necessary to allow for some room in the cockpit, to give occupants space to stretch their limbs, shift their weight, and so on. Otherwise, panic-inducing claustrophobia could easily set in.

Not so with lucid-controlled mechs. The space could be devoted instead to more artillery and more fuel.

Slipping into lucid, Gabe didn't just interface with the mech—he *became* the mech, standing just as tall as it did, and feeling just as powerful.

He would also feel what it felt. The designers had decided to render damage to the mech as physical pain to the occupant, which was easily accomplished using lucid.

That had been a controversial decision, and it almost hadn't happened, except for Gabe's ardent support for the idea.

A good soldier knew how to use pain to stay aware—of their situation, and also of their limitations. Plus, the knowledge that actual pain would accompany damage to the mechs would also force the pilots to use them as judiciously as they used their own bodies.

Which was good, because right now, the mech *was* Gabe's body. Its wicked artillery protruded from *his* metal flesh. And when he stepped toward the space elevator's opening aperture, toward the widening slice of star-speckled space, it was Gabe's heavy metal foot that moved.

Standing on the edge of the platform, looking down on the world, he felt like a god. All-powerful. Invincible.

He leapt. Which quickly reminded him of his humanity, and the accompanying mortality.

At first, there was barely any sensation, as he hadn't entered the atmosphere yet and so there was no air resistance. The planet also didn't seem to get any closer. He was so high up, it didn't feel like he was falling at all.

Then, his ablative heat shield deployed automatically, just before he hit the atmosphere. The shield lowered the temperature to a survivable level by carrying the heat away using convection, but Gabe could see the flames that licked at it, and he felt their heat, too. He was really sweating, now.

It occurred to him how insane jumping from the elevator had been, without having tested the process first. Darkstream considered it worth it to gamble with their soldiers' lives in this particular situation, and Gabe hadn't said a thing about it.

He'd become just as reckless as the corporation he worked for, apparently. This type of thing never would have gone ahead, back in the UHF.

Of course, if he'd been in the UHF all this time, he would have been court-martialed several times over for the things he'd done.

At last, the fires receded, and now wind whipped past his metal frame, threatening to freeze his—well, technically he didn't have those right now, did he?

In an attempt to distract himself from Eresos' surface, which now grew gradually larger, he thought of an old story he'd heard just before leaving the Milky Way, about that pansy Vin

Husher, taking a leap down to the surface of the Winger home-world in nothing but a Darkstream reentry suit.

Ten credits says he wet himself on the way down. He accepted his own bet, though he wasn't sure how the logistics of that would work.

To be fair, in just a suit, Husher would have had a much worse time than Gabe was having now. The drop weight was much lower in a reentry suit, meaning the number of Gs your body was subjected to ratcheted way up.

Either way, Husher wouldn't have been able to handle this much machine. Of that, Gabe felt confident.

"How's everyone doing?" he subvocalized to his team. "Check in."

"Doing fine, sir," Jake said.

"As good as can be expected," said Henrietta.

One after another, his entire team sounded off. Which only served to distract him for around thirty seconds.

He thought of Jess, but quickly stopped himself. No need to show up for battle a sobbing wreck.

Come on, Gabe. This isn't a big deal. You've entrusted yourself to the laws of physics, that's all. And to Darkstream engineering.

Which, admittedly, wasn't always the most dependable.

There was nothing to get overly excited about. This was only the first mech space jump performed in history.

Probably this was a very, very stupid idea.

His mech's heat shield had dissolved, and now Eresos' landscape expanded below him, its details growing sharper and sharper. Before long, a parachute would deploy, designed to disengage well before landing. After that, aerospike thrusters would take him the rest of the way.

He spotted Ingress below, surrounded on all sides by teeming masses of indistinct purple dots. As those dots grew larger, they became vaguely recognizable as Quatro.

"Sir?" It was Ash.

"Yeah?" he croaked, his voice coming out mangled. He cleared his throat. "Yeah?" he repeated, more confidently.

"Are you sure we calculated our entry angle correctly?"

Gabe blinked, trying to clear his head. He studied the ground. To do this, he didn't need to tilt the mech's head down—the machine had sensors all over, and it fed their data to his implant, which relayed it to him in lucid.

As he considered Ash's question, his parachute deployed.

He cleared his throat again. "Uh—it seems we're going to come down directly in the middle of the Quatro, everyone. Stay frosty and remember your training."

In the meantime, Gabe's chest tightened with panic, and he struggled to calm himself down.

Breathe. Just breathe.

CHAPTER 36

Heavy Ordnance

Jake's mech crashed to the ground.

More accurately: *Jake* crashed to the ground, his metal legs buckling to absorb the shock.

Rearing to his full height of two and a half meters, he retracted the mech's hands to reveal twin rotary autocannons, which he leveled at the Quatro who charged at him from all sides.

Inside the mech's forearms, the guns began to rotate, sending heavy ordnance tearing into the beasts' flesh, flinging them back as they yelped or barked throatily.

As he'd fallen toward the planet, his anxiety over the coming battle had quickly mounted, but that hadn't prepared him for the level of sheer terror he experienced now. Even within the dream, he could feel his nostrils flare widely as he sucked in each ragged breath, and he became intensely aware of everything around him, wary of potential threats.

The autocannons weren't enough to keep the enemy at bay. A Quatro pounced on him from behind, knocking him forward, making him stagger a couple of steps.

This can't happen. I won't let it.

As his hands reassembled themselves in front of the autocannons, blades sprung from his wrists, and he spun around, slashing wildly at his assailant.

Steel found alien flesh, and scarlet droplets flew through the air, but another Quatro crashed into him from the side, sending him stumbling again, and then another tackled him head-on.

Jake was sent sprawling onto his back. The Quatro piled onto him, tearing at his skin, racking his entire body with waves of pain.

This was nothing like training—even lucid hadn't prepared him for this. Lucid, where even though his brain accepted the simulated reality, on some level he'd still known it to be a simulation.

This...this was real. Each claw mark left searing lines along his body. The aliens weren't bothering to use their guns; they seemed content to tear apart his mech and rip Jake from it bodily.

Even before applying to become a mech pilot, Jake had considered himself among the best—the quickest kid in the Belt; one of the best lucid gamers in the system. Wasn't that supposed to count for something? *Can this really be it?*

Some of the Quatro had long bayonets with wicked blades, and they gouged Jake with them, working at his joints, scoring his casing.

When Jake glimpsed the sky between the giant aliens covering him, it flashed blood-red—the dream's way of reflecting the danger he was in.

His fear did a good job of that, too. He was consumed with fear. The world seemed made of it.

But then and there, he decided he would refuse to let it paralyze him. Motivated more by terror than determination, he managed to roll onto his stomach and bring one of his knees between his chest and the ground.

Then, he shoved the ground, surging up through the hulking aliens that pinned him.

One of the Quatro went flying, leaving a patch of red-flashing sky in its place, and Jake sunk his blade into another.

Then, an idea struck him. He knew Darkstream had designed the mechs to withstand a grenade blast.

Time to test that.

Pointing his grenade launcher directly at the ground, he fired.

He didn't have to wait long for the explosion.

Searing heat washed over his body, making him cry out in the dream, and sound replaced fear as the universe's main ingredient.

The Quatro smothering him were blown apart into several pieces. Time seemed to slow as alien limbs and torsos and heads went soaring away in all directions, streaming blood and sinew.

Jake watched in awe at the utter carnage he had wrought.

Then, he looked around for his comrades.

He felt confident one of them was very nearby. Not taking the time to consult his HUD to figure out who it was, he instead charged at the dogpile of Quatro covering his teammate.

Grabbing one of the beasts with enormous metal hands, he flung the creature away, sending it several meters into the air, yelping, before it landed with a sickening *crunch.*

The thing started spasming, but Jake didn't take the time to watch. Instead, he plunged his blade into the next Quatro, ripping it open all down its body, and then he stabbed the next, over and over.

The Quatro turned to face him, lessening their pressure on the downed mech, and Jake retracted his segmented hands to let loose with his autocannons once more, backing up as he did. This gave him enough room to mow down the aliens as they came at him, and the mech they'd been holding down rose up behind, joining Jake in the slaughter.

It was Ash.

"Thanks for the assist," she said, her voice echoing a little in the dream.

"Assist?" he said, chuckling, though his laughter sounded somewhat manic in his ears. "I *saved* your ass."

"Oh, God. It's going to be like that, is it?" Ash leveled her heavy machine gun at Jake and fired.

His stomach dropped, but then he realized what had happened—she'd downed a Quatro that had been charging at him from behind.

"Are we even now?" Ash said.

"Hardly. I could have taken that one."

"Right." Ash turned, striding toward Roach, who was just gaining his feet himself, and starting to visit havoc on the Quatro surrounding him.

Jake joined her, and together they waded into the war for Eresos.

CHAPTER 37

Crumbling

Gabe loosed a rocket, picking off a group of three Quatro charging toward him.

We're turning the tide. We're going to win this thing.

His HUD alerted him of another enemy coming at him from his seven o'clock, barreling across the little minimap. Alongside that, the HUD also gave him a readout that listed the Quatro's velocity and estimated mass, but Gabe didn't have time to *read.*

Instead, he turned in time to roast the thing with twin gouts of flame to the face.

The Quatro yelped, and the smell of charred fur and flesh reached Gabe's nose.

Whoa. I didn't know this thing had olfactory sensors.

Darkstream R&D truly had thought of everything.

Turning just in time to impale another Quatro on the point of his right-hand bayonet, Gabe stumbled as a vivid flashback hit him, of walking through a blackened cave.

The Quatro slid off his blade and onto the ground as he lost himself in memory, the images just as sharp as they'd always been.

A charred Quatro corpse lay prostrate near the bottom of a cave wall, the wall itself smeared with blood where it had cracked off its claws in its futile struggle to escape.

Snap out of it, Gabe.

He turned to confront another group of three Quatro that had almost reached him, firing his autocannons at full bore, his shooting sloppy, this time. Two of the Quatro did go down—but the third crashed into Gabe, knocking him backward.

Another flashback. A mother curled protectively around her pups, all of them charred black as coal.

Another: two Quatro that had died locked in combat, driven mad by the fuel air explosive, which had turned their oxygen to fire.

Why? Why now? Is the dream amplifying it somehow?

Struggling to keep it together, Gabe kicked up with his legs, sending the Quatro pinning him flying over his head. Turning as he rose, he picked off the alien before it hit the ground. It didn't move again.

Another memory took over his vision: a white shape, a summer dress, stained with the scarlet smear of blood.

Jess.

A gunshot. Jess's father, Mayor Sweeney, driven to take his own life by the horror of it all.

Your fault. It's your fault, Gabe. Admit it.

The sound of cheering reached his ears, jerking him from his dark reverie. It was his team, Oneiri Team, celebrating.

Why? We're still surrounded by Quatro.

Then he saw: the rest of the reserve battalion had arrived. It felt like the mechs had hit the ground less than an hour ago, but now that he thought about it, he realized he'd killed a lot of Quatro.

Armored personnel carriers, tanks, infantry—they all poured out of the city's open gates, giving it to the enemy, hard. Darkstream snipers fired on the aliens, from positions all along Ingress' walls.

"We're doing it, sir," Jake said. "We're beating them!"

Glancing to the right, Gabe saw Jake's mech, its fist raised in victory. Blood smeared its twin blades, and fragments of viscera covered its metal skin.

"Get back to work," Gabe rasped. Turning, he fired up his autocannons, barrels rotating as they sent round after round of hot lead into the enemy, who were swiftly crumbling.

CHAPTER 38

First Words

Given that the only macroscale organisms Lisa knew to exist on Alex were humans, and now Quatro, she worried about the source of the meat the aliens had left for them. Eventually, her hunger overcame her worry, and she ate it, as did Tessa and Andy.

"The Quatro haven't actually done anything to hurt us," she reasoned out loud. "Screwed with us, maybe, but not hurt us."

"That's probably coming," Andy said, ever the optimist.

"I'm just saying," Lisa said as she chewed, holding the remainder of her haunch of succulent...whatever it was. "I'm sure this food is fine."

"Huh?" Andy said. "What do you mean, fine? It tastes good. What are you worried about? You think they might have poisoned it or something?"

"Uh...never mind." She'd assumed they were all thinking the same thing, but apparently not. Lisa exchanged glances with Tessa, and they all returned to dining in silence.

Two days after their ordeal in the puzzle room, the hatch flew open to reveal a Quatro in the enormous corridor, staring at them with bright orange eyes.

For the first time since they'd been transported from the strange, puzzle-filled room, the invisible force seized them, dragging them into the corridor, where four more Quatro awaited.

This time, the force did allow Lisa to walk on her own—but only in the direction the aliens seemed to want her to move in. If she attempted to head another way, it was as though a brick wall was stopping her.

They entered a part of the ship she hadn't seen yet, and Lisa's internal compass told her they were heading deeper into the subterranean vessel, though she had no idea of its actual size.

The corridor gradually opened up, until it became a cavern of a chamber, terminating in a multi-level dais covered in furniture similar in shape to the pieces the humans had been sleeping on, though these were much more sumptuous.

Twenty more Quatro studied them from atop that furniture, enormous paws drooping from lush upholstery, forty pairs of eyes studying them—ranging from orange, to pink, to green, to one Quatro with midnight eyes the likes of which Lisa had never encountered.

Without warning, the Quatro rose as one, and the dark-eyed beast pounced, crashing to the deck right in front of Lisa.

The beast loomed over her, body bunched, its feline face terrifying in its fierceness.

Am I about to die?

It seemed likely. Tortured, at least.

Something's about to happen. And I doubt it will be pleasant.

Something did happen, but it turned out to be nothing like her fears.

It was no less shocking, however.

The Quatro spoke.

"Hello. Human."

That done, it continued to peer down at Lisa, and she realized that what she'd mistaken for ferocity was actually curiosity. It was waiting for her to speak as well.

"Um...hi," she said.

CHAPTER 39

Our Planet Now

Gabe walked the fields outside Ingress in his **MIMAS**, helping to clear away Quatro corpses, as well as a few that belonged to human beings.

The latter would receive proper funeral ceremonies and burials. The former would be piled in a heap and burned.

Perhaps one of the mechs would be the one to light the pyre.

Once his team had regained their footing and started fighting the Quatro in earnest, the battle had shifted quickly, with the aliens falling in droves. When the rest of the Darkstream battalion arrived, it had quickly become a slaughter.

The Quatro ranks, such as they were, had broken, and the enormous quadrupeds had begun to flee into the hills surrounding Ingress.

Oneiri Team hadn't taken that as a cue to relent. Instead, they'd run the beasts down, metal feet pounding across the hard-packed dirt surrounding Ingress, guns blazing. They hadn't wasted any more rockets on the fleeing Quatro, but they hadn't been shy about pouring hot lead into their retreating backsides.

And so the hills, too, were littered with Quatro corpses.

The battle had been a rout, in short, and the MIMAS mechs' first outing had confirmed Gabe's high estimation of his team's skill, as well as the power of the mechs themselves.

Still, the Quatro had shown up in numbers they were not known to have, with a level of cohesion that also had never been seen before.

Sure, the aliens' behavior had always suggested Quatro packs were tight-knit, but an attack of this scale required a level of social intelligence that surprised every analyst Gabe had heard from so far.

It was worrying. From a number of perspectives.

Something else worried him—a thought he kept wanting to suppress. Mostly because it made a little too much sense, based on what he knew about the company he worked for.

From a distance, he spotted Jake Price loping across the killing field toward him. He could see Price's mech in as much detail as he would have close-up, thanks to his own mech's enhanced visual sensors. As with everything else, while in lucid, his mech's sight was his sight.

He hadn't gotten out of his mech since they'd jumped from the space elevator, and what was more, he had no desire to. In fact, the idea of returning to his lesser, human form filled him with reluctance; even a low-level dread.

His mech periodically injected him with an REM sleep-inducing sedative. Just enough to keep him in the dream.

A dream from which he had no desire to wake.

It would take Jake fewer than ten seconds to cross the intervening space, though he'd been quite some distance away when Gabe had first spied him. At a jog, the mechs ran faster than a horse at full gallop.

A soldier helping with the cleanup was outside his speeder momentarily, and directly in Jake's path. She noticed that fact too late to jump out of the way, and her body language suggested extreme terror, but Gabe knew she wasn't in any danger.

He watched as Jake leapt several meters into the air, crashing to the ground on the other side of the soldier without breaking his stride.

Just like that, he was at Gabe's side, saluting. Gabe saluted back.

"Sir, have you had a chance to inspect the weaponry the Quatro were using against us?"

Sniffing, Gabe felt a flash of annoyance at the question. Annoyance, because it drilled straight to the heart of his paranoia about what Darkstream might be up to.

"What are you here to report, Seaman?" Gabe asked.

"The guns, sir...I've found countless SL-17s on this field, as well as a bunch of others I recognize. This is all Darkstream-issue weaponry, sir."

"So is every gun in this system. Did you think the Quatro manufactured the guns themselves?"

"No, sir. But it does raise the question of where they got the guns."

"By invading villages, probably. By overwhelming their garrisons and raiding their arsenals."

Jake shook his head—or rather, his mech did, and the motion looked surprisingly natural. "Village arsenals tend to be small, and we know they haven't invaded that many villages anyway. Not enough to allow them to conduct a battle on this scale."

Gabe sighed, taking care to prevent his implant from transmitting it. "You're right, Price. It's unusual. I'll talk to Bronson about it." The captain had been put in charge of overseeing and directing Team Oneiri.

"Thank you, sir."

"Get back to work."

Jake did, sprinting away to help a nearby group of soldiers struggling to hoist a Quatro corpse onto a trailer.

Bronson soon answered the call. Inside the dream, instead of just the captain's grizzled face, the man actually appeared alongside Gabe on the battlefield. His hands were folded behind his back, and his mouth twisted slightly, as though he'd eaten something that hadn't agreed with him. It often did that when Gabe contacted him.

"Roach. What can I do for you?"

"Sir, one of my pilots has noticed something odd. The Quatro used Darkstream guns to fight this battle."

"So? Those could have come from anywhere. Raiding villages, probably. What are you suggesting, Roach?"

"Nothing, sir. I'm seeking your perspective on the matter. That's all. I speculated about the Quatro obtaining arms from the villages they hit, but the combined arsenals of the ones we know they've invaded...it doesn't seem like that would amount to as many guns as we saw here today."

"Well, what about the bands of marauders? We have no records of how many times *they've* fought the Quatro. They don't tend to share data with us, and it's been a while since I've sat down with a marauder for afternoon tea. You?"

"Same, sir," Gabe said, indulging Bronson's need for a certain level of absurdity in any given conversation.

"There's our answer, I suspect. The Quatro probably attacked some marauder camps before moving on to bigger prizes."

"What do you think is the Quatro's aim in all this?"

"It seems pretty straightforward to me. The Quatro want their planet back. But unfortunately for them, it's our planet now."

CHAPTER 40

Fullerenes

"**I** apologize for the lacking communication," the Quatro said, its lips pulling back from its teeth as it spoke.

But after a second, Lisa realized the alien wasn't actually speaking the words. Probably it lacked vocal cords suited to human language. Instead, a device hanging from its neck like a collar emitted the sound. Even so, the timbre of the device's tones were deep and rich. It reminded Lisa of the way her family's fat tabby cat back in Hub would purr—except, you'd have to turn up that purr several octaves to achieve a sound nearly as resonant as the Quatro's.

"That's...fine," Lisa answered, reluctant to get too pushy with a couple dozen giant aliens. She wasn't sure why the Quatro had chosen to address her in particular. *Just go with it.* "Is that a universal translator?"

"With sufficient time, yes. But the device is also needing of enough data to translate with big enough utility. Probably you find the structure of sentence and word choices clumsy, even so."

"A little bit," Lisa admitted. "But I can understand you."

The Quatro paused, probably waiting for the device to parse her words. In the meantime, now that they were getting friendly, Lisa tested to see whether the invisible force still prevented her from moving backward.

Shifting her elbow to nudge the air behind her, she found that indeed it did. The Quatro were clearly interested in communicating with them, but just as clearly, the idea of restoring their freedom did not yet appeal.

"The device will improve over time," the Quatro said, and nothing else. It continued to stare at her.

Maybe it's as nervous as I am. Somehow she doubted that, but things *were* getting a bit awkward, so she ventured another question.

"So...how did you collect this data on our language? Have you been spying on the Habitats?"

"We have monitored *your* talking," the Quatro replied.

"Ah." That made more sense. "Is that what that room with all the puzzles was about?" she asked, reasoning things out as she spoke.

"Indeed. It was the purpose of stimulating you to speak. We generated a series of unique situations, so that you would use words particular only to them, and all the while our program interpreted the meaning and assembled. Before, progress was compromised because of the rate you spoke—we needed you to speak more, faster."

"Why'd you bring us here?" Andy said, less amiably than Lisa. "Why treat us like this?"

The Quatro swung its massive head to peer at Andy. Its expression looking menacing, but Lisa doubted any expression would exactly look comforting on that large, panther-like face. "We have treated you with hospitality, have we not? No harm was brought to you."

"You've dragged us all around this station using some sort of magic trick, is what you did. How'd you do that?"

"Easy, boy," Tessa said. "We're not in the best negotiating position, right now."

Even a glance from the Quatro seemed a momentous gesture, and Lisa thought she saw Tessa flinch a millimeter away when the beast looked at her. "There is not a need for negotiating. We hope to request your help."

"Request away," Tessa said. "What is it you think you need?"

"Short time will bring *your* answer. Now, I will answer that of your friend. Your question as to how we manipulated your bodies and other things—it is by way of our minds."

"Wait," Lisa said. "Like telekinesis?"

The Quatro's onyx eyes met her. "This word is not one known to the translator device."

"You, uh...you can move things with your thoughts?"

"Not with thoughts. This poses difficulty in terms of explaining with the human words available, but I will make a try. We Quatro—I know that is your word for us, and ours is not translatable into your words, so we will say Quatro—we Quatro have developed brains that channel and focus the energies of our bodies. This ability works better in proportion to how colder the surroundings are. In warmth, the ability is very weak, but here in this coldness of underground, it is powerful indeed. We use it to attract, push, or otherwise control anything containing metal. Our ability to move you comes from the metal in the suits you wear."

Andy cursed. "It's been the pressure suits the whole time," he spat. "If we'd taken those off, we could have taken them."

"I highly doubt that, boy," Tessa said. "Especially considering we would have frozen to death without the suits' heating systems. It might be time for you to shut your mouth. This is the first communication between humans and Quatro in history, and you aren't improving it."

Seeming to take the hint, Andy shut up.

Facing the hulking alien once again, Tessa said, "I think I can give you the words you need to explain your ability. It sounds like your brains contain fullerenes—organic superconductors, which you use to generate the strong magnetic fields needed to manipulate metals as you describe. For a long time, evolutionary biologists have speculated whether nature could produce such a structure, and now it seems we know. If I'm right, it would make sense that the ability weakens with warmth. Typically, superconductors only work at extremely low temperatures, and to function even at the temperature of this ship, the fullerenes evolution has given you must be very advanced indeed."

Surprising Lisa, Andy spoke again: "How in Sol do you know all that?"

The white-haired woman shot him an annoyed look. "Your implant gives you access to almost every book ever written by humans, including plenty written by more advanced species, like the Tumbra and Kaithe. I suggest you take advantage of that sometime." She studied the Quatro again, eyebrows twitching upward. "Now, about answering *my* question. You said you need our help. Why?"

"We have observed your people since your arrival on this world." For the first time, Lisa noticed how still the alien stood as it spoke. All the Quatro did, actually: other than the occasional flick of an ear or—more disconcertingly—a lick of the lips, they barely moved at all.

The Quatro continued: "At first, we assumed you were just an additional tool of the..." Pausing, the alien swung its head toward Lisa. "What is a word for one who interferes?"

Blinking, Lisa gave it a moment's thought. "Uh, how about 'meddler?'"

"Then we will now call them the Meddlers. It is the Meddlers that stole the capability of flight from my drift's ship."

"Your drift?" Lisa asked.

"Wait a second," Andy said, in a tone that suggested he was having some sort of epiphany. "Are you even *from* this star system?"

"Our first home is far away from here," the alien said. "Many, many stars away. We came here to establish a second home, and at first, this system seemed like the perfect one for that. Like you, we took advantage of the moving devices that carry valuable metals and other materials to holding containers."

"You mean the Gatherers?" Lisa said.

"It does seem likely we are talking of the same thing. Yes. Gatherers. We did not question their existence, also like you, except to worry about whether their makers would return at some time. But we thought that the makers must have these Gatherers in systems elsewhere. We even thought about the chance that the makers might have fallen a long time ago, leaving their devices to continue working."

The dark-eyed Quatro turned to exchange looks with another, who had orange eyes. That Quatro raised its paw slightly. Lisa wasn't sure what the exchange signified, but the midnight-eyed Quatro continued its explanation.

"At some time, we noticed something about the deep reservoirs where the Gatherers deposited their materials. We noticed they would soon be filled up. Not all of them—many of the reservoirs did not fill, because we were taking the materials for our own use instead, as we have seen you do. But the ones that had been left alone were close to full.

"It was when they filled that the Meddlers came. They loosed great machines on us, which strode the surface of this planet, as well as that of the other planet in this system hospitable to living. Those great machines prevented us from gathering resources at the levels of before. Worse, they attacked our ships, destroying most. This one crashed to the planet, its moving ability destroyed, though its armor kept it mostly intact. Our drift was driven underground, and over time, we went quietly onto the surface at night and dragged our ship below the surface, piece by piece, to reassemble it here, so that we could have a living place."

"How have you survived?" Lisa asked. "How did you...how do you eat?"

"We had sufficient food to last until we reassembled our ship's lab. After that, we synthesized what we needed."

Lisa nodded slowly. *Synthesized meat. I see. Well, that's a relief.* "There are walking machines like the ones you describe on Eresos—that's what we call the system's habitable planet. We named those machines Amblers. But no one has ever seen an Ambler on Alex. This planet, I mean."

"The machines you call Amblers disappeared very soon before your arrival. We thought you to be another agent of the Meddlers, and so we chose to hide ourselves from you. The Meddlers diminished our drift greatly—we have no more than the forty-two Quatro you see before you—and so we have exercised extreme caution over the last two decades. But when we realized that you three had entered danger on the planet's surface, we made a decision to bring you here, where you could safely breathe. We could also learn whether you are truly of the Meddlers, and we have decided to base our future actions on the idea that you are not."

"This is all very informative," Tessa cut in, "but you still haven't told us why you need our help."

"That is simple," the Quatro said. "The Meddlers came when the reservoirs filled, and they will be filled again in fewer than two orbits. That is when the Meddlers will return, and you can expect to lose your ability to fly through the stars when it happens. We are scared of that day, and we believe that you should be scared also."

CHAPTER 41

Collectivist

The conversation with the Quatro inside their vessel's audience chamber had only gotten more interesting after they'd mentioned the Meddlers, who seemed likely to be the creators of the Gatherers and Amblers.

"We're not really in a position to help anyone," Lisa had said. "In fact, we were on our way to seek help ourselves—from Habitat 1, one of the four permanent human settlements on this planet. We come from Habitat 2, where a criminal element called Daybreak has taken control. We aim to take it back."

"Then we will both improve our respective situations," said Rug, which was the name the midnight-eyed Quatro leader had chosen for herself. "We will do so by helping each other. If we help you retake your home, then perhaps you can help us reach our starship."

"Wait," Lisa said. "Starship?"

"Yes. Even though we Quatro took full advantage of the resources collected by the Gatherers, just as you have, we also took caution. Knowing the creators would likely return some day, we concealed a ship in the outer comet belt, as a contingency. If you can help us reach it, then we all can escape."

"What if we don't want to escape the Steele System?" Andy said. "What if we decide we kind of like this place, after all?"

Rug looked at Andy for a prolonged period of quiet. "You will want to leave, when the Meddlers come. You will want to leave very quickly."

After a brief huddle, Lisa, Tessa, and Andy had decided that the deal the Quatro had proposed was much better than they were likely to get. Much better than suffocating on the surface of Alex, certainly.

"And we don't *have* to leave Steele," Lisa said. "As long as we help them reach their ship, we'll have kept up our end of the bargain. In return, we get Habitat 2 back."

"How exactly are we going to help them reach the Outer Ring, Lisa?" Andy said. "Do you have that part figured out yet?"

"No," Lisa said, a little sullenly. "But I will. We have to figure it out, don't we? This is our only option, now, and to be honest we're lucky to have it."

That had decided it. Two days of hasty preparations later, the Quatro vessel's airlock opened, letting them out into the dark tunnel once more.

So began a very interesting journey.

For one, the Quatro refused to travel by day.

It was summer on Alex, and near the equator as they were, the temperature got as high as twenty degrees Celsius during the day. That level of warmth turned the fullerenes inside the Quatro brain from superconductors into fridge magnets.

Well, not exactly that bad. But near enough.

The Quatro assured Andy that they would be able to fix the beetle's wheels once they reached it. They were used to repairing things that broke down—it had been the only way they'd survived all these years. Once the beetle was fixed, together the humans and Quatro would press on toward Habitat 2.

Lisa spent the journey mostly exhausted, since Tessa had decided to renew their training program, driving her even harder than before.

She began to incorporate more lucid simulations, and now that Lisa's implant was properly calibrated to reflect her actual abilities, they were much more challenging and generally more intense.

Even so, after months of Tessa's tutelage, she found herself way better equipped to grapple with whatever Tessa sent at her, whether it was a whole platoon of Ixa or an Ambler that had malfunctioned and gone on a rampage.

The older woman had totally eradicated the Quatro from the simulations.

"Doesn't seem right, anymore," Tessa said, and that was all she had to say on the subject.

It's all she needs to say.

The Quatro leader spent a lot of time walking alongside Lisa, talking to her over a wide channel, teaching her about their culture as well as giving her a crash course in the nature of the aliens' powers.

"Incredibly collectivist" was the word Tessa used to describe Quatro social organization, after listening to the leader speak to Lisa enough.

According to the white-haired ex-soldier, "collectivist" meant that individuals of a society placed the interests of their group—"drift," in this case, Lisa supposed—before even their own needs.

"The polar opposite of the society we've set up in the Steele System, basically," Tessa said. "No wonder our two species don't get along."

Lisa had to admit that the Quatro were quite different. Part of her wanted to respect the fact that theirs was a totally alien culture and had no doubt taken the shape it had for a reason.

But on the other hand, she found them extremely odd. The Quatro were so "collectivist" that they didn't even have names, to begin with!

Once the Quatro realized that having a name was important for communicating with humans, they each chose one for themselves, an exercise they seemed to view as an amusing game.

"What call you the object that covers a floor?" asked the black-eyed Quatro.

"Uh, carpet?" Lisa said. "A rug?"

The Quatro paused, seeming to consider Lisa's offering.

"Rug," she said. "I will be Rug."

The other Quatro chose similar names, after everyday objects. "Table." "Faucet." "Lamp."

Other than being hilarious, the names also made sense, in a way. They reflected how the Quatro saw themselves: as unremarkable entities that sought to be useful to those around them.

"They're totally selfless," Tessa said. "Some people would call that admirable. Although, most of those people live in the Milky Way."

Even though Lisa thought of Rug as the Quatro "leader," she wasn't, not really. The Quatro had no leaders. They each mulled endlessly over what was best for the drift, what the drift needed, and then they spent the rest of their time trying to fill that need as best they knew how. No leader was required for that, apparently.

Lisa's father had always taught her that selfishness was actually a virtue, which kept a society running smoothly. If everyone pursued their own rational self-interest, then the economy worked itself out, and everyone prospered. Everyone who deserved to, anyway.

In fact, people back in the Milky Way hadn't properly valued selfishness, and that was a big part of why Darkstream had been forced to leave.

The Quatro don't have a selfish bone in their bodies, and look how they ended up. Stranded underground on an inhospitable planet, barely kept alive by technology that constantly seemed to be breaking down.

Take the turtle-shaped Quatro vehicle that trundled along behind them as they crossed Alex, which Andy had taken to calling "the Dome."

It broke down twice during the journey—once because it stalled out while trying to get up a particularly steep hill, and a second time because of a faulty engine part.

The aliens seemed used to occurrences like this, though, since they carried around a considerable store of spare parts, from which Lisa assumed they would attempt to fix the beetle.

The Dome also featured an oxygenated compartment that could hold two Quatro in tight quarters, should their pressure suits fail. The blue Quatro pressure suit *was* a thing of wonder, even Lisa had to admit. In addition to preventing the wearers from suffocating, it also supplied their bodies with nutrients on the move, kept them hydrated, and converted their waste into energy, which was efficient but also kind of gross.

Even so…

"You're clearly doing something wrong, to have ended up stranded on Alex," Lisa told Rug point-blank. "These Meddlers sound like real jerks, but they must have been stronger than you, and that's probably because they looked out for themselves instead of worrying about the needs of others so much."

"Do you truly believe strength means ignoring the needs of others? If so, perhaps we should have left you and your friends to suffocate on the surface of Alex." The Quatro translator was getting a lot better, as it collected more data on human language.

"Well, sure," Lisa said. "But you needed us, or so you said. The Meddlers probably had no need of you."

"They need us now."

"They do? For what?"

"To show them mercy."

Lisa shook her head. "I don't understand. What do you mean?" Maybe the translator wasn't working as well as she thought.

"For them to continue living, they will need us to show them great mercy. Because currently, we intend to kill them."

That, Lisa hadn't expected to hear from Rug. It sent her into a thoughtful silence, which the Quatro eventually interrupted. "Our first objective is to escape this system, before the Meddlers return. We cannot beat them with our current might. But we *can* return with more weapons, more ships, and when we do, we can look for clues that will help us track them to their home and make them pay for what they did to us."

The next day, they found the beetle, which was already covered by an inch-thick layer of blue dust.

Without hesitation, the Quatro got to work.

CHAPTER 42

Red Company

The entire battalion rolled out from Ingress as dawn lit the land with shades of gray.

They'd received word of Quatro moving toward a nearby settlement, called New Gower, and luckily for the settlement, they had a long-standing contract with Darkstream.

While the entire strike force deployed to intercept the Quatro, nothing could travel faster than the mechs, which bounded over the terrain with virtually limitless energy.

That energy worried Gabe, who'd ordered his entire team out of their mechs after they'd finished helping with clean up after the Battle of Ingress. Before bed, he'd subjected them to two hours of hard PT.

The dream did simulate effort and exertion when controlling the mech, however that was balanced out by the mech's immense power, so that you only felt as taxed as a being the size and strength of a MIMAS mech would feel.

Either way, those actions required nothing of your body, beyond what calories its basil metabolic rate burned through. That meant their bodies would wither away, if they let them.

And part of Gabe *wanted* to let them. Part of him never wanted to leave his mech, where he dreamed he was mighty, without peer—a dream that happened to be true.

When he looked in the eyes of his team, he saw that sentiment reflected in them, and that only made him even more adamant about making sure they spent ample time actually using their bodies to get some damned exercise.

Originally, he'd only planned to make them do ninety minutes. But after Henrietta took it upon herself to mutter, "Thought we were done with this after training," Gabe heaped on another thirty.

"I told you I planned to maintain total authority," Gabe barked, pacing up and down the line of them doing push ups. "Did you think that meant I'd hold your hand while reading you bedtime stories?"

He'd gotten no more complaints, and that satisfied him. So he dropped to the ground and joined them.

Now, the ground rushed past beneath his exquisitely engineered feet, which had better balance than his human ones. They were molded for peerless locomotion.

When the team encountered a copse of trees, instead of bothering to run around, they charged through. A tree of middling size reared up before Gabe, which would have forced him to choose another path, if he hadn't been willing to barrel straight into it, splintering it into a shower of a thousand fragments.

The Quatro would not stop them, and neither would Eresos. He felt like he'd already bent them both to his will.

Ahead, the tips of the settlement's buildings crested the horizon, and less than a minute later, they arrived.

The village was surrounded by a ring of Quatro corpses.

Oneiri Team slowed, wary of running into whoever had killed the Quatro, but also of causing undue damage to the property of a Darkstream client as they strode between the buildings.

A village green sat at the center of town, and there they found a foursome of men in motley dress, sitting at a picnic table, each heavily armed.

"Who are you?" Gabe said, the mech amplifying his voice so that it became a deafening bellow. The other mechs spread out, servomotors buzzing as they surveyed the surrounding buildings.

The largest of the men—which was saying something—rose to his feet, hands on hips. Pistols hung from crisscrossed holsters not far from those hands, and the barrel of an SL-17 poked over his shoulder.

"Well, I'm Saul. As for these others, all you need to know is that we're all soldiers of Red Company."

"Never heard of it," Gabe said.

"And I'll never have to listen to you say that again, will I? You've heard of Red Company now, you big metal bastard, and you'll *keep* hearing of us. We just finished saving New Gower from the Quatro, and we're just getting warmed up."

"New Gower has a contract with Darkstream."

"Wrong. They *had* a contract with Darkstream. Now they have one with us."

"Bull. Why would they break a deal with the leading defense contractor in the system?"

"Little thing I like to call market competition. I know you haven't had to experience that since arriving in this system, but you'd better get used to it, because our terms aren't nearly as ridiculous as yours."

"Our contract contained some pretty serious repercussions for violating it. New Gower's council knows that."

Reaching behind his back, Saul unlimbered the assault rifle, holding it casually across his chest. "They also know that we'll protect them from you, too, if need be."

Gabe laughed. "You can't withstand Darkstream. We'll crush you."

"Actually, with a war brewing between you and the Quatro, I expect we probably can. But go ahead. Try to fight us. We have contingents stationed all over Eresos. See what happens to the contracts we haven't poached yet when you leave your clients to the Quatro while you attempt to put us down."

The other three joined Saul in standing. One of them held a rocket launcher, which he leveled straight at the face of Gabe's mech.

Richaud stepped forward, leveling twin autocannons at the man threatening Gabe. "Let's waste 'em, sir."

"Before you do," Saul said, "you may want to have another look around."

Gabe did, and so did the other mech pilots. Men and women as shabbily dressed as the four before them revealed themselves from positions all around—narrow alleys, doorways, rooftops.

Most of them bore heavy artillery, including rocket launchers, grenade launchers, and at least two heavy machine guns on tripods.

Gabe turned back to glare at Saul, though of course the man wouldn't see the expression.

"You haven't seen what the MIMAS mechs can do," Gabe growled.

"Neither have you, I expect," the man said, as calm as ever. "You haven't experienced their full potential, and neither have you learned their limitations. If you want to see how you do against the heat we're packing, be my guest. We're eager for the challenge. But consider what kind of message it'll send to the clients you have left, when you tear New Gower apart in an effort to get all of us. Consider what Bronson might have to say to you, if you don't have the brain cells to put it together yourself."

"How do you know Bronson?"

"We know a lot more about you than you do about us, evidently."

Even in the dream, Gabe's body felt hot with anger. But Saul was right. Engaging here, now, without seeing how the board felt about it...it wasn't a good idea.

"Wait until the Quatro come in force," Gabe said. "See how cocky you feel then."

"We'll take them."

"You'll die. You don't have mechs."

Saul smiled. "Maybe we'll end up with some soon enough. Where do you think we got these guns?" The burly man hefted his gun a little. "Stay safe, you hear?"

As Oneiri Team jogged out of New Gower, followed by the raucous laughter of Red Company, Gabe got in touch with Bronson. The man appeared, and the dream rendered him hovering along the ground near Gabe to keep pace.

He flushed scarlet when Gabe told him the news—a rare departure from his usual sarcasm-laced calm.

"How *dare* they," he seethed. "They have no idea what's coming to them! Way tougher men than them have gotten what they deserved after screwing with me."

"Their leader seemed to imply they got their artillery from Darkstream. I recognized an SL-17 strapped to his back."

Bronson grimaced, but seemed to take a deep breath, regaining some of his composure. "Like hell they got it from Darkstream. They got theirs the same way the Quatro got theirs—by killing. We'll deal with this Red Company soon, but we can't just yet. There are reports of Quatro massing near Plenitos, Roach. We're expecting an attack—the worst one yet. I need you to assemble the reserve battalion and start making preparations to begin the journey there."

CHAPTER 43

So Long as the Walls Hold

It had taken a week and a half to get the battalion marshaled and ready for the journey south to Eresos' capital, with the supplies that such a trip would require.

After that, their nonlinear route through the complex system of Gatherer paths combined with the distance between the two cities meant the journey south lasted nearly two months.

By that time, the siege of Plenitos was already well underway.

Plenitos had been built on a lake, which, Gabe had read on the system net, was larger than the biggest Great Lake back on Old Earth.

Trying to access it by land would have been stupid, given the legion of Quatro that surrounded it, but the aliens had no water craft, giving the mech pilots full access to the city—along with any other human who cared to cross the water. The crossing would take four days, but it was better than getting intercepted by the enemy.

As a barge neared the beach where they waited, Gabe smirked within the dream.

If the Quatro wanted to pull off an actual siege, they'd have to surround the entire lake. No matter how many numbers they have, there's no way they can support that.

His smirk soon faded, however.

That could mean they don't expect their siege to last very long. Meaning they think they have a way inside the city.

The city had been built atop solid rock, making tunneling difficult. Maybe the Quatro were too stupid to have figured that out in advance.

And not so long ago, he would have believed that. But not now. The aliens were proving themselves to be more formidable with every passing day.

And the sheer *number* of them that had gathered to pressure Plenitos—that was the truly staggering thing. On the satellite images of the city and the surrounding area, which Bronson had sent Gabe to review on his implant, the Quatro presence appeared as a single dark mass.

As he stepped onto the sturdy barge, he was surprised to notice Arkady Black standing near the bow.

The man was a fellow Darkstream employee, a captain, and also head of the security force charged with protecting Plenitos. Of every contract the company held in the Steele System, this one was the most lucrative, and the board had trusted Black with its execution.

Gabe strode over to the man, coming to attention and saluting.

"Not so close," Arkady said, holding up a warning hand. "Back up a step, Roach. You don't know how imposing you are inside that thing."

"Sorry, sir." Gabe took a step back, bumping into Henrietta Jin, who'd followed too closely behind.

"Hey!" she yelled. "There's not much room on this tub, you know. Not with all of us here."

"Shut up," he muttered, then turned back to face Black. "I'm surprised to find you aboard, sir. We could have easily conducted a war meeting via lucid, or even using our implants."

Arkady Black barked laughter. "I suppose I should have expected a man who signed up to be a robot would place that much trust in technology. Here's how this is actually going to go: you're going to step out of that mech and switch off your implant. Then you're going to join me belowdecks, in a chamber I've had swept for bugs."

Gabe tried not to sound as hesitant as he felt: "I don't think the Quatro have the tech to intercept our communications, sir."

"We don't know *what* they have, Roach. They've already surprised us a hundred times since last Tuesday. Plus, we have this infernal Red Company to contend with, now, and we already know how crafty humans are." Black's bushy eyebrows knitted together. "I'm confident you'll follow the order I've given you, Roach, but I'm beginning to wonder about promptness. Has living inside a hunk of metal made you forget about the importance of the chain of command?"

"No, sir." Gabe ordered the mech to inject his body with the sedative's antagonist, and then he crawled backward down the ramp that unfurled to let him out, his legs moving rather stiffly. After spending the journey to Plenitos inside the mech, other than nightly PT with the rest of Oneiri, Gabe had developed a distinct reluctance to leave the machine. Outside it, he felt diminished.

That's dangerous. After this battle, we need a long break from the MIMAS mechs.

Black met him at the side of the mech, saluting for the first time. Gabe saluted back, which made the captain smile.

"Good to see an actual salute, from an actual human being." The smile faltered, then, as he caught sight of the track marks dotting Gabe's bare forearm. "You look like a junkie, son."

"Part of the job, sir."

"Hmm."

The chamber Black had selected for their meeting must have been pretty easy to sweep for bugs, considering how tiny it was. A school desk of a table made for the only furniture, and both men loomed over it, studying a single-use tablet where Black called up battle plans.

"So long as the walls hold, we're fine, in theory," Black said, running his finger along the thick, dark line that indicated them. "The Quatro can't tunnel here, as I'm sure you've figured out already, and the walls are strong. But they must be gathering for a reason."

"Yeah."

"Either way, we can't very well let them camp out in front of the walls of Plenitos. The citizens are feeling pretty spunky right now—we've rallied them with talk of resistance, justice, and a little vengeance sprinkled in. Even the beggars are getting into the spirit of things. It won't last, though. Letting Quatro trample the fields in front of Plenitos is a sign of weakness, and one we can't afford to let go on for long. Darkstream must continue to be seen as the dominant force in the system, which is doubly important with these cursed mercenaries springing up like weeds."

"Why do you think they're acting now, sir? They've always just roamed the countryside, attacking the weakest villages— the ones too poor to do anything but provide for their own defense."

Black nodded. "Such as it is. But I'm surprised to hear you asking *me* this question, Roach. The reverse seems much likelier. You have Bronson's ear more than almost anyone, and Bronson has the board's."

Shaking his head, Gabe said, "You know as much as I do, sir."

"I see. Well, either way, in my view, the only thing strange about the mercenaries' behavior is that it no longer serves Darkstream interests."

Black's eyes tracked Gabe's carefully as he answered. "How do you mean?"

"Do you really not know, or are you just playing dumb, son?" Shaking his head, Black said, "Doubt you'd tell me either way. Back when the raiders were roaming the countryside, it served to drive Darkstream contracts, not to mention increasing the money they made from those contracts. Considering that reports say the mercenaries wield mostly Darkstream weaponry, it all kind of fits, doesn't it?"

"I don't know about that," Gabe said with a shrug. "Where else does anyone get guns? The system's flooded with Darkstream-issue weaponry, sir. We have to make money, meaning we can't discriminate too much between buyers, though we do run background checks, as you know. But it's easy enough to fudge a background check. Other than firearms brought to the system from the Milky Way, Darkstream' s the only game in town when it comes to guns."

Black nodded. "The company line just rolls off your tongue, doesn't it? I suppose it would. You have a reputation."

"For being the first one to step foot on a planet that isn't located in the Milky Way?"

"For being a brutal dog controlled by Darkstream, who does anything the company demands of him. Absolutely *anything*, the rumors say."

Gabe stiffened. "I have a code."

"Yes, and a pretty easy one to recite, I'd wager. If it makes money, you'll do it. That about right?"

This time, Gabe answered with only silence. He found himself wishing for his mech.

"Has all that started to catch up with you, yet, son? Everything you've done? Because it usually does, for all but the most soulless men. Which are you? Soulless, or do you have a scrap of one left?"

Continued quiet, on Gabe's part, though he clenched his fists. Usually, others found even his silence intimidating, but not Black. He just stared and stared.

With a glance down at Gabe's clenched fists, Black nodded, as though having confirmed something. "Yes, I think you probably have a scrap of a soul left. Which means you're headed for a crash. Try not to bring the rest of your team down when it happens, all right? And if you can muster up the strength of spirit, try not to order them to do something that will damn them forever."

Without another word, Black exited the tiny chamber, leaving Gabe alone with his scarlet-tinged thoughts. If he'd been inside the dream, everything would have been flashing the color of blood, just as it had at the peak of his bloodlust during the Battle of Ingress.

Gingerly, he dredged up a memory from that same battle, of the flashbacks he'd experienced. Tattered Quatro corpses, strewn across a cave floor. Quatro families. The smell of burnt fur and flesh.

Then he thought of Jess—not of finding her dead, but of the way her hair flicked when she whipped her head around to smile coyly. The faint whiff of perfume whenever he'd passed her on the village green.

He realized, then, exactly why he missed her so much, when no other woman had made him feel that way:

After two long, dark decades of committing atrocity after atrocity for Darkstream—acts that were apparently starting to catch up with him at last—Jess had been the first person to ever make him experience something pure and uncomplicated and good.

He hadn't deserved to experience that, not since he'd been a child. But Jess had made him feel it all the same. And now the Quatro had taken it from him.

Gabe knew the Quatro had at least some justification for attacking the human settlements on Eresos. Hell, he'd personally provided a fair amount of that justification.

But he didn't care. The Quatro had also taken Jess from him, and for that reason, he would carry out at least one more horrible act.

He would slaughter every last one of them.

CHAPTER 44

Shut Up and Shoot

While startling, the satellite images did no justice to seeing the Quatro horde with his own eyes.

Persistent neutralization fire from the city defenders kept the Quatro away from the walls, forcing them to linger near the edge of the area Plenitos' council kept cleared of trees.

But now, they had begun to mill about, the mass of them writhing like one gigantic, purple beast.

"They're about to strike," Gabe remarked. The surface of the wall's parapet was barely large enough to accommodate his mech.

Jake Price stood nearby, and now he turned to face Gabe. "There's no way they can breach the wall...is there?"

"They're here, aren't they? And I just told you they're preparing to strike. So they must *think* they can, at the very least. That should trouble us."

The idea was worrying to everyone, which Gabe could see in the way the soldiers of the garrison shifted their weight from foot to foot, occasionally exchanging nervous glances.

The occasional Quatro attack was the reason Eresos' two cities had built walls in the first place, and until now, they'd proven fully effective.

Quatro weren't supposed to be smart enough to try tunneling under them, as they had at Ingress. But they had, and they also made full use of human firearms.

Now, Gabe wondered whether they might have acquired the artillery necessary to bring down Plenitos' walls.

"We need to be out there," Price said.

"You're right," Gabe said. "Round up the others and meet me outside the walls, now."

"You're serious?"

Gabe could only see the outside of Price's mech, but his very posture conveyed his surprise. "Maintaining total authority doesn't mean I'm closed off to good suggestions, Price. You should try making them more often."

"Yes, sir," Price said, turning. He didn't bother to make for the long set of stairs they'd used to get up here. Instead, he simply leapt from the wall, crashing to the earth below with a *thump* that was audible even from sixty-five meters up.

Gabe hailed Arkady Black using his com, who accepted the call. He hadn't quite forgiven Black for the uncalled-for verbal assault, but the man remained his superior officer, and they still needed to work together as well as they could.

Inside the dream, the man appeared alongside Gabe, atop the parapet.

"Sir, I'm taking my team out onto the field."

"You'll be crushed. Incredible," Black said, shaking his head. "I knew those tin cans had filled you with hubris, but I had no idea how much."

"I haven't finished speaking. The Quatro will charge soon, and I want to do everything we can to try to break that charge—or at the very least, take down as many of them as we can. I'm contacting you to request that your men stand by to open the gates at my signal, in time to admit us before the Quatro reach the walls."

"Ah," Black said, expression unchanged. "That makes more sense."

"I imagine it does. But sir, I promise you that you are grossly underestimating the capabilities of the MIMAS mechs. You haven't seen them in action."

"I don't need to," Black said, raising both hands. "They're nothing but a gimmick—a marketing gimmick. There's a reason no one developed them until now."

"You're right, there is. But it's not the reason you think. Unfortunately, the true reason is classified, and unlike me, you're not authorized to know it."

"There's that hubris again. Let's you and I limit our communication to only what's needed, shall we, son? I doubt either of us need our blood pressure raised any more than necessary."

"Works for me," Gabe said—growled, in truth.

"While we're at it, why don't you try acting your age? Black out." The officer vanished from the parapet.

The sky over Plenitos darkened, and it took Gabe a moment to realize that it was merely a reflection of his mood, and not the weather.

Without further ceremony, he stepped onto the wall's crenellations and then let himself drop.

Sixty-five meters' worth of air whistled around his mech's sensor-covered frame, and his HUD registered the otherwise unnoticeable increase in speed caused by acceleration due to gravity.

He absorbed the force of the fall by instinctively bending his legs, but it was hardly necessary. The mech's complex system of shocks would have kept him perfectly safe without the maneuver.

The Quatro apparently hadn't yet noticed his departure from Plenitos.

They will in a second.

Though he knew he should wait, the conversation with Black had once again dredged up unwanted thoughts and memories. The man got to him far more than he should, far more than made sense. But the fact of Gabe's rage remained, and across the grassy expanse waited the perfect object for it.

Striding forward, he loosed a pair of rockets, then pivoted slightly to loose two more.

They struck seconds later, explosions blossoming from the ground, tossing burnt and mangled Quatro through the air as though they were toys.

That done, he fired six grenades in quick succession. By now, the Quatro were surging across the field toward him, meaning it was virtually impossible for his grenades to have anything but a devastating effect.

And indeed they did. More freshly-made Quatro corpses. Gabe laughed, and in the dream, his laughter shook the world.

All around him, his team began to crash to the ground, one-by-one.

Price shot him a look. "Trying to hog all the fun to yourself, sir?" The comment was delivered as a jest, but Gabe heard the note of concern it contained.

"Shut up and shoot," Gabe said, running ahead, autocannons spinning faster to send hot lead screaming across the battlefield.

Explosions tore up the ground all along the loose formation of rushing Quatro, tearing the aliens apart, sowing chaos and confusion.

But still they came.

"Sir," Price shouted a short while later, loud enough for all of them to hear over the explosions and the yipping of the oncoming aliens. "We have to go back!"

Gabe didn't answer. He continued to visit death upon the enemy. Nothing would stop him from avenging Jess.

Suddenly, Price was at his side, placing a metal hand on Gabe's bicep. "If we wait any longer, our window will vanish, sir. The guards won't open the gates."

Shaking off the seaman apprentice's hand, Gabe turned back toward the Quatro to continue firing. "Go back, if you want. I'm staying."

"They'll overwhelm you, sir. Besides, none of us are going back if you don't, so they'll overwhelm all of us. We'll do a lot more damage in the long run by surviving this opening scuffle, right?"

Mentally shaking himself, Gabe inclined his head. "Yeah. You're right. Let's go."

Together, Oneiri Team ran back toward the gleaming steel walls, where the gates were already open and waiting. But as they neared, those gates started to close, and as the last one through, Beth Arkanian almost got trapped outside.

The gates clanged shut. Overhead, the garrison fired nonstop into the Quatro force.

But down here, just inside the city, his team just stood around and stared at Gabe.

They're wondering about my ability to command. And they can cut that out right now.

"Remember who maintains total authority over your asses," he bellowed. "Get back on that wall and rain down hell!"

"Yes, sir!" they said in unison, turning to speed toward the nearest stairwell.

CHAPTER 45

Act Fast

After the Quatro drove Oneiri Team inside the walls of Plenitos, Gabe had expected the aliens to have a swift followup.

"What is this?" Ash Sweeney said over the team-wide channel as she reined havoc on the Quatro below with her grenade launcher. She'd turned out to have a keen sense of where the enemy *would* be once each grenade exploded, not where they were when she launched it.

Probably from her lucid gaming, Gabe reflected reluctantly. As much as he and other old-school Darkstream operatives liked to look down their noses at it, lucid did teach an undeniable level of situational awareness and ability to prioritize targets.

"What is what?" Tommy Tomlinson asked, and Gabe decided not to interject with his view.

He was still in observation-mode when it came to the dynamics and abilities of his team, and he expected to remain in it for some time. Possibly forever. A good leader only stepped in when absolutely necessary. Constantly micromanaging only taught soldiers to rely on that micromanagement.

"I get that Chief Roach was trying to bait the Quatro by firing on them, but can that really be the only reason they charged? Surely they had a followup plan?"

Inside the mech—inside the dream—Gabe winced. They really needed to come up with some nicknames for everyone on the team, including himself. Having his team refer to him by his rank in battle created too much distance. Nicknames were more valuable for team cohesion than most people assumed.

But I have to let them emerge naturally, too. His old unit had called him Pioneer, but it didn't feel right to simply order his team to call him that.

"Maybe the Quatro really are as dumb as we thought," Tommy said.

Maybe. But Gabe doubted it. Still, the Quatro's behavior made no sense. He'd expected them to have enough knowledge of the terrain to not try digging into the city, so the fact that they hadn't done that didn't surprise him, but they didn't seem to have *anything* else, other than milling about in front of the city walls and trading shots with the defenders.

Either way, the Quatro offered no shortage of targets, and as he swept their ranks with his autocannons, he watched them bend and fall and break. Part of him rejoiced at the injury and death he dealt, and part of him recoiled in horror.

God, I'm a mess.

Through it all, he could see Jess's face, and he couldn't tell whether the expression she wore was approving or disappointed.

Either way, her memory enraged him, driving him to continue exacting his vengeance, no matter how she would have felt about it, no matter whether it was right or not. The madness of battle was upon him, and reason had no part of it.

As he stowed the autocannons by instructing the mech's hands to reform in front of them, he used those hands to rip his rocket launcher from his back, just in time to loose a rocket at a particularly dense cluster of Quatro.

As he did, the Quatro revealed to him their plan.

The charge *did* have a purpose, after all. The sea of Quatro that had crashed against Plenitos' walls was meant to conceal the heavy artillery-bearing individuals among them.

Individual Quatro wearing multiple rocket launchers of their own strapped to their backs leapt over the heads of their fellows with powerful limbs, loosing multi-rocket barrages straight at Plenitos' walls before landing among their brethren and getting lost in the seething throng.

"Watch where they fall," Gabe barked at his team. "Anticipate their trajectories. *Take them out!*"

But try as they might, the Quatro's tactic was too effective. They were fast, and their fellows maneuvered to give them leeway to quickly change their position once they landed to continue running up and down the battlefield, firing barrage after barrage from random positions.

In the dream, Arkady Black appeared beside Gabe, hands clasped behind his back, looking strangely calm as he peered down at the battlefield, in full view of the enemy.

Or at least, it looked to Gabe like the enemy could easily sight and snipe him.

But he isn't truly there.

"We seem to have a problem," Black remarked.

"You don't say," Gabe said, following another rocket-launching Quatro's path and loosing a rocket at where he expected it would be. It didn't come back up again, and he felt fairly sure he'd finally taken one down.

Of course, another could easily take up its launchers.

Without the benefit of opposable thumbs, Gabe didn't know how a Quatro could manage to strap the launchers onto its back, but then, they'd clearly managed to get them there in the first place. And the firing mechanism continued to remain a mystery.

"How much punishment like that are these walls built to take?" Gabe asked.

"Not very much at all," Black said. "The builders never expected the Quatro to have access to rocket launchers, or to have the ability to use them if they did. You need to act fast, Roach."

With that, Black vanished.

Thanks for the insight, Gabe said, racking his brain for how in hell they were going to prevent this city from falling.

CHAPTER 46

How Many Teeth

The journey back to Habitat 2 hadn't been as eventful as the journey away from it. They weren't returning with the reinforcements Lisa had hoped to secure, but...

At least we aren't coming back alone.

Still, she wondered about just how effective the Quatro would prove against the drug lords' fighters. They seemed to consider Lisa, Tessa, and Andy as part of their drift, now. And although the Quatro had avoided contact with humans for almost two decades, fearing they were agents of the Meddlers, the quadrupeds' gentleness and geniality made it hard for Lisa to imagine them waging fierce combat against a determined foe.

If they proved just as friendly and accommodating toward Daybreak, then regaining Habitat 2 simply wouldn't happen. Daybreak's leader, Quentin Cooper, would crush them.

No matter how big the Quatro are...or how many teeth they have...

The Quatro did have incredibly bulky guns that they mostly carried using their Dome. The aliens were fairly closed-mouthed about the nature of their weaponry.

As for the Quatro themselves, they never seemed to tire—either of loping across the landscape of Alex alongside the beetle, or of engaging in long discussions about their culture.

Despite those long, informative talks, Lisa could never quite get an answer out of them about why they'd ended up in the Steele System in the first place. Or about what the home was like that they'd left behind.

Lisa soon tired of trying to sate her curiosity. Despite their politeness, the Quatro could be incredibly evasive when they wanted to, and she knew they used the language barrier to their advantage, even though that was dwindling as the translator got better and better.

Either way, as they drew closer to Habitat 2, she switched to talking about tactics. They would need a plan to retake her home from Daybreak, after all. She hadn't realized that she actually thought of Habitat 2 as home until someone had taken it from her.

Funny how that works.

"We don't have the sort of artillery that'll let us blow open the side of the city," Lisa said to Rug as she reclined inside their inflatable habitat one morning, following a strenuous PT session under Tessa's ever-appraising eye. Strenuous, but they didn't exhaust her like they'd once done. Lisa had gained a new layer of lean mass during her months of training. She hadn't "bulked up" too much, but she liked how much more toned her body looked in the mirror now, and when she moved she could *feel* her increased strength in the way her muscles shifted, and the way everything had become much easier.

Rug wasn't inside the habitat with her—the Quatro were much too large to fit through the airlock. They'd spent the entire journey in their self-sustaining pressure suits, supplemented by their dome-shaped supply vehicle. Lisa communicated with her via radio.

"Even if we did have that sort of firepower, I wouldn't want to use it," Lisa went on. "The idea is to retake the city, not kill its inhabitants by blowing open its side in a way that can't be fixed quickly."

"The city subsists on the yield of the Gatherers. Does it not?"

"Well, that's the whole reason for its existence. To intercept the Gatherers and harvest their contents. As far as basic survival...what Habitat 2 can't grow hydroponically, it gets from the constant supply runs to and from the space elevator."

"Suffice it to say, then, that if the Gatherers ceased to come with their bounty, those who control Habitat 2 would become upset."

"I'd say that's an understatement," Lisa said. "Cooper would have a fit, according to what Tessa says about him. He'd be ready to kill something. Do you have a way to disrupt the Gatherers, somehow?"

"We do. Before your arrival, we learned to reprogram them. In fact, our doing so is why your Habitat 2 has proven so lucrative. Have you not noticed that the site receives a disproportionate number of Gatherers?"

"We have," Lisa said, shifting her position on the air-filled couch, which she could never quite get comfortable on. "It's the entire reason we built the city there."

"Yes. We also constructed a settlement there, once. And we reprogrammed the Gatherers to come to it in great numbers."

"Wait a second," Lisa said, sitting up, the overinflated couch as hard as a rock beneath her. "The Quatro used to have a base where Habitat 2 is now? Why was there no trace of it?"

Rug paused briefly, and then said, "I would posit two theories. One, the constructors of your city concealed from you the remnants of our settlement, which was destroyed by the Meddlers. Two, the Meddlers themselves cleared away all evidence of it ever existing."

"Why would they do that?"

"I'm not aware of why the Meddlers meddle. But it is how they came to receive the name we gave them."

"If we reprogram the Gatherers to deliver their payloads to somewhere else, we could starve out Habitat 2 permanently," Lisa said. "It would become useless to my employer. I can't do that to the people who live there. A lot of them are my friends, and most of the rest are good people."

"Worry not. This can be a temporary measure, to remain in effect only until we have forced this Cooper to emerge from your city to confront us. Once we have retaken it, we will help you to increase Gatherer traffic to Habitat 2 even further, and you'll become wealthy beyond your wildest imaginings."

"Oh. That sounds pretty good, then." She also liked the increasingly aggressive language Rug had begun to use.

When they finally reached Habitat 2, they approached it at the time of night when Alex was darkest—a time that changed throughout the year, and one which the Quatro kept careful track of. At this hour, the habitat was just a sprawling, dark silhouette against Alex's sapphire terrain, devoid of detail.

Under that blanket of darkness, Lisa and her two human companions joined the Quatro in surrounding Habitat 2, to intercept every Gatherer that approached it.

In the frigid air, the Quatro's powers were at their height. They seized the Gatherers with their superconducting brains, stopping them and forcing them open.

That done, they deposited a very specific amount of Terbium inside each Gatherer.

"This will cause every Gatherer to begin mining from a Terbium deposit fewer than ten kilometers from here," Rug said. "We have measured these amounts carefully—a single milligram more or less, and the Gatherer would not heed our command."

"Why will they go to that deposit in particular?" Lisa asked. "Is that the only one on the planet?"

"No. The amount required to indicate a particular deposit is always relative to that deposit's size. The Gatherers appear to have perfect knowledge of the planet's composition, but we do not, and determining the correct amounts took tremendous trial and error. Mostly error. But if we knew the correct amount, we could instruct the Gatherer to travel to a deposit on the other side of the planet. And it would."

"Incredible," Lisa said. She could appreciate the simplicity— the elegance, even—of the Gatherers' functionality.

Hopefully retaking Habitat 2 will be that straightforward.

Somehow, she doubted that. Over a week ago, her stomach had begun churning at the thought of the coming battle; her first one, outside of lucid sims. She didn't count fighting the thugs who'd stolen their beetle as a battle.

That said, she *had* killed that day, and now, she broke into a cold sweat at the thought that she would soon be called on to do so again, many times over.

Am I ready for this?

She didn't know. But tomorrow would bring the answer.

CHAPTER 47

Parabola

"I don't get it," Tommy Tomlinson said as another rocket hit Plenitos' walls, shaking it worryingly. He shifted his position on the parapet, gleaming legs flashing in the sun, and answered with rockets of his own. "The MIMAS mechs were supposed to help us win against the Quatro." Tension and exertion made his voice waver as he continued to pepper the alien horde with explosives. "So why are they about to break through?"

"Doesn't exactly work like that, Tommy," Ash said, grunting a little as she ran along the wall to get a better vantage point before spraying a line of Quatro with bullets. "In these mechs, we can take on twenty Quatro each, probably more. But we can't defeat an army like this by ourselves. Not in enough time to stop them from breaching the walls. The walls were supposed to hold."

"Shut up," Gabe barked, annoyance at his pilots' chatter amplifying his stress. "We don't have time to stand up here and philosophize about it. We have to do something, now."

"What would that be, Chief?" Jake Price asked.

"We need to stop defending and start attacking."

"But Ash just pointed out—"

"I don't care what she pointed out. I don't submit my orders to a committee—I give them, and you follow them. Everyone off the walls and follow me into the city."

"But I thought—"

"*Off the walls and into the city!*" Gabe yelled, turning to leap from the parapet. The asphalt rushed up to meet him, yet he barely felt a thing upon impact, and he hit the ground running.

Behind him, the team charged after him, finally having ceased their babble.

Within a few minutes, they reached Plenitos' only launch site, which was intended for situations where someone needed to reach Valhalla fast—like in the event the city was overrun, for instance, and the council felt moved to evacuate without delay.

"We left the battle," Tommy said, in the tone of someone who'd just spilled his soft drink and had to buy another.

"We'll be back there very soon," Gabe said. "Each of our mechs has the launch capacity to escape a planet's gravity well and achieve orbit."

"What does that have to do with the siege?" Henrietta Jin asked.

"Well, if we can attain orbit, then we can definitely launch ourselves over the city walls and come down directly behind the Quatro. From there, we'll be much closer to the ones with rocket launchers. We can fight our way to them, put them down, then launch ourselves back to safety."

"Probably singe some Quatro in the process," Ash said. "I like it. But can you modify the function in time, sir?"

Gabe nodded. "Just need to tweak a few parameters. Give me a second."

It took more like a minute, which was a minute they couldn't afford to lose. But given the circumstances, it was pretty quick, and he was proud of how fast he arrived at calculations describing a shallow parabola that would take them over Plenitos' walls.

"Sending it to your implants now," he said. "Everyone spread out around the site. That's against regular procedure, but we need to go together to cut down the Quatro's reaction time, and our mechs' armor is strong enough to handle a little rocket exhaust."

Oneiri Team spread themselves across the launch site in a roughly even distribution. *Good enough.*

"All right," he said. "Engage rockets on my mark. One...two...mark!"

The thrusters in his mech's legs flared to life, and Gabe left the ground with startling speed. He barely cleared the roof of a warehouse, and then the city hurtled past below him.

Within seconds, his flight crested, directly over the wall.

Then, he passed the teeming mass of Quatro.

Then...

Then, he descended into the woods, having overshot his target.

Damn it, he thought as he crashed through the foliage, hitting the ground and rolling several meters before coming to a rest against one of Eresos' countless leafless trees.

He'd sorely miscalculated. All around them, the other mechs collided with the ground, making it rumble.

"Back!" Gabe ordered. "We have to go back!"

But the Quatro had seen them land—and heard them, probably. Dozens of them charged into the woods in chase, and soon Oneiri was fighting them among the trees, desperately trying to push back toward Plenitos.

CHAPTER 48

Makeshift Tank

As shadows lengthened rapidly all across Alex's landscape, Andy drove the beetle toward Habitat 2 at a stately pace. Lisa sat beside him, the intercom raised to her lips, ready to broadcast over shortwave.

Finally, a form of communication that doesn't rely on satellite.

Although she'd accepted that Darkstream maybe didn't have the situation in Habitat 2 completely under control, she was still an employee of the company, and she intended to invoke that authority now.

They crested a rise that brought Habitat 2 into sight, and Lisa could make out more of it in the twilight. She hadn't seen it from outside very often. Few did, other than the beetle drivers. It wasn't built with aesthetics in mind, not the outside view anyway, but even so, Lisa thought it was beautiful.

The way its gunmetal gray flowed into Alex's blue in the waning light. The way it sprawled across the terrain, with antennae, satellite dishes, and observation towers distributed across it at random intervals—the spires mostly offered a view of the planet itself , not of the habitat, though you could catch glimpses of it from them.

You couldn't see it like this. Not like she was seeing it. And in that moment, Lisa came to love and miss her home even more.

I'm so close, yet regaining Habitat 2 will not be easy.

The beetle rolled to a halt, and Lisa depressed the slim red button that would broadcast her voice to Daybreak—and to any Habitat 2 inhabitants listening over the wide channel.

"This is Seaman Lisa Sato. I have M-level Clearance and I operate with the full authority of Darkstream Security to dispense and execute justice as I deem necessary. You have unlawfully captured Habitat 2, a settlement in which Darkstream Security possesses a controlling interest. I hereby order you to surrender and turn Habitat 2 back over to company constables and also to the council. You have five minutes to reply."

Replacing the intercom, she glanced at Andy, who offered a small grin that didn't hold much heart. "Think they'll listen?"

Lisa paused. "No. But I have to give them a chance."

"Do you? I don't recall anything in the employee handbook about showing mercy to gangsters who mess with company property."

"You're right...but I have to anyway. For me."

"I see."

Five minutes passed, during which Daybreak failed to contact them. She raised the intercom once again, and was about to speak when the dashboard speaker crackled to life.

"How did you survive?" a gruff voice said.

"Who am I speaking to?"

"Quentin Cooper. Answer my question."

She pressed the red button. "I'm not inclined to give you any information, Cooper. Submit to my requirements, or face the consequences."

"What consequences? You're out there. We're in here. You can suffocate, for all we care."

But Lisa heard the note of uncertainty in his voice. She drew a deep breath. "No doubt, by now, you've noticed the total shutdown of Gatherer traffic to Habitat 2. *We* did that. If you won't surrender, if you want the flow of resources to resume, then you'll at least have to come out here and face us. Without the Gatherers, you'll have no leverage with Darkstream at all. They'll devote considerable resources to exterminating you."

Another silence—and this one lasted almost twenty minutes. Andy kept the beetle at the top of the rise.

From where they sat, they could see two vehicle bay doors, and at last, one of them opened to admit a beetle that had been outfitted with heavier armor than was usual for the transport vehicles, along with plenty of artillery.

Alongside that makeshift tank marched an entire platoon of pressure suit-clad figures, who also carried their share of guns.

"All right," she said, her voice a little breathless. Her skin had begun to crawl with the prospect of imminent battle, and she felt like she couldn't inhale enough oxygen, no matter how deeply she breathed. "We need to move."

CHAPTER 49

Steam

A Quatro charged at Jake, leaving a faint trail behind it inside the dream—an effect he hadn't noticed before, which he attributed to the alien's speed.

He pivoted behind an unusually large tree, with a quickness that still surprised him, given the mech's bulk. The maneuver forced the Quatro to veer to the right, leaving its muscular haunches exposed to Jake's heavy machine gun.

It made short work of the beast.

He heard the next attackers before he saw them. They hit him from two new angles, outside his field of vision, and for a moment, he couldn't move enough to bring one of his weapons to bear.

Screaming with the effort, he shoved his weight to the right, knocking one weighty alien aside and extending his right bayonet to drive it into its flank. As fast as he could, he stabbed it twice more before pushing it away.

The other Quatro pounced on him from behind, pinning him to the ground while it raked knife-like claws across Jake's pack, sending spasms of pain through his body.

Nothing seemed effortless, inside the mech—the dream saw to that. Yes, his strength was increased a hundredfold at least, but he still experienced every exertion as though it was his own.

Because it *was* his own.

He pushed against the ground, flashing back to the intense PT Roach had subjected them to, trying his best to make them wash out.

The strain made him grunt. *You're going to wash out if you can't do this,* he told himself, and it occurred to him then that making Oneiri Team had been just as important as his own survival. More important, maybe. Because being an ongoing part of Oneiri ensured his sister would get the medical attention she so sorely needed.

He heaved upward, shifting the Quatro enough that Jake got his left leg underneath him.

That did it. Surging upward, he turned to aim a flamethrower at the beast—better suited to close-range than the autocannon, which would require time to engage and spin to life.

A gout of fire took the Quatro in the side and belly, causing it to recoil, screeching as its flesh sloughed off. Jake finished it with his heavy machine gun.

Scanning the trees for his next opponent, Jake noticed that the patches of sky between the forest canopy were flashing red.

That's me, he realized. *I'm doing that. The sky is reflecting my anger.*

Most of his anger wasn't for the Quatro, either—it was for Gabriel Roach. Twice now, the chief had miscalculated, landing the team in a position that detracted from the battle effort rather than enhanced it.

He didn't care whether that was due to the newness of the mechs. If that was the case, Darkstream should never have deployed them this early, and Gabe should never have supported them in doing so.

To Jake, Gabe represented Darkstream. As far as he was concerned, they were one and the same in their eagerness to push new technologies before they'd been properly tested.

As a result, here they were, too far from Plenitos' walls, which were about to fall.

Almost on cue, the sound of a rocket hitting the walls reached him, followed by a prolonged screeching sound. Another rocket exploded. Then another.

"What was that?" Tommy screamed over the team-wide as he grappled with a Quatro nearby, finally managing to throw the thing into a tree before turning to confront the next. The first Quatro snapped the tree clean in half.

Before answering, Ash drove her bayonet deep into an alien that had reared up before her on its hind legs. She eviscerated it.

"Pretty sure that was Plenitos' walls," she said.

Ash was between Jake and Tommy. Three more Quatro emerged from the trees, then, all converging on her.

Jake ran as fast as he could toward her, but as he approached, she fended off one with a savage swipe of her bayonet while peppering the next with her heavy machine gun.

The first Quatro balked, giving Ash a window to turn her gun on it, planting her next round into its skull. When the third Quatro charged, she ducked low, and the alien soon found itself flipping through the air.

By the time it hit the ground, Ash was already opening fire with both autocannons.

"Damn," Jake said as he reached her. "Nice going."

"Oh, that? I was just blowing off some steam."

"Hey," Tommy said. "Maybe that can be your nickname, Ash. Steam. You sure moved through those Quatro like you were steam, or smoke or something."

"Steam." Ash's mech cocked its head to its side. "Could be worse."

"Uh huh," Jake said. "We need to get to the walls, you two. Pronto."

The trio dashed through the trees, and when they emerged from the tree line, they found Gabriel Roach standing just outside it, massive hands at his sides, staring at a quickly emptying field.

A wicked rent had opened in the city walls, splitting it almost in two, with only the topmost portion still joined.

The gap was wide enough for three Quatro to charge through abreast, and the massive horde was bunched at the walls, waiting their turn to enter, ignoring the smattering of gunfire from those defenders that had managed to retain their posts.

But that wasn't what caused Jake's ears to start ringing with rage. It was the fact that Roach just stood there, staring, not even bothering to fire on the bunched-up Quatro.

"Come *on!*" Jake growled, barreling toward the gap, both autocannons spinning up to send twin streams of hot lead across the field.

CHAPTER 50

A Losing Engagement

Commander Benjamin Clifford fought to retain his battle calm as Quatro after Quatro poured through the opening they'd made with their endless rocket barrage.

The original plan had been for Clifford's battalion to push out of the city gates once Roach and his team had managed to neutralize the Quatro rocket launchers. They'd expected that effort's success to enrage the Quatro, turning their focus on the mechs.

But when they'd overshot their mark, Clifford had known immediately that the walls would be breached. With that in mind, he made the snap decision to keep his battalion inside Plenitos, ready to deploy to wherever the Quatro managed to break through.

And so here they were—a significant portion of Darkstream's reserve forces, known through the company as the Force Multipliers, all arrayed in a wide arc to gun down the Quatro as quickly as they came through.

Or at least, to attempt that. The aliens were proving just as resilient as always. At first, the combined fire of five mortars, ten heavy assault weapons, two tanks, and three platoons' worth of soldiers with fully replenished kits had managed to keep the Quatro at bay.

Soon, though, the aliens began to use their dead fellows as cover, crouching behind them to fire on the defenders.

One of the tanks tried switching from kinetic penetrators to explosive anti-tank rounds. Clifford thought that seemed like a good idea, on the surface at least. The Quatro certainly had tank-like qualities.

And the first round did significant damage to the massive Quatro, obliterating one of them in a spray of viscera while debilitating two more.

The second shot missed its target, however, hitting the city wall instead and widening the gap even further. That made Clifford curse under his breath.

Just what we needed.

It was especially vexing, since Darkstream's tanks were known for their pinpoint accuracy, especially at relatively close range like this.

That means the gunner screwed up.

A Quatro with a rocket launcher made it through, then, getting off two shots before Clifford's people put the thing down.

The first shot went high, crashing into the upper floor of a supply depot, but the second took out a squad's worth of tightly bunched soldiers.

That seemed to do it. The Force Multipliers were highly trained, and they'd seen plenty of fighting during the initial colonization of Eresos. Hell, a lot of them had once been UHF soldiers, with long histories of fighting insurgents in the Milky Way's Bastion Sector.

Still, they knew a losing engagement as well as anyone, and as more and more Quatro made it into Plenitos, the line started to buckle, and the Force Multipliers began to lose their superior firing arc.

If I don't do something right now, this is going to turn into a rout, and I'll be commander of nothing but a corpse pile.

"Fall back!" he screamed over the battalion-wide channel.

The reserve forces did not need to be told twice. They began retreating to the protection of the buildings behind them, the tanks rolling backward while firing off round after round, and the soldiers inching backward, doing their best to keep the Quatro at bay all the while.

CHAPTER 51

Attack Angle

They'd chosen the angle of their approach to Habitat 2 carefully, and as the Daybreak force neared, Andy inched the beetle backward through a shallow valley, gradually picking up speed.

The valley was already completely dark, and within minutes, so would be the rest of Alex. Parallel rows of hills comprised the valley, one side higher on average than the other, which formed a corridor between them. It was through that corridor that Andy now accelerated backward.

The drug lord's cronies obliged them by following.

"You'd better get going," Andy said. "If you wait any longer, they'll have a firing solution on you. Plus, the beetle's only picking up speed."

"Where'd you learn the term 'firing solution?'" Lisa said, grinning at him.

He smiled back, and this time it wasn't as half-hearted as before. "Maybe I've been listening in on your sessions with Tessa."

She laughed, surprised to find herself enjoying a conversation with Andy. "I imagine that was tiring all by itself. All right. Crack open the hatch."

Double-checking her pressure suit, she made her way to the vehicle's rear, where a sliver of waning sunlight had already appeared.

She'd tried to seem nonchalant to Andy, but she'd used her joking to cover up how terrified she felt. Her stomach was performing flip-flops as she grasped the handholds halfway up the beetle's hatch and hoisted herself up.

Head emerging, she swallowed hard as she eyed the terrain, which suddenly seemed pretty far below.

What if I screw up the landing? What if my suit gets compromised?

But she couldn't wait any longer. If she did, it wouldn't just be her suit that got compromised.

Pulling herself up the rest of the way, she balanced on the lip of the beetle's hatch before leaping sideways, plummeting two meters before tucking into a roll and coming up unscathed, other than an aching shoulder—the one that had borne the brunt of the fall, since she'd had to lean that way to prevent the sniper rifle strapped to her back from digging into the ground and botching the maneuver. Still, the forward momentum had spared her any serious injury.

No time to stand around congratulating myself.

She sprinted toward the nearest hills under the cover of what was now total darkness, to find a suitable vantage point as fast as she could.

The Quatro were distributed all along the hills on both sides of the valley, though Lisa didn't encounter a single one as she slipped out of sight of the approaching enemy.

She swept the terrain with her gaze, spotting at least three places that offered good cover.

None of them held the hulking aliens.

Maybe those places don't offer quite enough cover for a giant quadruped.

That was possible. But the fact that she couldn't see any of her allies only heightened her tension, making the base of her throat clench, as it usually did when she felt extremely stressed.

Of course, Tessa had stressed her out plenty of times—during PT in the cramped beetle, during target practice, and especially inside the panicked lucid sims she was so good at concocting.

This is just like that. I didn't let Tessa get the best of me. And I won't let Quentin Cooper, either.

Instead, she ran for the cover closest to the approaching enemy, unlimbering her sniper rifle from where it was slung across her back—they'd recovered it from one of the thugs she'd killed in the firefight out in the middle of Alex's nowhere.

She also had her SL-17, though she hoped to prevent the enemy from getting close enough to make her use that.

Carefully raising her head just enough to see the approaching soldiers, as well as the modified beetle they surrounded, Lisa settled the rifle directly on the rock, peering into the scope and covering one of the lead soldiers with her crosshairs.

The enemy was nearing the location that she, Tessa, and Rug had identified as the optimal spot to engage them.

Lisa's first shot would serve as the signal to the others to commence firing. But if the Quatro had truly abandoned her...

If that had happened, Lisa would surely die.

But she had to trust someone, and she knew she didn't trust Darkstream quite as much as she once had. She loved her job, and she loved the work the company did, but she'd truly expected them to help the people of Habitat 2. Instead, they'd done nothing. So far, at least.

And she knew if she let fear prevent her from firing, or even just from firing on time, this battle would not end well.

I need to trust someone. Don't I?

She exhaled steadily, slowly squeezing the trigger, just as Tessa had taught her.

Her bullet took the soldier in the neck, and he dropped like a sack of rocks. That caused the other soldiers to tense up, peering around wildly.

Some of them drew closer to the beetle, but they didn't seem to know which direction the shot had come from, so they couldn't figure out which side of the beetle offered actual cover.

As Lisa smoothly switched targets and fired again, the enemy began to figure out where the preparation fire was coming from.

Where are the Quatro?

The answer to that question came as quickly as she asked it. Crackling beams of energy lanced out from multiple locations, lighting up the darkness all along the hills. Five soldiers went down in quick succession, their pressure suits charred where they were struck. With any luck, the suits were also compromised.

Energy weapons. So that's what those strange guns were.

She was relieved that the Quatro had begun to engage, and also pleased by the disorienting effect it was having on Cooper's fighters, who milled around the beetle, firing wildly into the hills at random.

Her relief was short-lived, however, as the enemy beetle's main gun turned toward her.

They figured out my location, she realized, just as the beetle began to fire.

CHAPTER 52

Beating Heart

Jake pounded through the city streets, frantically searching for Quatro to kill. He'd just finished dealing with a group of five of them, but it had taken way too long, and he'd narrowly dodged a direct hit from a rocket in the process. Even though the MIMAS mech had withstood a close-proximity grenade blast just fine, he still wasn't eager to find out whether it could endure quite the level of punishment a rocket would provide.

I can't believe *this. They're inside Plenitos...*

The city was the de facto capital of the Steele System. Sure, maybe an argument could be made for Valhalla claiming that title, but no one outside the space station was likely to accept that.

No, Plenitos was the place that had the most ordinary people, living together, working together—and now, dying together.

As Jake hunted through the city streets, he encountered an alarming number of human corpses. Most of them weren't soldiers, either. They were just normal people who'd been caught outdoors when the Quatro breached the walls. Many of them wore clothes that were little more than rags.

If Plenitos falls, we lose Eresos.

Jake didn't know that for sure, but it made a lot of sense. Sure, Ingress had the space elevator, but this was the capital. Plenitos was the beating heart of the human presence on the planet.

"Help us!" a voice cried out, echoing between the buildings. "Someone, please!"

He had difficulty discerning the source of the plea, but his implant dutifully assisted, indicating the direction by assigning a green haze to a nearby alley mouth while washing the rest of the world in blue.

Jake didn't wait. He pounded toward the alley, turning the corner to find two Quatro trying to get at four survivors halfway up a fire escape: a family of four, with two small children huddled against their parents in fear.

The fourth flight of stairs had been blown apart, probably by a Quatro rocket, and the pair of aliens were trying their best to access the family, with one of them leaping and snapping with its jaws while the other attempted to squeeze between the narrow railings.

Both had guns strapped to their backs, but for some reason they weren't firing. Probably, they were out of ammo.

Jake didn't waste time trying to figure that out. Wary of damaging the fire escape further, he decided to forego his artillery in favor of bayonets, which he extended fully, locking them in place as he sprinted toward the Quatro.

He screamed as he ran, which served to divert the aliens' focus onto him. The one that had been attempting to jump high enough to catch one of the humans in its jaws now turned to face Jake, squaring its shoulders.

Jake crashed into the beast, sending it back into the fire escape, which groaned worryingly.

So much for not endangering it. He still wasn't as used to the mech as he would have liked. Nor was he used to its power.

Grabbing the Quatro by one of its forelegs, he swung it around, tossing it down the alley and forcing it to scrabble for purchase on the cobble before charging at Jake again.

He moved to meet its charge, but the other alien had extricated itself from the fire escape, pouncing on him from behind. For a moment, he was sandwiched between the snarling creatures.

His blade found the first Quatro's leg, quickly cutting to the bone. It yelped, backing off enough for Jake to whip around and hack at the other.

The alien dodged the first blow, but Jake pivoted to plunge his bayonet deep into his adversary's shoulder, following it with the other blade, which he buried in the Quatro's head.

Wrenching both weapons from his defeated foe, he turned to find the other Quatro had left the alley, leaving a trail of blood behind.

Above, the adults studied him warily, while their children buried their faces in the folds of their clothes and refused to look at Jake's mech.

"Come with me," Jake said, as gently as he could. "I'll see you to safety." They hesitated, and he added: "Come on, now. We don't have much time."

Finally, they listened, the dark-haired mother and father carefully descending the stairs to join Jake on the ground. "Thank you," the woman said. From their parents' arms, the children still wouldn't look.

Before the battle, Roach, Black, and Clifford *had* developed a plan for safeguarding Plenitos' citizens, which had been based on a modified version of a scheme the council had already had. It involved shepherding everyone inside nuclear-hardened shelters, where they would hide until the Quatro were rooted out.

But no one had actually expected the aliens to breach the city walls, least of all its citizens, who had always felt more or less invincible inside Plenitos.

Not anymore.

And that wasn't all. The city also had an ample helping of homeless people, be they mentally ill, disabled, or just elderly and alone. It was highly likely that many of them hadn't even been aware of the attack until the Quatro were already in the streets. They were Plenitos' abandoned people, and now they paid the most dearly for the failings of the city's so-called defenders.

The city council had certainly been well aware of the Quatro threat. Forty minutes before, Jake had spotted them leaving in an emergency evacuation rocket, bound for Valhalla, where they would no doubt wait in comfort until this was all over, one way or another.

The family he'd saved didn't seem poor—just unlucky.

They could have been unluckier.

Jake had memorized the locations of the city's ten shelters, and as he led them to the nearest one, they didn't encounter any more Quatro.

"Thank you," the mother repeated, just before they entered the safety of the shelter. The father just stared at him, hollow-eyed, and the children continued to cower.

"Make sure those doors are secure when I leave," Jake said, turning to sprint through the streets in search of his next target.

Or, more likely, another family to save.

"Price," Roach said to him inside the dream, and Jake could tell it was a reconstruction of his voice, derived from a subvocalization.

"Yeah?"

"You're out of position. There's a host of Quatro in the northwest quadrant. I need your help taking them out."

Roach seemed to have recovered from the trance Jake had found him lost in, outside Plenitos. Around twenty minutes ago, Jake had glimpsed the chief across one of the city's squares, engaging a group of six Quatro with a savagery Jake hadn't witnessed from his commanding officer before.

"Sir," Jake said, "there are people still outside the shelters. Families. I just helped a family of four to safety, and I was about to look for more."

"Price, get your ass over here *now.* I'm aware you think you know battle better than I do, but if we waste our time trying to escort individuals to safety, the Quatro will burn Plenitos to the ground. Do you get that?"

Jake took a deep breath. He wanted to call Roach out, but he knew his CO was right. *All* of Plenitos' families would die if they couldn't retake the city from the Quatro. Fighting them was how he could serve its citizens best. Roach obviously knew that.

Better than I do, clearly.

Jake claimed to want to help his sister get better, and yet he was playing fast and loose with his career by bucking Roach's orders. Sooner or later, he realized, that would catch up to him—it could even result in his mech getting taken away, no matter how high his skill level.

That prospect frightened him almost as much as the idea of his sister dying—a comparison that was frightening in itself.

I need to start doing as I'm told more. Even if the orders seem like they suck sometimes.

It didn't mean he intended to go along with what his superiors wanted every time...but he needed to choose his battles, at the very least.

"I understand, sir," he said to Roach. "I apologize. I'll be right over."

CHAPTER 53

Fear and Revulsion

The shot from the beetle's main gun sheared off half of Lisa's cover, showering the rest with rubble big enough to crush her skull.

Luckily, she was elsewhere when it hit— several meters to the left, to be specific, where she'd leapt as the beetle fired.

She didn't stop there, though, knowing that any shrapnel could easily tear a hole in her pressure suit. Instead, she continued scrabbling away, breaking into a run once certain she was completely out of the enemy's view.

Remembering the other vantage points she'd scouted before engaging the enemy, she ran toward the farthest one, judging that the nearest was far too close. The Daybreak fighters would probably expect her to pop up near her original position. Instead, she ran as fast as she could across the uneven, hilly terrain—blue dust kicking up all around her.

Her heart hammered away in her chest, partly from exertion, partly from her ongoing terror. On top of that, her throat clenched so tightly she worried about airflow, though that was probably irrational.

What isn't irrational about today? Nothing. The fear and bloodlust that gripped her, the fact that she was called upon to shoot and kill human beings—none of that made any sense.

Nevertheless, it was how the universe had shaken out today, and the death she dealt would mean freedom for her neighbors inside Habitat 2.

Providing I deal enough of it.

As she reached her destination, after a headlong dash that had seemed to last far too long, she realized that she would never overcome the fear and revulsion battle caused her to feel. Being an effective soldier meant fighting on in spite of those feelings.

And administering justice meant becoming nearly as monstrous as those to whom you meted it out.

Maybe just as monstrous.

She settled her sniper rifle atop the rock at her new vantage point and surveyed the carnage in the valley. The Daybreak fighters still didn't seem to know quite what to do.

Some of them still circled their beetle, seeking safety where there was little to be had. Others stood in full view, returning fire until a Quatro energy beam cut them down.

Others charged for the hills, to seek cover themselves, no doubt—and to root out their assailants.

Something *crunched* behind Lisa, and she turned to behold an enemy soldier, combat knife in hand.

She had no time to draw her SL-17. Instead, she whipped the sniper rifle around as he sprang toward her. The long barrel caught him in the chest, and she pulled the trigger, blowing him back to land on the sapphire ground, where he ceased to move.

Taking a deep breath, she studied him a second longer. He had a pistol, which she would collect from his corpse on her way to the next vantage point, but no doubt he'd foregone using it for the sake of remaining stealthy.

A miscalculation, as it turned out.

Turning back to the battle, Lisa drew a bead on a soldier who was running toward the hills on the opposite side of the valley. She fired, missed, then took a moment to steady her breathing.

She fired again. Her target dropped.

A bullet hit her in the chest, and it was her turn to fly backward, landing partially on the man she'd downed. Darkstream pressure suits were woven with para-aramid fiber in areas that covered vital organs, and so unlike her late adversary, she survived.

Sure hurts like hell, though.

She struggled to her feet, wheezing, but willing herself to stagger on in search of more cover from which to fire. There was nothing else she could do.

"Lisa," Tessa's voice said, reconstituted from a subvocalization.

"Yes?" she grunted. "What?"

"Just checking you're safe. And warning you."

"Warning me?"

"Another group just came out of Habitat 2. Just as big as the first. Get ready, girl. This isn't nearly over yet."

CHAPTER 54

Sharing

Phineas Gage did not like to stand idle behind his bar. He always tried to be doing something, whether it was wiping down the counter, cleaning out a glass or—better—pouring someone a drink.

He realized that made him the most stereotypical alien-planet sealed-habitat bartender in history, but he didn't care. A few stereotypes existed for a reason. Not many, but a few. And the cheerful, hardworking bartender was one of them.

So he didn't like to stand idle.

But that was exactly what he *was* doing. Ever since Bob O'Toole walked into the Dusty Bucket bristling with guns.

"Where'd you get those?" was his first question.

"Where does anyone get them in the Steele System?" O'Toole grunted. "Found them under a bush. Dug them out from between the cushions of my couch."

"There aren't any bushes in Habitat 2," Phineas muttered.

"You know what I mean."

He wasn't sure he did. But that wasn't unusual, when it came to Bob O'Toole. What *was* unusual—highly unusual—was that O'Toole seemed as sober as a Mormon judge.

Phineas decided to try another line of inquiry. "What are you doing with all those guns in my bar?" he asked.

"Sharing," O'Toole said. Shifting some of his load from one arm to the other, he held out a rifle by its stock.

"And why would I want to take that from you, Bob?"

"Because we're going hunting, you and me. Hunting us some Daybreak asshats."

"You're crazy. There are two-hundred of them and two of us. If we start taking out Daybreak members, we'll get gunned down faster than we can say boo."

"There *were* two-hundred of them. At least a quarter of them are dead by now, and most of the rest are out on Alex, fighting."

"What in Sol are you talking about?"

"My girl Lisa Sato. She's done it."

"She's not *your*—" Phineas stopped himself, shaking his head. *One thing at a time, Phin.* "What do you mean, done it? What has she done?"

"Brought back reinforcements, is what she's done! I heard her over the short-wave, giving an ultimatum to those Daybreak jerks, real steely like. Reminded me of Tessa Notaras, and I wouldn't be surprised if she's out there, too. We're taking back this town, Gage. Now take the damned gun."

Still, Phineas hesitated, studying O'Toole's gap-toothed grin, trying to decide whether the old lech had finally lost it.

"How do you know a quarter of Daybreak's people are dead?"

"Got a nerd to hack the exterior feed. They got one hell of a battle brewing out there, Gage. It's time we got one started in here."

He'd heard enough. Phineas pushed away the rifle O'Toole was offering him. "Get that away from me," he said.

Then he plucked another firearm from where it dangled at O'Toole's hip. "I'm taking the Uzi."

CHAPTER 55

Take No Prisoners

The Battle for Habitat 2 dragged on through the night.

Darkstream pressure suits could hold three doses of stims, and well before the eastern sky began to brighten, Lisa used them all.

How long have we been fighting? It seemed like eight hours at least, and it probably was. *Maybe more.*

The Daybreak beetle had trundled up and down the valley for the first part of the battle, providing a focal point for the ene-my's defense against Lisa, Tessa, and the Quatro.

The second group of fighters to emerge from Habitat 2 had no beetle—probably they hadn't modified a second one, and unmodified beetles were next to useless in traditional combat, which was why Andy had long since driven to safety.

The Daybreak reinforcements moved to back up their lone beetle, but shortly after, Lisa had finally managed to secure a vantage point close enough to make a move against it. She'd ripped a grenade from her suit's waist, pulled the pin, and lobbed it as hard as she could, spraying the Daybreak soldiers with bullets as it flew.

They returned fire, and she ducked, but then they realize what she'd done, and the shooting stopped.

Peeking over the rise, Lisa saw them fleeing from the beetle as fast as she could.

Did I...?

Fire had blossomed from underneath the enemy beetle, spreading across the ground and lighting up the night. The rear hatch opened, and three figures leapt free of the vehicle, two of them landing upright to join the others in fleeing. The third went sprawling on the ground, leg twisting, followed by an attempt to crawl away from the fire as fast as possible.

The enemy beetle hadn't exploded, but it was clearly disabled, and it had ceased to be an effective rallying point for the Daybreak fighters.

After that, they scattered into the hills.

Lisa strapped her sniper rifle to her back once more, after that. It was useless, but she didn't want to abandon it, for fear that the enemy would pick it up and use it to their advantage later.

That had been hours ago. Now, she stalked through the hills, suit audio jacked up to amplify any and all sounds.

On her way down a shallow hill, she nearly stepped on a Daybreak thug hiding in a crevice. He spotted her around the same time she did him, and he managed to get his gun out, but Lisa put a round each in his neck and chest before he could fire. He slumped back into his hiding spot and moved no more.

When she picked up his pistol, she found that it had a silencer, and so she clipped her assault rifle to her pressure suit, holding the pistol before her instead.

This part of the battle was the tensest yet—the protracted creeping through pitch-dark hills, forever hunting for an enemy that was hunting her. Every sound made her twitch. Including her own footfalls.

A noise made her spin around, and she tried to track the source with her pistol's muzzle.

Just some skittering rocks.

Then another Daybreak fighter appeared before her. The woman got a round off, but she was clearly as excited as Lisa, and the shot went wild.

Lisa took full advantage, bringing her pistol up and firing twice. One shot missed, but the other took her target in the shoulder.

Staggering backward, the woman managed to raise her gun once more.

A shot went off, and Lisa dropped to the ground at the same time, so that the bullet went over her head.

On her stomach, she couldn't raise the pistol's barrel enough to hit any vital organs, but she fired at her target's shins, and one of her bullets must have hit. Her adversary fell to the ground, clutching at her right leg. Lisa regained her feet.

"Please," the woman said over an unencrypted channel. "Mercy."

"I—" Lisa shook her head. "I can't. We don't have the ability to take prisoners, and I have no reason to trust you. I can't just leave you here."

"Take my guns. What am I going to do? Look at me. I'll probably die anyway, if my suit doesn't manage to seal the holes you put in me."

Lisa raised her gun to point at her enemy's head.

I'd be letting everyone in Habitat 2 down by not doing this.

Her finger shifted on the trigger, began to squeeze...

She eased up. "Toss away your weapons, slowly, so I can see what you're doing."

"Okay. Yes. Thank you." The woman did as she was told, and Lisa stepped forward, kicking away the weapons even farther.

"Is your suit sealing properly?"

"I—I think so."

"All right." Lisa sighed. Again, she'd almost let her fear push her into doing something that wasn't her. Her fear of defeat, of failing everyone she knew.

That wasn't enough to compromise who she was. It couldn't be. Yes, she'd fought hard today. Yes, she'd killed people, for the first time in her life. But she still clung to the belief that she was a good person.

She glanced around at their surroundings, keeping her pistol leveled at her prisoner, ready to swing it around to point at a new target if one appeared.

Now what?

She couldn't carry the woman's weapons. Not while continuing to fight. And she couldn't leave her here with them.

In the east, the sky had begun to brighten. At first, that made Lisa glad, but then she realized...

Oh God.

The Quatro would be rendered useless during the daylight. They wouldn't be able to bear the weight of their enormous weapons, nor could they repair their pressure suits if they tore. If Lisa, Tessa, and the Quatro couldn't end this battle fast, at best they would lose their only chance to save Habitat 2.

At worst, they'd die.

Indecision tore at her. She glanced at the woman again. *Should I have...?*

No. No matter what happened, killing an unarmed person was not the right move, even if that person had helped to terrorize Lisa's friends and neighbors.

Still, her heart rate spiked as she continued to scan her brightening surroundings.

Then, Tessa's voice was inside her helmet, and this time, it wasn't a reconstructed subvocalization.

It was just Tessa, and she sounded relaxed: "Lisa. It's over."

"What? How?"

"The people of Habitat 2...they rose up. They took their home back from Cooper. And once the ones we're fighting realized they're stranded out here..."

"They gave up."

"Yeah. They were probably already pretty stressed out as it is. Cooper fled in a beetle less than an hour ago, apparently. I doubt he was expecting to fight Quatro on Alex."

"Hey, Tessa?"

"Yes?"

"You didn't call me girl. You called me Lisa."

"So I did," Tessa said, and Lisa could hear the smile in her voice. "So I did."

CHAPTER 56

Clutch

When Gabe had first seen the Quatro pouring into Plenitos through the rent in the walls they'd made, he'd frozen, stricken by the thought that this was surely karmic retribution for the things he'd done in Darkstream's name during the taking of Eresos almost twenty years ago.

Then the flashbacks had begun anew, just snippets at first, their impact amplified tenfold by the dream.

He'd been riveted in place by them. They'd shattered his drive to continue fighting.

How embarrassing that Jake Price had been the one to snap him out of it.

"Come *on!*" Price had bellowed, charging across the battlefield, and the effect had been akin to a church bell on Sunday, ringing with Gabe's head inside it.

Price had sprinted toward the teeming Quatro, opening up with both autocannons, followed closely by Ash Sweeney and the rest of the team.

Sweeney. Jess's sister. Ash still didn't know Gabe's connection with her. But the thought of Jess rekindled his rage—his lust for vengeance.

And he'd charged after them.

Now, the last of the Quatro stalked the city's northwest quadrant in a pack three-hundred strong, which stretched across four streets at any given time. They made short work of anyone in their path, as well as every glass storefront they encountered.

The store windows weren't meant to withstand bullets, or even a fully grown Quatro leaning against it with its front paws. Other than building the shelters, no one had planned for the Quatro ever getting this far.

And yet here they were.

Gabe had already given the order for what was left of Darkstream's reserve battalion to muster in a square directly in the path of the alien horde. In the center of the square sat a gigantic, circular fountain that gushed water several meters in the air before it came back down to splash into a large basin.

His team gathered in the square, too. Everyone except Price.

"Where is he?" Gabe yelled over the team-wide, and even he could hear the manic edge in his own voice.

He saw Ash raise a metal hand to point.

Following the gesture, he saw Price, emerging from between two buildings.

The ground began to tremor, and on the opposite side of the square, the Quatro were beginning to step out onto the square as well.

"Form up," Gabe barked over the battalion-wide. "This is it."

"Clutch," Ash said.

"What?" he said, whipping around to face her.

She was still looking at Price.

"That should be Jake's nickname. Clutch. Because he seems to always arrive at the last minute, and that last minute always seems to be the one that matters most."

"Clutch it is," Gabe muttered, striding to the front of his forces' formation.

The moment he arrived, the air beside him flickered, and Captain Black appeared beside him.

"I saw you fall to pieces outside the city," Black said, his eternal calm apparently intact. "If it happens again, well...I doubt I need to outline the consequences. If you survive this, you'll be discharged, probably dishonorably."

"It won't happen again," Gabe said flatly.

"Good," Black said, vanishing.

"Hit them," he ordered over the wide channel. "Now."

His team of mechs had assembled directly behind him, at the very front of the Darkstream reserve forces.

They surged forward as one, a single fist of steel and death that swung forward to smash the Quatro apart.

"Grenades first," Gabe subvocalized. "Then bayonets, once we're among them."

The volley of grenades sailed overhead in a wide arc, creating a crescent of explosions deep within the Quatro ranks.

The enemy enveloped Gabe's team, then, surrounding them, swarming between them.

That suited Oneiri well. It gave them room to bring their bayonets to bear. Soon, each mech was covered in fur and flesh and blood.

Driving his blade into hide after hide, opening wound after wound, sending arc after arc of scarlet spurting into the air, Gabe lost himself in the dance of battle.

The roar of the remaining tanks' guns, the mortar shells, the automatic gunfire...it sounded muffled, to him. Everything did. His world was made of his blades and the Quatro flesh they found and the sky that flashed over and over with his rage, in colors that matched the viscera covering everything.

Soon, the mortars and tanks stopped firing, since to do so would endanger friendly units, locked as they were in close combat with the aliens.

Gabe wouldn't have been able to say how long it lasted. Hours, days, minutes.

At any rate, it ended. He whirled to find his next target and found nothing but a square littered with corpses, both Quatro and human.

Other than his team of mechs, Darkstream's reserve force was significantly diminished. The tanks remained, but few soldiers were left, and that included the mortar teams' numbers.

Gabe strode over to a petty officer he recognized. "Where's Commander Clifford?" he rasped.

"Dead, sir," the petty officer said. His name was Hayworth, if Gabe remembered correctly.

Nodding, Gabe turned, striding through the sea of bodies to reach the massive fountain in the center of the square. Without ceremony, he mounted it with a single step, turning to face what remained of his forces.

He spread his metal hands wide, taking in the entirety of the square, which soon would acquire the stink of death. Insects had already begun to light on the bodies.

Soon, they'll cover them.

"These beasts are evil," Gabe said. "Plain and simple. Today, we beat back evil—barely. We prevented them from taking what was most dear to us—barely. But they'll come again. They've tasted success. They've tasted human blood. And now that they have the taste, for as long as they live, they'll never stop hungering for it."

"So let's make sure they don't live much longer!" shouted Hayworth.

"I agree," Gabe said, nodding at the petty officer. "Let's." He swept those gathered with his gaze, metal head creaking softly as it turned. The battle haze was still leaving him, which the dream rendered by making the faces of his audience shimmer slightly. "Let's hit the Quatro in their home, now, with everything we have. Let's do to them what they just tried to do to us. Let's make it so they can never hurt us again."

That was it—all he had. The speech brought ragged cheers and a grim resolve, which Gabe could see etched in the face of every soldier. He could even see it in the posture of his team members.

Since before the battle, he'd suspected that the Quatro must have had a reason for hitting Plenitos. Possibly, they'd been provoked—they'd certainly been provoked twenty years ago, when Darkstream's forces had first driven them deep underground, using the most devastating weaponry they had access to.

He no longer cared. Provoked or not, the Quatro had taken everything from him that had given his life the paltry meaning it had had. His love, as well as his pride.

They'd taken everything that had driven him. And now, nothing drove him, except his desire to kill every last Quatro on Eresos.

The sky stopped flashing, settling into a red the color of blood.

That seemed fitting. The sky mirrored the ground, and soon the ground itself would be soaked through.

CHAPTER 57

A Troop of Giant Aliens

The Quatro couldn't fit through the regularly sized airlocks, and so Lisa had to order the vehicle bay airlocks opened for them.

Normally, the decision whether to open up the vehicle bays for a troop of giant aliens would have fallen to Chief Lannon, head of security for Habitat 2, but unfortunately he was unable to dispense his usual duties due to languishing in an eight-by-six cell. As for the other Darkstream employees, it turned out the company had negotiated with Daybreak for their release from Habitat 2, and they were long gone.

So Lisa had made the call, and now forty-two Quatro roamed Habitat 2's wider streets, leaving narrow lanes on either side of them—enough space for little more than a hoverbike to pass.

The aliens seemed totally unconcerned about blocking traffic, unless it was the part of traffic that consisted of Lisa, Tessa, and Andy, and the vehicles they drove.

Before the Battle for Habitat 2, Lisa had doubted whether the Quatro had it in them to be as vicious as battles tended to require.

Now, they surprised her in the opposite direction, with their cold demeanor toward every human that wasn't one of the first three they'd spoken with.

The communication barrier wasn't the problem. The Quatro translator had progressed to the point where their speech was basically indistinguishable from colloquial English.

Basically.

No, the Quatro simply didn't seem to like the majority of the human species. Or at least, the majority of the portion they encountered.

When she asked Rug about it, the alien paused pensively. "How best to explain," she muttered, midnight eyes staring into the distance. Before she spoke again, those eyes locked on to Lisa's, unwavering.

"In providing you succor while you were stranded on the barrens of Alex, we signaled that you were part of our drift—to you, and to ourselves. As far as we are concerned, you, Andy, and Tessa are Quatro as well as human."

Lisa blinked. "What is everyone else in Habitat 2, then?"

Rug snorted, sounding like a horse, or at least like the recordings of horses Lisa had heard. "They are potential Meddler agents."

"But...they're humans, too. They're my neighbors, friends. If they're agents, then wouldn't we likely be agents as well?"

"We have already taken that gamble, Lisa. It was a necessary one, and there is no going back."

"Then why not take it with the others?"

"That would represent a foolhardy risk."

Frowning, Lisa took a turn to stare into space. There was a gap in either Rug's logic or her own, and the Quatro's circuitous semantics had her doubting which it was.

Of course, there were other reasons for the Quatro's distress. Soon after the surviving Daybreak fighters were squared away in holding cells, along with the few Three Points members they'd kept alive, Lisa and her companions had learned of the war on Eresos, which seemed to shock the Quatro.

"Our species does not engage in gratuitous conflict," Rug said, flanks heaving. She was the only Quatro in sight at the time, and Tessa and Andy stood nearby as well. The Quatro were too large to fit inside most Habitat 2 structures, so they mostly remained in the climate-controlled out-of-doors. "They would not have engaged without provocation," she said.

"The reports say they attacked two cities, Rug," Tessa said, her tone gentle. "And that they killed hundreds of innocent civilians."

"Plus, you *are* pretty lousy to humans who aren't us," Andy chimed in. Lisa glared at him, which he studiously ignored.

"It is one thing to regard someone with suspicion," Rug said, sounding scandalized. The translator was pretty good at converting Quatro inflections into spoken English, too. "It is quite another to do them harm.

"After the Meddler attack, we lost contact with the other Quatro that accompanied us to this system. We feared they had died. But this is almost as concerning as that prospect. If they've strayed so far from Quatro norms…" Rug shuddered, also like a horse, a gesture Lisa had come to think of as equivalent to a human shaking their head. "It is difficult to countenance."

Lisa felt for the Quatro. And whether they came to trust more humans or not, so long as they did no harm, they were welcome to remain in Habitat 2 indefinitely, as far as she was concerned.

That said, she didn't have the time to play therapist to them. The social fabric of Habitat 2 had been damaged badly, and now it fell to Lisa to ensure that damage got repaired.

"You've come a long way," Tessa said to her, without prompting, as they both worked through damage claims made by residents of Habitat 2. "I'm prepared to consider you graduated from my training program. Congratulations."

"Wow. Thank you." It truly did mean a lot, and it elevated Lisa's mood, which she sorely needed.

"Just don't put too much pressure on yourself. Right now, everyone's treating you like you're the city council and Darkstream's physical incarnation all wrapped up in one."

"It's just until a new council is elected, ma'am."

The older woman smiled. "You can call me Tessa again, Lisa."

It was good to have her old friendship with Tessa back—surprisingly intact, despite the rigors the former soldier had put her through.

She wished she knew where she stood with Andy, though. They'd been through a lot during their journey across Alex, and they'd even seemed to bond a little at the end of it. But now that he was back in Habitat 2, he seemed just as smug as ever, and possibly even more aloof than before. Lisa told herself that she didn't really care about that, but still, it would have been nice to think what they'd endured together had meant something.

Tessa was right about the pressure Lisa was under, and they couldn't hold elections for city council soon enough. Cooper had executed the entirety of the old city council on his way to seizing control.

With the exception of one man: Councilman Leonardo Fiore had not been executed, which Lisa found highly suspicious. It probably meant he'd been corrupted by Daybreak all along, but there was no actual proof of that—just some pretty damning reports of special treatment during Cooper's occupation.

I guess I should just be grateful that the drug problem isn't likely to resurface anytime soon.

Tessa had her own view on that, of course.

"The drugs will come back," she said. "They're a factor in every human society. Besides, Darkstream *needs* them around, so that they can continue policing the populace. Controlling them."

That had made Lisa repress a sigh. The star of the company she worked for had certainly fallen somewhat in her eyes, but she still had trouble swallowing Tessa's endless conspiracy theorizing.

And then, something happened that lent a level of credence to those theories that Lisa would never have anticipated.

Part of repairing the social fabric inside Habitat 2 involved investigating exactly what had led to Daybreak's insurrection, and then to putting on trial those who'd been involved. It would likely take months, but she figured that to properly recover from the crisis, they had to figure out exactly what had happened.

To speed up that process a little, she floated the prospect of leniency for any prisoner that offered information that either led to a conviction or was judged significant in uncovering the truth.

She wasn't sure how well that would work, since she didn't have the authority to decide on how much leniency could actually be given, or whether any could be given at all. A message she'd sent to Valhalla requesting guidance on the matter had not yet received a reply.

So it surprised her when one of the prisoners came forward, a man named Samuel Dalton, almost immediately.

He claimed to be a high-ranking member of Daybreak, and citizen reports seemed to confirm that—he'd been seen giving orders and generally bossing around some of the Daybreak underlings.

The guards brought the man before Lisa in shackles, inside her temporary office in the Constable Station near the center of town.

"Well?" she said, eyebrows raised, trying for a mix of skepticism and cool disinterest.

"Darkstream willingly allowed the takeover by Daybreak," he said. "Encouraged it, even."

That shattered Lisa's mask of detachment. She furrowed her brow and stared at the man. "Why would they do that?"

"Because they knew Daybreak would take away everyone's assets, along with their rights. They'd be slaves, basically, and that's what they were until you came back here with those savages."

Lisa's head jerked back, as though she'd been slapped. What the man had told her almost perfectly mirrored what Tessa had said on the day all of this had happened.

That doesn't make it true, she tried to tell herself.

But the thought rang hollow, and she began to sense that something fundamental had changed in her little world. Something that couldn't be repaired or put back in place.

CHAPTER 58

Retreat

Bronson lent his full approval to Gabe's crusade against the Quatro dens, sending most of Plenitos' garrison to accompany Oneiri Team, along with what remained of the reserve force the company had sent down the space elevator. The captain also gave command of the battalion to Gabe, given Clifford's death.

The fact that Plenitos was being left with a skeleton force of defenders bothered Gabe, on some level. It reminded him too much of Northshire.

But on another, more immediate level, he couldn't care less. The extermination of the Quatro was what mattered, and everything else was subordinate to that.

Everything.

The entrance to the Quatro tunnels was comprised of solid rock, and too tiny for the mechs to enter. They might have blasted it wider, but the claustrophobic conditions persisted for half a kilometer, and it would have taken them days to finish the job, possibly weeks.

The tunnels probably narrow again farther in, anyway.

It didn't matter. Each member of Oneiri was trained in every weapon Darkstream had ever made, along with several it hadn't. If the lucid network was good for anything, it was that. Preparing players in the basics of combat, priming them for being trained and molded by the company later.

In particular, Oneiri had focused on drilling dozens of scenarios it was likely to encounter on the surface of Eresos, over and over again, until they were etched into the surface of their brains. As a result, their instincts would guide them through much of any engagement, and training and conditioning would see them through the rest.

So when Gabe ordered his pilots out of their mechs, no one complained. No one even blinked.

They're ready. After Ingress and Plenitos, he doubted there was much they weren't ready for, actually.

The dead Force Multipliers had left behind plenty of weaponry, with which he outfitted his team now. Shotguns for Marco and Beth, assault rifles for Gabe, Ash, and Jake, a flamethrower for Richaud, and a heavy machine gun and tripod for Tommy and Henrietta to operate.

Hopefully we won't have cause to set that up. It would mean they were in the direst of straits, and frankly, Gabe did not expect to enter those.

Most of the Quatro are already dead. They have to be, after the battles we just waged.

Either way, the heavy machine gun was the most powerful artillery Darkstream had signed off on for this mission. Mortar shells would be useless in the caves. Rocket launchers and grenade launchers were invitations for friendly fire. And fuel air explosives...

Well, they weren't approved for use at all anymore. They'd been meant for clearing out the Quatro en masse, before any of Darkstream's noncombat personnel had colonized Eresos. The same personnel who had later mostly quit the company to become the planet's citizens, unaffiliated with their former employer, except via the equipment they leased.

Now that Eresos was more heavily populated, the Darkstream board considered the use of fuel air bombs too..."sensitive for the current environment," was how Gabe remembered it being put.

Oneiri Team led the way into the tunnels, scouting ahead for the rest of the force. They were the best-trained and best-prepared out of everyone on the mission.

And yet, outside of his mech, Gabe felt incredibly vulnerable. Incredibly small.

Not to mention, he suddenly felt somewhat divided about what he was about to do.

There's no going back now, he told himself. *This isn't the time to cut and run. You're the one who orchestrated this. See it to the end.*

Remember Jess, he told himself.

He did. And he advanced.

His body was somewhat stiff as he did, probably from being inside his mech for so long. He tried to work it out as he walked, as best he could, taking overlong strides to stretch his muscles a bit.

The implants had night vision capability, obviating the need for lights. The Quatro would have no warning. And Oneiri would give no quarter.

Tommy and Henrietta were on point. At the first sight of Quatro, they would begin setting up their tripod and gun while the others charged ahead to engage, seeking to push the aliens back. If things went south, they could fall back behind the heavy machine gun, which would tear the beasts to shreds.

The tunnel they walked along continued for fifteen minutes without splitting, and barely changing direction by more than a few degrees here and there.

"Contact!" Tommy shouted after twenty-five minutes of walking along the same tunnel, his voice cracking, and he began fumbling with the tripod.

Gabe, Jake, and Ash surged forward, raising their SL-17s to sight along the barrels, firing at the pair of Quatro standing side-by-side fifteen meters in. The gun muzzles flashed, creating a strobing effect in the gloom.

Nothing happened. The Quatro stood there, completely immobile.

"Wait," Jake said. "Are they, like, statues?"

They weren't. A series of clattering noises followed, which Gabe quickly realized was the sound of bullets falling to the rock.

Then the Quatro took a step forward in tandem. Another.

"Fire!" Gabe yelled, and they did again, all three of them sending a volley of lead directly at the aliens.

Again, nothing. Again, the bullets hit the ground with dozens of *clinking* noises.

The Quatro stepped forward.

Suddenly, Gabe's gun was wrenched from his grasp, and so were Ash's and Jake's. The weapons flew through the air toward the Quatro, disappearing into the dark behind them.

Then the aliens charged.

"*Back!*" Gabe barked. "Fall back behind the tripod! Tomlinson and Jin, prepare to fire!"

They retreated behind the heavy machine gun, which commenced its staccato roar, a blinding starburst spouting from its muzzle.

The effect was exactly the same, with the Quatro continuing their charge. One of the aliens pulled ahead of the other, reaching Tommy to swat his face with a paw larger than the boy's head.

Tommy flew into the tunnel wall, neck twisted at an unnatural angle, staring back at the rest of his team, rivulets of blood dividing his face into vertical segments.

"*Retreat!*" Gabe screamed over the battalion-wide channel, running from the Quatro as fast as his stiff body permitted. "Everyone out of the tunnel, now! Get out! *Get out!*"

CHAPTER 59

Quaduped

Gabe was one of the last to rush out of the tunnel mouth—not due to some valiant instinct, but only to his position in line.

His breathing came hot and ragged, and his innards felt like they were vibrating. Without the mech dream separating him from the world, he'd been completely certain he was going to die down there.

If I'm being honest, I have no idea why I didn't.

"Get into some kind of formation," he ordered over the wide channel. "Prepare to send everything we have against those Quatro."

For his part, he made a beeline for his mech, using his implant to send it his unique signature. It detached its back, lowering it to form a ramp for him to climb.

He reached into the mech, groped the pocket just inside and to the right, and sighed with relief when he found the sedative he used to enter the dream and control his machine.

Popping it, he climbed into the claustrophobic confines of the mech, trying not to let the closeness increase his sense of panic.

At last, he slipped into lucid, and a dream-replica of the world replaced reality.

In that dream-replica, Gabe became his mech once more. Its limbs were his limbs, and so was its bristling artillery.

But the tunnel mouth remained empty. The Quatro did not pursue them onto Eresos' surface.

Why didn't our bullets affect them? The Quatro are invincible!

But invincible or not, the aliens did not emerge.

All of Oneiri were inside their mechs now, pacing back and forth in front of the tunnel mouth, but always facing it.

Their confidence had returned, now that they had resumed control of their mechanized colossi, and they positioned themselves between the tunnel and the rest of the battalion, ready to protect their fellow soldiers from whatever the Quatro had become.

Still nothing. *Why don't they come?*

"What happened to Tommy?" Richaud asked.

"The Quatro got him," Henrietta said, her voice quavering slightly. "One swipe was all it took."

Richaud shook his head, silent.

"Sir?" Jake said.

Gabe turned to look at him, and when he did, he found Price facing away from the tunnel. Following the seaman apprentice's gaze to the horizon, he saw...

Nothing.

"What is it, Price?"

"I—maybe it's nothing. I thought—"

Something streaked across the sky, toward the surface of the planet, and when it met the horizon there was a brief, faint glow before darkness returned.

"There!" Price said. "That was it."

Another meteorite fell as he said it, and then another. Except, these did not behave like regular meteorites. A fourth fell, much closer, and this time it was followed by a rumble that Gabe felt from inside his mech, from within the dream.

"They look like they're coming down pretty close. Think we should check it out, sir?"

"Yeah," Gabe said. "Just you and me. You others, stay here and guard the tunnel mouth. Notify me immediately if you detect any movement at all."

"Yes, sir," his team responded in rough unison.

Gabe and Price loped toward the low hill where the meteorites had seemed to fall, not saying anything else, both presumably lost in their thoughts.

Eresos' landscape sped by, and it occurred to Gabe that he was finally starting to take it for granted—even the weird, leafless trees, and maybe even that constant mildew smell.

Maybe this *was* home.

Or maybe it's just a suitable place to fight the Quatro till I find an early grave.

At the top of the grassy hill, they found a wide area that had been flattened, and at its center was a perfectly circular crater, no doubt caused by one of the things that had fallen.

Adjusting his night vision and using his implant to magnify his sight, Gabe studied the spherical object lying in the exact middle of the fresh crater.

He approached it.

"Sir, do you really think...?"

Price trailed off, probably after realizing Gabe intended to continue ignoring him. When he reached the sphere, which was easily five meters across, he noticed several crescent-shaped crevices. He stuck his hand into one, tugging at it, but not expecting it to do anything.

So it surprised him a fair bit when something did happen.

"Sir, get back! It's opening up!"

Gabe didn't need to be told twice. He danced back, then leapt backward into the air, coming to land on the rim of the crater beside Price.

"Is that...?" Price trailed off again, apparently hesitant to classify the object that the sphere had opened to reveal.

The surface of that object was very similar to that of the Gatherers, of the Amblers...

And of the mech Price and his father had found on that comet.

In fact, it clearly *was* a mech. But just as clearly, it was not one that had been designed for human use.

"Quadruped," Gabe muttered, his voice hoarse. "Someone built this for the Quatro to use."

"Who's sending these here?" Jake wondered aloud. He clearly didn't expect an answer.

Which was good, because Gabe didn't have one for him.

"Could it be a species that lives in one of the nearby star systems?" Jake went on.

"We don't know for sure that those systems are occupied by anyone."

"Okay, but it seems pretty—"

"*Sir!*" It was Ash, apparently forgetting to subvocalize. She sounded panicked.

"Report!" Gabe barked.

Exertion strained her voice as she continued. "We're engaging the Quatro. There are fifty of them up here already, and they're showing no sign of stopping!"

Gabe turned to Price to find the boy looking back at him.

"If we let those creatures get to these things, we're done. Humanity is done—on Eresos, at the very least. You ready, boy?"

"Yes, sir. I'm ready."

"Then let's head back to that cave. See if we can contain them there. If not, we'll fall back to here, and do what we have to in order to keep the Quatro from accessing these things. Let's go."

Gabe sprinted back toward the tunnel mouth, and behind him, he heard Price pounding across the earth.

Acknowledgments

Thank you to Jeff Rudolph for offering insightful editorial input and helping to make this book as strong as it could be.

Thank you to Tom Edwards for creating such stunning cover art.

Thank you to my family - your support means everything.

Thank you to Cecily, my heart.

Thank you to the people who read my stories, write reviews, and help spread the word. I couldn't do this without you.

About the Author

Scott Bartlett was born 1987 in St. John's, Newfoundland, and he has been writing since he was fifteen. He has received various awards for his fiction, including the H. R. (Bill) Percy Prize, the Lawrence Jackson Writers' Award, and the Percy Janes First Novel Award.

In 2013, Scott placed 2nd in Grain Magazine's Canada-wide short story competition and in 2015 he was shortlisted for the Cuffer Prize. His novel *Taking Stock* was also a semi-finalist in the 2014 Best Kindle Book Awards.

Scott mostly writes science fiction nowadays, though he's dabbled in other genres.

Visit scottplots.com to learn about Scott's other books.